每日生活英語會話

Everyday English!

Carolyn G. Choong／著

笛藤出版

目次 / Contents

delighted

pride

sorrowful

worried

angry

MP3 音檔連結

Part 1

上下班通勤

Commuting

上下班通勤

COMMUTING

MP3 001

情境會話

辦公室 同事 解釋遲到

Annie Why weren't you here this morning? This is only the start of the month. You won't get (the) full attendance bonus.

Bill I dreamed of a typhoon day's off today. I didn't know it just issued a sea alert for the typhoon.

Annie You didn't need to take the half day off.

Bill When I took the MRT, there was an accident. The MRT stopped working for almost two hours.

Annie It seems you are out of luck today.

Bill Oh, don't even mention it.

Annie：你今天早上為什麼沒來？這個月才剛開始耶，你的全勤不就沒了？
Bill　：我夢到今天放颱風假，不知道才發布了海上颱風警報而已。
Annie：那也不至於請半天假？
Bill　：搭捷運的時候，又遇到捷運事故，列車停了將近 2 個小時。
Annie：看來你今天運氣不太好。
Bill　：哎，別再說了。

今天很早起

我今天很早起床。	I woke up really early today. ★ wake up 清醒；get up 醒後起床。
今天要穿什麼呢？	What should I wear today? ◎ What should I wear ？= 我要穿什麼？
我無法決定要穿什麼。	I can't decide what to wear. ◎ I can't decide … = 我無法決定…。
今天有重要會議，要穿正式服裝。	I have an important meeting today, so I have to dress formally. ◎ formally (ad.) = 正式地。
先看天氣預報再決定穿什麼。	Let's check the weather forecast to decide what to wear. ◎ weather forecast = 天氣預報。
天氣轉涼，要記得帶外套。	The weather is getting colder. Don't forget to bring a coat. 文 *Don't forget +to+Vr(原形動詞)* *= 別忘記…。*
我還有充足的時間可以準備。	I still have enough time to prepare. 文 *have enough time+ to+Vr (原形動詞)* *= 有充分的時間…。*
我吃完早餐才去上班。	I go to work after having breakfast.
每天早上喝杯咖啡後才真的醒來。	A cup of coffee every morning wakes me up.

今天下大雨，我要早點去上班。	It's raining really hard today, so I should leave for work earlier. ★ hard 的形容詞和副詞一樣。 ◎ leave for … = 前往…。
我總是準時上班。	I always get to work on time. ★ 頻率副詞 always (總是) > usually(通常) > often(時常) > sometimes(有時候) > seldom(鮮少) > never(從不)。 ◎ on time = 準時。
早睡早起身體好。	Keeping early hours is good for health. ◎ be good for… = 對…有好處。
我沒辦法熬夜到很晚。	I'm not the type of person who can stay up late. 文 *be not [the type / that kind] of …* *= 不是…類型。*
我一熬夜隔天就爬不起來了。	Once I stay up late the night before, I'll have difficulty getting up the next day. ◎ once = 一旦…，此處為連接詞。 ◎ stay up late = 熬夜。

早睡早起有益身心，如果沒什麼事，就別黏在電腦電視或手機前，不妨早點休息，隔天精神會更好喔。

不小心睡過頭了！

昨晚沒睡好。	I didn't sleep well last night.
昨晚做了惡夢。	I had a nightmare last night. ◎ nightmare (n.) = 惡夢。
好想睡回籠覺。	I want to fall back to sleep again. ◎ fall back to sleep = 睡回籠覺。
再睡 5 分鐘。	I'll sleep for just five minutes.
慘了，睡過頭了！	Damn, I overslept! ◎ oversleep (v.) = 睡過頭。
天哪！鬧鐘竟然沒有響！	Gosh! The alarm clock didn't go off! ★ go off 除了可當「響起」，也有「東西變質」和「進行」的意思。
不！再十分鐘就八點了。	Oh no! There's only 10 minutes to 8. ◎ 數字 minutes to 數字 = 再…分鐘…點。
我的眼睛好腫。	My eyes are puffy. ◎ puffy (a.) = 腫脹的。
我的頭髮亂七八糟。	My hair is a mess. ◎ mess (n.)= 混亂。mess up = 把事情搞砸。
我嚴重宿醉。	I have a terrible hangover. ◎ hangover (n.) = 宿醉。
我的識別證在哪裡？	Where is my staff ID? ◎ staff ID (n.) = 員工識別證。 ◎ Where is / are …? = …在哪裡？

啊，我的機車沒油了。	Oops, my motorcycle is out of gas. ◎ out of gas = 沒油。
不，火車開走了。要等下一班了。	Oh no, the train just left. Gotta wait for the next one. ◎ Gotta = going to = 將…。
我再五分鐘就到公司了。	I'll be at the office in 5 minutes. ◎ in…minutes = …分鐘內。
我已經在路上了。	I'm on the way to the office. 文 *on [the / one's] way to… = 在…的路上。* *例：I saw a car accident on [the / my] way to work.*
今天是幾月幾號？	What's the date today? ◎ 也可以用 What's today's date ？
不會吧！今天端午節不用上班！	Holy cow! We're off today since it's the Dragon Boat Festival! ★ Holy cow！是感到驚訝時會用的口頭禪，也可以說 My gosh!。 ★此處的 since 為連接詞，有「因為」的意思。
今天放颱風假！	We got the day off today because of the typhoon. ◎ day off = 放假。because of + N= 因為…。

最好還是提早出門，才不會急急忙忙反而半途遇到狀況。

搭乘大眾運輸工具

星期一真讓人憂鬱。	Mondays are depressing. ◎ depressing (a.) = 憂鬱的、沮喪的。 同 discouraging；disheartened。
真想翹班一天。	I'd love to play hooky one of these days. ◎ play hooky = 翹班、翹課。 同 play truant；skive work；skip work。
噢，悠遊卡餘額不足！	Uh-oh, there's not enough money in my Easy Card!
我要加值悠遊卡。	I need to add value to my Easy Card. ◎ add value to = 加值。 同 top up。
差一點就沒搭上公車了。	I almost didn't make the bus.
公車上人擠人，沒有多的座位。	It's packed in the bus, and there aren't any seats left. ◎ It 's packed. = 很擁擠。
搭捷運上班的人真多。	So many people take the MRT to work. ◎ MRT = Mass Rapid Transit。
捷運車廂好擠喔。	The MRT carriages are so crowded.
車上有人在睡覺，也有人在玩智慧型手機。	Some people are dozing off on the train, while others are playing with their smartphones. ◎ doze off = 打瞌睡。

坐在旁邊的男生好臭。	The boy sitting next to me smells really bad. ◎ smell (v.) = 發出…氣味。
坐在旁邊的人一直在說話。	The people sitting next to me won't stop talking. ◎ next to = 旁邊、隔壁
站在前面的人音樂開太大聲了。	The person standing in front of me listens to music far too loud.
可以請你關小聲一點嗎？	Can you please keep it down? ◎ keep…down = 把…關小聲一點。
請將博愛座讓給老人。	Please yield the priority seats to the elderly. ◎ priority seat = 博愛座。
天哪！手機快沒電了！	GEEZ! My cell phone is almost dead! ◎ 手機沒電 = be dead。 反 有電 = be full charged。
我把錢包留在車上了。	I left my wallet on the train.
我的錢被偷了。	My money was stolen. ◎ steal (v.) = 偷竊。此處為被動式。 類 thieve = 偷竊；rob = 搶劫； burglarize = 破門盜竊。

搭乘大眾運輸工具時，除了要留心隨身物品，也請注意不要大聲喧嘩，以免造成其他人的困擾。

通勤二三事

你都怎麼來上班？

How do you get to work?

文 How do you get to + 地點？
＝你搭什麼交通工具去某處？

我都搭公司的交通車上班。
I always get to work by shuttle.

我 [男朋友 / 老公 / 女朋友 / 老婆] 載我上班。
My [boyfriend / husband / girlfriend / wife] drives me to work.

我平常都搭 [捷運 / 地鐵 / 火車 / 公車 / 計程車] 上班。
I take the [MRT / subway / train / bus / taxi] to work.
◎ take the + 交通工具 = 搭乘…。

我平常都 [騎摩托車 / 開車] 上班。
I [ride my scooter / drive] to work.

我今天搭同事的便車來上班。
I got a ride from a [coworker / colleague] today.
◎ get a ride = 搭便車。

我跟一個同事共乘上班。
I carpool to work with a [coworker / colleague].
◎ carpool (v.) = 共乘。

我 [走路 / 騎腳踏車] 上班，因為有益健康。
I [walk / bike] to work because it's good for my health.

你每天花多少時間通勤？

How much time do you spend a day on your commute?

◎ How much time do you spend
= 你花多少時間…？

公司有提供交通車嗎？

Does the company provide a shuttle?

◎ provide (v.) = 提供。

[捷運 / 公車] 幾分鐘來一班呢？

How often does the [MRT / bus] come?

你從家裡騎機車上班要多久？

How long does it take to get to work from home on your scooter?

◎ How long does it take + to …?
= 做…要花多久時間？

搭公車比搭捷運便宜。

Taking the bus is cheaper than taking the MRT.

你每天幾點出門上班？

What time do you go to work every day?

你一個月花多少錢在通勤上？

How much do you spend on commuting every month?

◎ How much… = 多少錢？

幾乎不用花錢。
Next to nothing.

每個月一千元。
NT$1,000 every month.

你有汽車駕照嗎？

Do you have a driver's license?

有，去年拿到的。
Yes, I got it last year.

有，但沒開上路過。
Yes, but I haven't used it yet on the road.

💬 有，但是我沒有車。
Yes, but I don't have a car.

💬 沒有，我不會開車。
No, I don't know how to drive.
◎ I don't know how to … = 我不會…

上下班途中的巧遇

啊！那裡有 [貓 / 狗] ！	Look! There is a [cat / dog] over there.
真可愛！跟牠們玩一下好了。	They are so cute! Let's have fun with them.
早阿，你平常不是開車上班嗎？	Good morning! Don't you always go to work by car? 💬 我的車昨天進廠維修了。 My car was being serviced yesterday.
要載你一程嗎？	Do you need a ride?
嗨！好巧哦。沒想到會在這遇到你。	Hi! What a coincidence! I am surprised to meet you here. ◎ What a coincidence! = 真巧！
你叫那麼大聲嚇死我了。	Oh, you shout too loudly! I was almost scared to death. ◎ scare to death = 嚇死。
好久不見，你變瘦好多。	How have you been? You've become so much thinner. ★好久不見的用法很多，也可以說 Long time no see，雖然這有點台式用法，但外國人也聽得懂，語言是非常靈活的。

聽說你換工作了？發生了什麼事？

I heard that you've changed your job. What happened?

★ hear 的相關片語：hear of = 聽說過；hear out = 聽完；hear from = 收到來信；hear about = 聽說。

除了碰到同事以外，你是否也巧遇過親戚、多年不見的朋友、前男友或前女友呢？啊，真尷尬（It's so embarrassing.）。

"Early to bed and early to rise, makes a man healthy, wealthy and wise."

– Benjamin Franklin

「早睡早起，聰明富裕身體好。」～*班傑明 ・ 富蘭克林（政治家、發明家）*

練習問題

選擇題 請選出正確的答案。

A) on my way	F) dead
B) overslept	G) leave for
C) off	H) skip work
D) out of gas	I) dozing off
E) on time	J) take

1. 我總是準時上班。
   I always get to work ________ .

2. 慘了，睡過頭了！
   Damn, I ________ !

3. 真想翹班一天。
   I'd love to ________ one of these days.

4. 唉啊，我的機車沒油了。
   Oops, my motorcycle is ________ .

5. 今天國慶日不用上班。
   We're ________ today since it's the Double Tenth Day.

6. 今天下大雨，我要早點去上班。
   It's raining really hard today, so I should ________ work earlier.

7. 天哪！手機快沒電了！
   GEEZ! My cell phone is almost ________ !

8. 搭捷運上班的人真多。

So many people ________ the MRT to work.

9. 有人在睡覺，也有人在玩智慧型手機。

Some people are ________ on the train, while some others are playing with their smart phones.

10. 上班路上有車禍發生。

There was an accident ________ to work.

單字填空 請填入適當的單字。

1. 今天是愚人節。

Today is ________ .

2. 要載你一程嗎？

Do you need a ________ ?

3. 我今天很早就起床。

I ________ really early today.

4. 早睡早起身體好。

Keeping early hours is good ________ health.

5. 喔噢，悠遊卡餘額不足！

Uh-oh, there's not ________ money in my Easy Card!

6. 糟糕，公車剛開走。等下一班吧。

Oh no, the bus just left. Let's ________ the next one.

7. 天氣轉涼，出門要記得帶件外套。

The weather is getting colder. Don't ________ to bring my coat out.

8. 我不是故意闖紅燈的。

I didn't ________ to run the red light.

9. 公車上人擠人，沒有多的座位。

It's ________ in the bus, and there aren't any seats left.

10. 我一熬夜隔天就爬不起來了。

Once I ________ late the night before, I'll have difficulty getting up the next day.

• 答案 •

Ⓐ 單字填空

①E ⑥G

②B ⑦F

③H ⑧J

④D ⑨I

⑤C ⑩A

Ⓐ 單字填空

① April Fool's Day ⑥ wait for

② ride ⑦ forget

③ woke up ⑧ mean

④ for ⑨ packed

⑤ enough ⑩ stay up

搭乘交通工具

表達搭乘交通工具到某處最簡單的說法是 by + 交通工具，例如：I go to work by bus.（我搭公車去上班。）若能記下這個用法，無論是日常閒聊、外國人問路或將來出國時都能用到喔。

以下是常見的交通工具：

機車 motorcycle / 汽車 car / 公車 bus / 接駁車 shuttle bus

計程車 taxi(cab) / 捷運 MRT / 火車 train / 高鐵 high speed rail

地鐵 subway / 空中列車 sky train / 飛機 airplane(plane)

上下班通勤

台灣國定假日

元旦	New Year’s Day (1 月 1 日)
春節	Chinese New Year (農曆 1 月 1 日)
和平紀念日	Peace Memorial Day (2 月 28 日)
清明節	Tomb Sweeping Day (春分後第 15 天)
勞動節	Labor Day (5 月 1 日)
端午節	Dragon Boat Festival (農曆 5 月 5 日)
中秋節	Moon Festival (農曆 8 月 15 日)
國慶日	Double Tenth Day (10 月 10 日)

歐美國家法定假日

元旦	New Year’s Day (1 月 1 日)
馬丁路德紀念日	Dr. Martin Luther King Jr. Day (1 月 21 日)
總統節	Presidents’ Day (2 月 18 日)
耶穌受難日	Good Friday (3 月 29 日)
復活節 (歐)	Easter (春分月圓後的第一個星期天)
五月節 (英)	Early May (5 月 6 日)
陣亡將士追悼日	Memorial Day (5 月 27 日)
美國國慶日	Independence Day (7 月 4 日)
勞動節	Labor Day (美國是 9 月第一個星期一；法國是 5 月 1 日)
萬聖夜	Halloween (10 月 31 日)
萬聖節	All Saints' Day =Hallowmas (11 月 1 日)
感恩節	Thanksgiving (11 月最後一個星期四)
聖誕夜	Christmas Eve (12 月 24 日)
聖誕節	Christmas Day (12 月 25 日)
聖誕節翌日 (歐)	Boxing Day (12 月 26 日)
新年除夕	New Year’s Eve (12 月 31 日)

Part 2

進公司

Arriving at the office

進公司

ARRIVING AT THE OFFICE

MP3 002

情境會話

辦公室　同事　電梯巧遇

Olivia	I just met the boss in the elevator. It was so embarrassing.
Alex	So you were the one who got stuck with the boss in the elevator for thirty minutes.
Olivia	You bet! I am out of luck.
Alex	Don't think too much. Today is Friday. Hold on! It will be a holiday soon.
Olivia	You are right. What are you going to do after work?
Alex	I want to invite you and Sarah to have dinner at a newly opened Thai Buffet. The beer is all you can drink during the trial period.
Olivia	It's a good idea. Wait… I forgot to punch in again.

Olivia：我剛剛在電梯裡遇到老闆，好尷尬。
Alex ：所以和老闆困在同一部電梯裡 30 分鐘的人就是你？
Olivia：對阿，有夠衰的。
Alex ：好啦，別想那麼多了。今天是星期五，再撐一下就放假了。
Olivia：說的也是。今天下班後有什麼活動嗎？
Alex ：我想找你和 Sarah 一起去吃新開的泰式 Buffet，開幕期間啤酒無限暢飲。
Olivia：這真是個好主意。等等…我又忘記打卡了！

搭電梯

請等一下，我也要搭電梯。	Wait a moment! I'd like to take the elevator, too. ★ take 可以換成 use。
你要到幾樓？	Which floor are you going? ★只說 Which floor？也 OK。
7 樓，謝謝。	The seventh floor. Thanks a lot.
不好意思，我要出去。	Excuse me. I' m getting out of here.

上班遲到被老闆唸

老闆有事找你。	The boss wants to see you.
小心點，老闆今天吃炸藥。	Watch out. The boss is in a bad mood today. ◎ watch out = 小心。同 be careful。
老闆對於員工遲到很生氣。	The boss gets mad when the employees are late. ◎ get mad = 生氣。
你知道現在幾點了嗎？	Do you know what time it is?
你為何常常遲到早退？	Why are you always coming to work late and leaving work early?
你這個月光是遲到就被扣了 1,500 元。	You got NT$1,500 taken out of your paycheck this month just for being late. ◎ take out of… = 從…扣除。

你今天為什麼遲到？

Why are you late today?

因為早上覺得不太舒服。
Because I felt sick this morning.
◎ feel sick = 不舒服。

因為我睡過頭了。
Because I overslept.

因為臨時有事情。
Because something came up suddenly.
◎ come up = 發生；開始流行。

因為沒搭到公車。
Because I missed the bus.

因為汽車半路拋錨。
Because my car broke down on the way.

因為道路施工。
Because there was a road construction.
◎ construction (n.) = 建造、施工。

因為上班途中有車禍發生。
Because there was an accident on my way to work.

你遲到的藉口很多。

You always have a ton of excuses for being late.

◎ excuse (n.) = 藉口。

文 *for + N / Ving =…的理由。*

塞車不是理由，是藉口。

Traffic is not a reason; it's an excuse.

◎ reason (n.) = 理由。

上班族應盡量避免遲到，太常遲到除了會被扣薪水，還會給上司不好的印象，得不償失。要是不小心遲到了，記得要誠實面對，千萬別因為怕被罵而想些誇張不實的藉口，弄巧成拙。

趕上最後一秒進辦公室

好險！差一點就遲到了。	That was close! I was almost late. ◎ That was close! = 好險！
不，我忘記打卡了！	Oh no! I forgot to punch in. ◎ punch in/out = 上 / 下班打卡。
怎麼啦？你今天很 [晚到 / 早到] 喔。	What's wrong with you? You got here [late / early] today. ◎ What's wrong with you? = 你怎麼了？
你永遠是 [第一個 / 最後一個] 到辦公室的。	You're always [the first one / the last one] to the office.

遲到不是病，但常常遲到可能會讓你被炒魷魚。試著想像這樣的畫面，某天在辦公室裡，當你聽到有人喊道：「遲到哥！遲到姐！」，而你只能不爭氣的回頭時，就表示你該檢討囉！

和同事閒聊

又是星期一，我討厭星期一。	It's Monday again…I hate Mondays.
星期一好難集中精神。	It's hard to pay attention on Monday.
距離週末還好遠。	The weekend is so far away.
終於星期五了。	It's Friday after all.
這個禮拜真長。	This week has seemed so long.
你今天晚上有什麼活動嗎？	What are you doing tonight?

今天請假的人好像不少。	It seems like a lot of people took the day off today. ★ take off 除了請假，還有「起飛」和「脫下」的意思。
我還有五天特休。	I still have 5 annual leave days left. ◎ annual leave (n.) = 年假。
我明天要請假。	I'll take a day off tomorrow.
你昨天有活動嗎？	Did you do anything yesterday?

昨天去幫我朋友慶生。
Yesterday I went to celebrate my friend's birthday.
◎ celebrate someone's birthday = 替某人慶生。

昨天去聽演唱會。
I went to a concert yesterday.
◎ concert (n.) = 演唱會。
★ a + 表演者 + concert = …的演唱會，例：a mayday concert = 五月天的演唱會。

昨天去看電影。
I saw a movie yesterday.
★ 也可以用 go to the movies。

昨晚去吃聖誕大餐。
I went to a Christmas banquet last night.

昨晚去酒吧喝酒。
I went out to a bar last night for drinks.

昨天去看統一獅對兄弟象的棒球賽。
I went to a baseball game between the Uni-President Lions and the Brother Elephants yesterday.

[派對 / 演唱會 / 電影 / 晚餐 / 棒球賽] 怎麼樣？	How was the [party / concert / movie / dinner / baseball game] ?
昨天球賽結果如何？	What was the final score of the base-ball game yesterday?
我懂你的感受。	I know the feeling.
週末過得怎麼樣？	How was your weekend? 很棒，但我現在好累。我完全不想工作。 It was great, but now I'm so tired. I don't want to work at all. ★ at all 用於否定句，有「一點也不」的意思。

進公司後，稍微和同事閒聊一下無妨，但可別聊過頭，忽略了工作哦。

每天都要吃早餐

你吃早餐了嗎？	Did you have breakfast yet? 我在家吃過了。 Yes, I ate my breakfast at home. 我沒時間吃早餐。 No, I didn't have time to eat breakfast. 我睡過頭所以沒吃早餐。 No, I skipped my breakfast because I overslept.
你想吃什麼早餐？	What would you like for breakfast?
要訂早餐嗎？	Would you like to order breakfast?

你早餐吃什麼？

What did you have for breakfast?

漢堡加中冰奶。
I had a hamburger and a medium cup of iced milk tea.

飯糰配大杯豆漿。
I ate a rice and vegetable roll and a large cup of soy milk.

不吃早餐除了整天沒精神、反應遲鈍外，也比較容易發胖或腸胃不適，長期不吃早餐甚至會罹患慢性病。吃早餐好處多多，再忙也別忘記吃早餐哦！

同事今天特別不一樣

你今天看起來很有精神。

You're full of energy today.

◎ be full of … = 充滿…。

你今天看起來很漂亮哦。

You look [great / pretty] today.

◎ You look … = 你看起來…。

因為我今天有化妝。
Oh, it's because I did my makeup today.
◎ makeup = 化妝。

你今天看起來不太一樣耶。

You look different today.

你是不是剪頭髮了？

Did you get a haircut?

你是不是染髮了？

Did you dye your hair?

你的新髮型很好看，看起來年輕多了。

Your new hair style looks good. You look so much younger.

你的新眼鏡很適合你的臉型。

Your new glasses fit the shape of your face nicely.

你的指甲看起來很漂亮。我喜歡這個顏色。

Your fingernails look fantastic. I like the color.

💬 謝謝！真是過獎了。
Thank you! You're flattering me.

你是不是睡眠不足啊？

You're not getting enough sleep, are you?

★本句是附加問句。敘述句是否定句時，附加問句要用肯定句。

怎麼了？你看起來心情不好。

What's wrong? You look like you're in a bad mood.

◎ in a bad mood = 心情不好。
反 in a good mood = 心情好。

什麼事情讓你生氣啊？

What is it that made you pissed off?

◎ pissed sb off = 激怒某人。
💬 沒什麼事啦。
Nothing special.

人難免有低潮，還是要盡量避免壞心情影響工作。如果一個人常常擺臭臉，會讓人感覺不好親近，久而久之，人緣也會變差。

"Nobody stands taller than those willing to stand corrected."

– William Safire

「沒有人比願意站起來承認錯誤的人更高。」～*威廉・薩菲爾（作家）*

練習問題

選擇題　請選出正確的答案。

A) in a bad mood	F) full of energy
B) felt sick	G) What's wrong
C) being late	H) came up
D) the movies	I) That was close
E) angry	J) take a day off

1. Oliver 遲到的藉口很多。

   Oliver always has a ton of excuses for ________ .

2. 我明天要請假。

   I'll ________ tomorrow.

3. 明天要去看電影。

   I will go to ________ tomorrow.

4. 什麼事情讓你生氣啊？

   What is it that made you ________ ?

5. 你今天看起來精神飽滿喔。

   You're ________ today.

6. 怎麼了？

   ________ ?

7. 好險！差一點就遲到了。

   ________ ! I was almost late.

8. 因為早上覺得不舒服。

Because I ________ this morning.

9. 老闆今天吃炸藥。

The boss is ________ today.

10. 因為臨時有事情。

Because something ________ suddenly.

單字填空 請填入適當的單字。

1. 因為機車半路拋錨。

Because my motorcycle ________ .

2. 不！我忘記打卡了。

Oh no! I forgot to ________ .

3. 我這個月光遲到就被扣了 1500 元。

I got NT$ 1,500 ________ my paycheck this month just for being late.

4. 你永遠是第一個到辦公室的。

You're always ________ to the office.

5. 我還有五天特休。

I still have 5 ________ left.

6. 塞車不是理由，是藉口。

Traffic is not a ________ ; it's an excuse.

7. 因為我沒搭到公車。

Because I ________ the bus.

8. 你要訂早餐嗎？

Would you like to ________ breakfast?

9. 請等一下，我也要搭電梯。

Wait a moment! I'd like to ________ , too.

10. 老闆對於員工遲到很生氣。

The boss ________ when the employees are late.

• 答案 •

Ⓐ 單字填空

① C	⑥ G
② J	⑦ I
③ D	⑧ B
④ E	⑨ A
⑤ F	⑩ H

Ⓐ 單字填空

① broke down	⑥ reason
② punch in/out	⑦ missed
③ taken out of	⑧ order
④ the first one	⑨ take the elevator
⑤ annual leave days	⑩ gets mad

藍色星期一？

每到星期一，就會聽到有人說「今天真是 blue Monday、我的心情好 blue……」你是否很疑惑，為什麼星期一是藍色的？為什麼心情很藍？這是因為 blue 除了「藍色」，還有「憂鬱的、沮喪的」的意思，blue Monday 正是指容易心情低落、無心工作的星期一。

此外，你是否聽過「black Monday 黑色星期一」呢？這個字源自 1987 年 10 月 19 日星期一，美國發生的嚴重股災，當時股市暴跌，間接造成了後續的經濟衰退，現在多用來形容星期一常常股市大跌的現象。

進公司

三餐的說法

早餐	breakfast
早午餐	brunch
午餐	lunch
下午茶	afternoon tea

晚餐	supper/dinner
零食	snack
宵夜	night snack

中式早餐

蛋餅	Chinese omelet
蘿蔔糕	turnip cake
飯糰	rice and vegetable roll
燒餅	clay oven rolls
油條	fried bread stick

饅頭	steamed buns
肉包	steamed meat buns
蒸餃	steamed dumplings
豆漿	soy milk
米漿	rice and peanut milk

西式早餐

三明治	sandwich
漢堡	hamburger
貝果	bagel
鬆餅 / 薄煎餅	pancake
格子鬆餅	waffle
穀片	cereal
吐司	toast
法式吐司	French toast

全麥麵包	whole-grain bread
優格	yogurt
牛奶	milk
咖啡	coffee
紅茶	black tea
綠茶	green tea
奶茶	milk tea
果汁	juice

memo

Part 3

會議

Meetings

會議

MEETINGS

MP3 003

情境會話

辦公室　同事　準備企劃案

Christina	It's your turn to present the ad project, isn't it? Are you ready?
Bill	Not yet. Honestly, I have no more ideas.
Christina	May I take a look? Perhaps I can do you a favor.
Bill	OK. Please give me some suggestions.
Christina	Your concept is great. You are too picky.
Bill	I hope so, I have worked overtime for several days in order to finish the project.

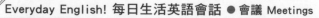

Christina：明天輪到你在會議上發表廣告企劃案，對吧？你都準備好了嗎？

Bill：還沒。老實說，我一點頭緒都沒有。

Christina：可以借我看看嗎？或許我能幫上忙。

Bill：好阿，給我一點意見。

Christina：你的想法很好啊，你太吹毛求疵了。

Bill：但願如此。為了這個企劃案我已經連續加班好幾天了。

開會前

通知大家開會。	Tell everyone we'll have a meeting. Tell everyone there's a meeting.
今天的會議由總經理主持。	The president will hold today's meeting. ★也可以說 Today's meeting will be held by the president. ◎ hold a meeting = 主持會議。
會議預定下午兩點開始。	The meeting is scheduled to start at 2pm. 文 *be scheduled + to Vr … = 預定…。*
會議時間預定為兩個小時。	The meeting is scheduled for two hours.
開會請穿正式服裝。	Please dress formally for the meeting.
開會時不能穿得邋遢。	You have to look sharp when we have meetings. 文 *S + have/has to + Vr…= 某人必須…。* ◎ look sharp = 看起來精明、時髦。
請準時到達會議室。	Please come to the conference room on time.
開會要提早十分鐘到達會議室。	You should come to the conference room 10 minutes before the meeting starts.

開會遲到很失禮。	It's really impolite to be late for a meeting. ◎It's really impolite to … = …是很沒禮貌的。
請事先準備會議資料。	Please prepare your materials before the meeting.
開會要準備什麼東西？	What should I prepare for the meeting? ◎ prepare for… = 為…準備。 你要準備投影機。 You should set up the projector. 每個人要帶筆記本和筆。 Everyone should bring their notebooks and pens. ◎ Everyone should… = 每個人都要…。 每個人要準備自己的提案。 Everyone should bring their own proposals. ◎ proposal (n.) = 提案。
今天會議要發表簡報，你都準備好了嗎？	You're going to present a briefing in the meeting. Are you ready? ◎ present a briefing = 發表簡報。
你有收到明天會議的議程了嗎？	Have you received the agenda for tomorrow's meeting? ◎ agenda (n.) = 議程表。

開會前做好充足準備，就不會臨時慌了手腳。報告時可以利用電腦、海報等工具加深大家的印象。講話時，目光請看著眾人，語調要有抑揚頓挫，否則講到最後，可能會變成眾人皆「睡」你獨醒哦。

會議時間變更

今天早上的會議取消。	This morning's meeting is cancelled.
今天的會議延到星期五。	Today's meeting has been postponed to Friday.
你知道開會時間嗎？	Do you know what time the meeting is? ◎ Do you know…? = 你知道…嗎？ 不確定。聽說時間好像更改了。 I am not sure. I heard that they changed the time. ◎ I heard that… = 聽說…。 知道阿，從 1 點半到 2 點。 Yeah, I know. The meeting is from 1:30 to 2pm.
星期五的會議很重要。	The meeting on Friday is very important.
不能參加要提前告知經理。	Those who cannot make the meeting should tell their managers.
星期五的會議有幾個人不能參加？	How many people cannot attend Friday's meeting? ◎ How many people ? = 有幾個人？
我無法參加星期五的會議。	I can't make it to Friday's meeting. ★此處的 I can't make it. 有「我無法（來不及）參加」的意思。

因故無法出席時，記得提前告知，即使無法口頭告知，也可利用其他通訊方式，如 e-mail 等等，並依公司規定完成後續請假事宜，千萬不要無故缺席。

開會中（主持會議）

會議開始。	Let's call the meeting to order.
既然大家都到齊了，那我們開始吧。	Since everyone is here, let's get started.
今天會議的主題是什麼？	What's on the agenda for today's meeting?
今天的會議主題是我們的行銷策略。	Today's agenda is our marketing strategies. ◎ Today's agenda is …= 今天的議題是…。
今天的會議要討論如何提升銷售量。	The purpose of this meeting is to discuss how to increase the sales volume. ◎ The purpose of this meeting is … = 今天會議要討論…。
別人在報告時請不要討論。	Please don't talk when others are giving their presentation.
有人有問題嗎？	Does anyone have any questions?
如果有任何問題，歡迎隨時提出。	You're welcome to bring up any questions at any time. ◎ bring up = 提出。
有問題請舉手發問。	Please raise your hand if you have any questions. ◎ raise (v.) = 舉起。
是誰的手機在響？	Whose cell phone is ringing?

請將手機轉為震動。	Please put your cell phone on vibrate. ◎ vibrate (v.) = 震動。
開會時請將手機關機。	Please turn off your cell phones during the meeting. ◎ turn off + 電器用品 = 關掉…。 ◎ during … = 在…期間。
現在休息十分鐘。	Let's take a 10 minute break. ◎ Let's take a break. = 休息一下吧。
由於時間的關係，我們先討論到這裡。	It looks like we've run out of time, so we'll finish here. ◎ run out of… = 用光、耗盡…。
結論保留到下次會議。	The conclusion will be carried over to the next meeting. ◎ conclusion (n.) = 結論。 ◎ carry over = 延續、推到。
謝謝各位的注意。	Thank you for your attention. ◎ Thank you for … = 感謝你的…。 ★介係詞用 for，是非常實用的句子。
謝謝大家的合作。	Thank you for your cooperation.

開會中（簡報發表）

這份簡報大約十分鐘左右。	This presentation is about ten minutes.
我將簡報分為三部分。	I've split up the presentation into three parts. ◎ split up + 事物 + into + … = 將…分成…。 ★ split up 除了劃分，還有「離婚、分手」的意思。split 的動詞三態皆為 split。
簡報完後，我很高興回答各位任何問題。	I'd be happy to answer any questions from you after the presentation. ◎ I'd be happy to … = 我很樂意…。
我的提議分為六大項。	My proposal is organized into six sections.
讓我為你們舉幾個例子。	Let me give you some examples. ★ give 也可以換成 show。
以下是我的建議。	My suggestions are as follows. ◎ as follow = 如下。
請仔細考慮一下。	Please take this into careful consideration. ◎ take into consideration = 考慮。
如果您能接受我的提議，我會感到十分榮幸。	I will be very honored if you accept my proposal.
現在換下一個人報告。	Now I'll pass my presentation to the next speaker.

發表意見

很抱歉打斷你，可以請你說得更具體一點嗎？	Sorry to interrupt, but can you be more specific? ★打斷別人時先說 Sorry to interrupt. 比較有禮貌。 ◎ interrupt (v.) = 中斷、打斷。
我不懂你的意思。	I don't understand what you mean.
不好意思，我可以發問嗎？	Excuse me, but can I ask you something?
還有其他問題嗎？	Are there any questions?
這個問題不好回答。	That's a tough question to answer. ◎ tough (a.) = 棘手的。
我恐怕無法馬上回答你。	I'm afraid that I'm unable to give you an answer right away. ◎ I'm unable to... = 我無法⋯。
我贊成你的想法。	I agree with you. ◎ agree with + 人 = 同意某人的意見。
我完全同意。	I couldn't agree with you more.
我不認同你的想法。	I'm sorry, but I don't agree with you.
我的看法有點不同。	I'm afraid that my opinion is somewhat different. ◎ I'm afraid that ⋯= 我恐怕⋯。
我可以發表不同的看法嗎？	May I say something different?

你的想法很好，但是要做到並不容易。	You have a good point; however, it's easier said than done.
你的意見很寶貴，我會想想。	I value your opinion and I will think about it.
我們來投票表決。	Let's get a vote by ballot. ◎ ballot (n.) = 投票。

不認同別人意見時，婉轉的表達會比直接否定更恰當。即使對方的論點令人無法苟同，也不該馬上批評，若能好好討論，說不定反而能激發出更棒的想法。

會議之後

終於開完會了，我都要睡著了。	Finally, the meeting is over. I almost fell asleep. ◎ fall asleep = 睡著、入睡。
公司一天到晚在開會，都沒時間做事了。	Our company has so many meetings that I don't have enough time to do my job. ◎ so … that… = 如此…以致於…。
簡直浪費時間和精力。	It was a complete waste of time and energy.
我討厭沒有效率的會議。	I hate ineffective meetings. ◎ ineffective (a.) = 沒效率的 。
會議從來沒有準時開始。	Meetings never start on time.
老闆根本不聽別人的意見。	Our boss never listens.

上司很愛打斷別人發言。	My direct supervisor usually interrupts others.
老闆在說話，他在打瞌睡。	The boss was talking while he was dozing off. ◎ doze off = 打瞌睡。
他看起來心不在焉。	He looked absent-minded. ◎ absent-minded (a.) = 心不在焉的。
他又在開會時亂講話了。	He said something stupid during the meeting again.
他又在開會時說錯話了。	He said the wrong thing during the meeting again.
我習慣在開會時畫畫，有助於集中注意力。	I'm used to [drawing / doodling] during meetings because it helps me focus. 文 *be used to Ving = 現在習慣⋯。*
你知道新專案的事嗎？	Do you know about the new project?

抱怨歸抱怨，會議中交待的事情還是要好好完成。開會時，即使千百個不願意，也要仔細聽，不要錯過任何重要事項，否則就失去開會的意義了。

"It's lack of faith that makes people afraid of meeting challenges, and I believed in myself."

– Muhammad Ali

「人們因為缺乏信念而害怕面對挑戰，而我相信自己。」～ *穆罕默德 ・ 阿里（拳擊手）*

練習問題

選擇題　請選出正確的答案。

A)	as follows	F)	giving their presentation
B)	vibrate	G)	raise your hand
C)	Thank you for	H)	bring up
D)	is scheduled to	I)	It's really impolite
E)	think about	J)	I am not sure

1. 會議預定下午兩點開始。

   The meeting ________ start at 2pm.

2. 請各位將手機轉為震動。

   Please put your cell phone on ________ .

3. 如果有任何問題，歡迎隨時提出。

   You're welcome to ________ any questions at any time.

4. 謝謝各位的注意。

   ________ your attention.

5. 你的意見很寶貴，我會想想。

   I value your opinion and I will ________ it.

6. 開會遲到是很不禮貌的。

   ________ to be late for a meeting.

7. 別人在報告時請不要討論。

   Please don't talk when others are ________ .

8. 有問題請舉手發言。

Please ________ if you have any questions.

9. 不確定。聽說時間好像更改了。

________ . I heard that they changed the time.

10. 以下是我的建議。

My suggestions are ________ .

單字填空 請填入適當的單字。

1. 明天會議由總經理親自主持。

The president himself will ________ tomorrow's meeting.

2. 今天早上的會議取消。

This morning's meeting is ________ .

3. 開會要準備什麼東西？

What should I ________ for the meeting?

4. 現在休息十分鐘。

Let's take a 10 minute ________ .

5. 開會時請將手機關機。

Please ________ your cell phones during the meeting.

6. 知道啊。會議時間從 3 點到 4 點半。

Yeah, I know. The meeting is ________ 3 to 4:30.

7. 我完全同意你的意見。

I couldn't ________ you more.

8. 每個人要準備自己的提案。

Everyone should bring their own _________ .

9. 我討厭沒有效率的會議。

I hate _________ meetings.

10. 我將簡報分為三部分。

I've _________ the presentation _________ three parts.

• 答案 •

Ⓐ 單字填空

① D	⑥ I
② B	⑦ F
③ H	⑧ G
④ C	⑨ J
⑤ E	⑩ A

Ⓐ 單字填空

① hold	⑥ from
② cancelled	⑦ agree with
③ prepare	⑧ proposals
④ break	⑨ ineffective
⑤ turn off	⑩ split up; into

更有效率的會議

想要有效率的開會，以下幾點一定要注意：①事先決定會議主題。②提前告知討論的議題。③準備好開會用的資料及用品。④提早到達會議室。⑤準時開始與結束。⑥報告簡短扼要。⑦不偏離主題。⑧不打斷別人。⑨不私下交談討論。⑩不談私事。⑪對事不對人。⑫非必要不使用智慧型手機。⑬確保所有人都參與討論。⑭以尊重的態度提出反對意見。⑮事後追蹤討論過的項目。

會議

開會單字

會議室	conference / meeting room
出席會議	attend a conference / meeting
主席	chairman
與會者	attendant
議程	agenda
提案	proposal
專案	project
簡報	brief
報告	report
結論	conclusion
會議紀錄	minute
通知	notice
白板	whiteboard
白板筆	whiteboard pen
投影機	projector
投影片	transparency
雷射筆	laser pointer
麥克風	microphone
擴音器	speaker
插座	socket

會議種類

週會	weekly meeting
月會	monthly meeting
年會	annual meeting
檢討會	review meeting
記者會	press conference
臨時會議	unscheduled meeting

緊急會議	emergency meeting
視訊會議	videoconference
董事會議	board meeting
員工會議	staff meeting
團隊會議	team meeting
銷售會議	sales meeting

memo

Part 4

工作分際

Daily Work

工作分際

DAILY WORK

MP3 004

情境會話

辦公室 同事 請求協助

Tony	Are you available now, Miss Wang?
Miss Wang	Yes. Do you need any help?
Tony	Please contact the guests on the list, and check if they will attend the event tomorrow night.
Miss Wang	No problem.
Tony	By the way, please tell Mr. Lin the exact number of people who will come.
Miss Wang	OK. I will.
Tony	Thank you. You are doing me a big favor.

Tony： 王小姐，妳現在有空嗎？

Miss Wang： 有啊。你需要幫忙嗎？

Tony： 請妳幫忙聯絡名單上的人，並確認他們是否會出席明晚的活動。

Miss Wang： 沒問題。

Tony： 順便幫我把出席人數告知林先生。

Miss Wang： 好，我會的。

Tony： 謝啦，真是幫了我大忙。

一般公事

這個企劃案由你負責。	You're in charge of this project. ◎ in charge of = 負責。 同 be responsible for。
你的企劃進行得怎樣了？	How's your project going?
一切還好嗎？	Is everything OK?
一切都在掌握之中嗎？	Is everything under control? ◎ under control = 掌控之中。 反 out of control = 失控。
你明天去談代理權的事宜。	You're going to negotiate the distribution right tomorrow. ◎ negotiate (v.) = 協商、洽談。
這次一定要拿到代理權。	You have to get the distribution right this time.
我會教你談代理權的技巧。	I will teach you some skills to negotiate the distribution right.
有問題可以請問王秘書。	If you have any questions, please ask the secretary Ms. Wang.
如果有任何問題請馬上和我聯絡。	If you have any problems, please contact me immediately. ◎ If you have any questions/problems, please …= 如果有任何問題請…。
請將客戶名單全部列出來。	Please make a list of all of our clients. ◎ make a list of = 列出清單。

請把資料統整成圖表。	Please put the data into a chart. ◎ chart (n.) = 圖表。 同 graph。
有空請把檔案整理好。	Please organize the files when you have time.
這些文件要在今天下午兩點前整理好。	These documents need to be ready by 2 this afternoon.
請把這些文件全部列印出來。	Please print all of the documents out. 黑白還是彩色的？ In black and white or in color? 單面還是雙面？ Single-sided or double-sided?
請在所有文件上簽名，下午五點前交給我。	Please sign all these documents and have them ready for me by 5pm. 沒問題。我會照做。 No problem. I'll do that. 恐怕有困難。 I'm afraid that will be difficult. 會延遲一點時間。 It will be a little late.
請在星期一前將資料補齊。	Please have all the materials complete by Monday. ◎ by (prep.) = 在…之前。 ★ complete 可以換成 ready。
你打錯太多字了。	You made too many typos. ◎ typo (n.) = 打錯字、筆誤。

資料不齊全。	The data [is / are] insufficient. The file is not complete. ◎ insufficient (a.) = 不足的 。 反 sufficient (a.) = 充足的。
這些數據有問題。	There's a problem with these numbers.
你犯了很嚴重的錯。	You made a huge mistake. ★ make 動詞三態： make-made-made。和 make 相關的片語：make a mistake = 犯錯；make a decision = 做決定；make a friend = 交朋友；make up = 化妝。
我們的活動安排好了嗎？	Are our activities all planned out? 恐怕還沒。 I'm afraid not. 文 *be afraid of + N/Ving = 害怕…。* 一切都準備就緒了。 Yes, everything is ready.
我明天把申請表交給你。	I'll give you the application tomorrow.
你的檔案都放哪裡？	Where do you keep your files?
請在簽呈上簽名。	I need your signature for approval on the proposal.
上班請專心一點。	Please focus when you're at work.
你要懂職場倫理。	You should follow the career ethics. ◎ career (n.) = 職業。 ◎ ethics (n.) = 倫理、道德。

必須要看是誰負責。

We need to see who is responsible for this.

◎ be responsible for = 為…負責。

處裡公事要注意簽名和聯絡人的部分，以免發生問題時找不到負責人。

請求支援幫忙

你下星期一能代理我的職務嗎？

Can you fill in for me next Monday?
Can you be the substitute for me next Monday?

◎ fill in for someone = be the substitute for someone = 代理某人的職務。

你下星期一能幫我代班嗎？

Can you take my shift next Monday?

◎ take one's shift = 代班。

- 當然可以。
  Of course.
- 好阿，如果你請我喝飲料的話。
  OK. If you buy me a drink.
- 我那天有事。
  Sorry, but I have something going on that day.
- 我不確定。
  I'm not sure.
- 看情形再說。
  We'll have to see.

我們這裡人手不足。

We don't have enough people working here.

你可以調派幾個人幫忙嗎？	Can you send some people over to help?
這些資料可以幫我印五份嗎？	Can you make five copies of these materials?
可以幫我列印嗎？	Can you print it out ?
可以幫我打這份文件嗎？	Can you type up this document for me?
可以幫我修正我的英文嗎？	Can you help me correct my English? ◎ correct (v.) = 訂正。
幫我把這封電子郵件翻成英文。	Help me translate this email into English. ◎ translate (v.) = 翻譯。translate…into… = 將…翻成…。
請幫我寄這份文件。	Please help me mail this document.
麻煩你幫我傳真這封信。	Please fax this letter for me.
有電話請幫我接一下。	Please help me with the phones for a while.
請幫我聯絡這幾個同事。	Please help me contact these coworkers. 文 *help + 人 + (to) + Vr = 幫某人做某事，to 可以省略。help + 人 + with + 物 = 在…方面給予協助。*

麻煩你打掃一下會議室。

Please clean up the conference room.

◎ clean up = 打掃。

請別人幫忙要注意禮貌，明明需要幫忙態度卻很差的話，小心沒人想幫你喔。

主動伸出援手

需要幫忙嗎？

Do you need a hand?

Do you need any help?

有什麼我能幫忙的嗎？

Is there anything I can do for you?

謝謝你。麻煩你幫我聯絡客戶。
Thank you. I'd appreciate it if you could help me contact the clients.

謝謝，真是幫了大忙。
Thanks. That would be a great help!

多謝啦，但不用了！
Thanks a lot, but that's ok.

謝謝你的關心，但不用了。
Thank you for asking, but I'm fine.

這主意不錯，但我可以自己來。
Nice thought, but I can handle it myself.

如果需要幫忙請儘管說。

Feel free to let me know if you need any help.

好，我會的。
OK, I will.

主動幫忙的前提是手邊的工作已經完成，別熱心過頭忘了自己該做的事喔。

練習問題

選擇題　請選出正確的答案。

A)	take my shift	F)	keep your files
B)	send; over	G)	signature for approval
C)	clean up	H)	typos
D)	in charge of	I)	under control
E)	type up	J)	contact me

1. 一切都在掌握之中嗎？

   Is everything ________ ?

2. 麻煩你打掃一下會議室。

   Please ________ the conference room.

3. 這個企劃案由你負責。

   You're ________ this project.

4. 這些資料請在今天下午兩點前打好。

   Please ________ these data by 2pm today.

5. 你下星期一能幫我代班嗎？

   Can you ________ next Monday?

6. 你可以調派幾個人幫忙嗎？

   Can you ________ some people ________ to help?

7. 如果你有任何問題，請和我聯絡。

   If you have any problems, please ________ .

8. 你的檔案都放哪裡呢？

Where do you ________ ?

9. 請您在簽呈上簽名。

I need your ________ on the proposal.

10. 你打字錯多字了。

You made too many ________ .

單字填空 請填入適當的單字。

1. 幫我把這封電子郵件翻成英文。

Help me ________ this email into English.

2. 你可以幫我校正英文嗎？

Can you help me ________ my English?

3. 幫我聯絡這幾個同事。

Help me ________ these coworkers.

4. 請將客戶名單全部列出來。

Please ________ of all of our clients.

5. 把這些資料全部列印出來。

Print all of the ________ out.

6. 記得跟人資部聯絡。

________ to contact human resources.

7. 請把資料統整成圖表。

Please put the ________ into a chart/graph.

8. 你犯了很嚴重的錯。

You made a huge ________ .

9. 恐怕有困難。

I'm afraid that will be ________ .

10. 你需要支援嗎？

Do you need my ________ ?

• 答案 •

Ⓐ 單字填空

① I	⑥ B
② C	⑦ J
③ D	⑧ F
④ E	⑨ G
⑤ A	⑩ H

Ⓐ 單字填空

① translate	⑥ Remember
② correct	⑦ data
③ contact	⑧ mistake
④ make a list	⑨ difficult
⑤ documents	⑩ support

將心比心

人與人之間的情誼是慢慢累積的，與其成天勾心鬥角，不如和睦相處，為彼此帶來正面的影響。平日多關心同事，若對方需要支援，記得適時伸出援手，或許會在過程中發現自己的不足或學到新的事物。當你忙不過來或無法處理某件事時，也別害怕開口請人幫忙。只要你是誠懇又有禮貌的詢問，相信大部分的人都很願意幫忙的。得到同事的幫忙後也別忘了說聲謝謝喔！

工作分際

例行工作

上班打卡	punch in
下班打卡	punch out
影印	copy
列印	print
掃描	scan
傳真	fax
寄件	send
整理	organize
把～歸檔	file
打成（電子檔）	type up

各類文件

合約書	contract
文件	document
資料	data / material
企劃書	proposal
報告	report
提綱	handout
估價單	estimate
報價單	quotation
訂單	order form
收據	receipt
帳單	bill
發票	invoice
影本	copy
申請書	application

Part 5

商業往來

Business Relationships

商業往來

BUSINESS RELATIONSHIPS　MP3 005

情境會話

客戶公司　客戶　拜訪客戶

Monica	Hi, this is Monica from DT Company. Nice to meet you.
Kevin	Nice to meet you, too.
Monica	I am here to introduce our company's new products. As my e-mail mentioned......
Kevin	I've read the information and proposal you sent to me. I think your products are great, but I don't think now is a good time to discuss the matter of purchasing new products. We don't have enough in the budget.
Monica	OK. Maybe next time. Thank you for your time.

Monica：您好，我是 DT 公司的 Monica。很高興見到您。

Kevin：　我也很高興見到您。

Monica：我來拜訪是為了介紹敝公司的新產品。如同 E-mail 上提到的……

Kevin：　你寄來的資料和提案我已經看過了。我認為你們產品很棒。但我認為現在不是討論購買產品的時機。我們沒有足夠的預算。

Monica：沒關係。也許下一次。謝謝您寶貴的時間。

關係發展

我們曾在上星期致函貴公司。

We had correspondence with you last week.

◎ correspondence (n.) = 聯繫、通信。

我們的產品以電器為主。

Our products are mainly electric appliances.

◎ electric appliance (n.) = 電器。

我們在這行已經三十年了。

We have been in this line of business for 30 years already.

我們想知道能不能和貴公司建立貿易關係。

We'd like to find out if we can establish a business relationship with you.

◎ establish (v.) = 建立。

我們希望和貴公司建立合作關係。

We hope to establish a partnership with you.

◎ partnership (n.) = 合作關係。

您是從哪裡得知本公司的呢？

How did you hear about us?

經由網路。
From the Internet.

經由報紙。
From the newspaper.

經由電視。
From TV.

經由其他公司推薦。
Other companies have recommended you to me.

	經由孫先生的介紹。 Mr. Sun introduced you to me. 我們是透過趙先生得知貴公司的電話。 We got your phone number from Mr. Zhao.
我們雙方想要建立業務關係的想法相同。	We both have ideas about establishing our business relationship.
我方願意和貴公司展開貿易。	We are willing to have trade agreements with you. ◎ be willing to = 願意⋯。
我們很樂意和貴公司發展合作關係。	We are pleased to start a partnership with you.
我們很期待與貴公司建立良好的業務關係。	We look forward to entering into a good business relationship with you.

發展關係是很重要的，用字遣詞上請特別注意，避免造成對方的反感。

拜訪客戶 & 客戶來訪：在接待處

您好，我是 DT 公司的山姆。	Hi, I'm Sam from DT Company.
請問史密斯先生在嗎？	May I speak to Mr. Smith?
我和史密斯先生約好下午 1 點見面。	I had an appointment with Mr. Smith at 1pm.

不好意思，可以請您出示證件嗎？	Excuse me, can you show me your ID card? ◎ ID = identification 的縮寫。
請稍候，我幫您確認一下。	Wait a moment, please. Let me check it for you.
史密斯先生在開會，麻煩您稍等一下。	Mr. Smith is in a meeting right now. Could you please wait a second? ★ S +be+ in a meeting = 某人在開會。
請跟我來，史密斯先生已經在 2 樓的會議室等您了。	Please come this way. Mr. Smith is waiting for you in the meeting room on the second floor. ★ Please come this way. 也可以說 Please follow me.

拜訪客戶時，要有耐心和禮貌，就連對待櫃檯接待人員也不例外。千萬不要讓對方感到壓力，否則下次再訪時，可能會吃閉門羹喔。

拜訪客戶 & 客戶來訪：初次見面

史密斯先生，很高興見到您，我是山姆 。	Mr. Smith , nice to meet you. I am Sam William.
我也很高興見到您。	Nice to meet you, too ★ nice to meet you 用於初見面、不熟的人。
請坐請坐。	Please have a seat. ★也可以說 Please take a seat，但是 have a seat 比較友善。

我來拜訪是為了向您說明合作企劃案的事。	I'm here to explain to you the collaborative project. 文 *I am here to+Vr = 我為了做…而來。* ◎ explain (v.) = 說明、解釋。
我來拜訪是為了介紹敝公司的新產品。	I'm here to introduce our company's new products.
如同 E-mail 中和您提過的…	As my e-mail mentioned before…
如同電話裡和您提過的…	As I mentioned on the phone before…
請考慮一下我的提案。	Please consider my proposal. ◎ proposal (n.) = 提案。
經過考慮，我們決定接受貴公司的提案。	After consideration, we've decided to accept your proposal.

> 討論提案時，要注意自己的用詞和態度。尤其是面對初次見面的對象，謙沖有禮的態度，對方才會願意傾聽你慢慢介紹。

代理權限：我方為製造商時

感謝您來信表示想成為本公司在澳洲的代理商。	Thank you for the e-mail in which you express your desire to act as our agent in Australia. ◎ act as = 擔任。
我負責洽談代理權。	I am responsible for negotiating the agency. ◎ agency (n.) = 代理權。

請說明貴公司成為本公司代理商的優勢。	Please tell us your advantages to become our agent. 我們經驗豐富。 We have a lot of experience. ◎ experience (n.) = 經驗。 我們的行銷策略很成功。 Our marketing strategies are successful. 我們在許多國家都有分公司。 We have branches in many countries. ◎ branch = 分公司。

代理商很重要，一定要慎選。

代理權限：對方為製造商時

我聽說貴公司正在找代理商。	I heard that you are currently looking for an agent. ◎ look for = 尋找。 ◎ currently (ad.) = 目前。
貴公司在台灣並沒有代理商。	You don't have an agent in Taiwan.
我們希望能拿到獨家代理權。	We hope we can acquire the exclusive agency. ◎ acquire (v.) = 得到、獲得。 ◎ exclusive (a.) = 獨家的。
我們對於成為貴公司的代理商很感興趣。	We are very interested in becoming an agent for you.

我們可以擔任貴公司在台灣的代理商。	We can act as your agent in Taiwan.
我們希望成為貴公司在法國的獨家代理商。	We hope to become your exclusive agent in France.
我們很樂意成為貴公司的銷售代理商。	We are pleased to become a sales representative for you. ◎ sales representative = 銷售代理。
我們可為貴公司拓展出口商品至美國的業務。	We can extend your export business to the U.S. ◎ extend (v.) = 擴大、擴張。 ◎ export (n.) = 出口。
敝公司在業界有多年經驗，足以為貴公司提供在台灣的代理服務。	We've been in this line of business for many years, so we can offer our services as your agent in Taiwan.
本公司在這方面已經建立良好關係，可以擔任貴公司在加拿大的代理商。	Our company has already established a network of good contacts, so we can take on the responsibility of becoming your representative office in Canada.
如果你能讓我們銷售貴公司產品，我們會讓您很滿意。	If you let us sell your company's products, I think you will be very satisfied with our company.

想要爭取代理權，除了做足功課表現誠意之外，也別忘了說明公司的優勢，給對方一個非選擇你們不可的理由。

代理權限：決定代理商

我們決定委託貴公司成為我們在日本的總代理。	We have decided to commission you to act as our general agent in Japan. ◎ general agent (n.) = 總代理。
我們指定貴公司為我方在巴西為期三年的代理商。	We have appointed you as our agent in Brazil for a period of 3 years.
很抱歉，我們已經找到代理商了。	I apologize but we have already found an agent. ◎ I apologize … = 很抱歉 … 。
我們認為現在不是討論代理權的時機。	We don't think that now is a good time to discuss the matter of the agency.
事實上，我們認為現在簽定代理協議時間太早了。	Honestly, we think that it is too early to sign the distribution agreement now.

> 經營公司不容易，負面新聞卻能在瞬間能讓努力白費，千萬要慎選代理商，以維護良好的形象。

其他商務常用句

歡迎參觀本公司。	Welcome to our company.
明天早上八點我會到貴公司拜訪。	I'll go visit your office at 8 tomorrow morning.

我要和負責人談。	I want to talk to the person in charge.
商場如戰場。	The market is like a battlefield.
我們要互信才能合作。	We have to have mutual trust to form a partnership in the business. ◎ mutual (a.) = 互相的。 ◎ form (v.) = 養成；組成。
品質勝於數量。	Quality is over quantity. ★ quality (n.) = 質量。quantity (n.) = 數量。兩個長得很像，別搞混囉。
我們的競爭對手很強。	Our competitors are really strong.
本公司有競爭優勢。	We have a competitive edge.
本公司將推出自有品牌。	We are going to come out with our own brand.

> 商務上有些常用的句子，不妨將它們背熟，需要時就能順口說出來，增加專業感。

"There is no substitute for hard work."

— Thomas A. Edison

「努力沒有替代品。」～湯瑪斯 · 愛迪生（發明家）

練習問題

選擇題　請選出正確的答案。

A) responsible for	F) act as
B) an agent for	G) marketing strategies
C) come out with	H) in charge
D) looking for	I) something wrong with
E) become our agent	J) exclusive agency

1. 我負責洽談代理權。

   I am ________ negotiating the agency.

2. 請說明貴公司成為本公司代理商的優勢。

   Please tell us your advantages to ________ .

3. 希望我們公司能拿到獨家代理權。

   I hope we can acquire the ________ .

4. 我聽說貴公司正在找代理商。

   I heard that you are currently ________ an agent.

5. 我們的行銷策略很成功。

   Our ________ are successful.

6. 敝公司可以擔任貴公司在台灣的代理商。

   We can ________ your agent in Taiwan.

7. 敝公司對於成為貴公司代理商很感興趣。

   We are very interested in becoming ________ you.

8. 這個商品的報價有問題。

There is _________ the quotation of this product.

9. 我要和你們負責人談。

I want to talk to the person _________ .

10. 我們公司將推出自有品牌。

We are going to _________ our own brand.

單字填空 請填入適當的單字。

1. 我來拜訪是為了向您說明合作企劃案的事。

_________ explain to you the collaborative project.

2. 敝公司希望和貴公司建立合作關係。

We hope to _________ a partnership with you.

3. 貴公司在台灣並沒有代理商。

You don't have an _________ in Taiwan.

4. 我們決定委託貴公司成為我們在日本的總代理。

We have decided to commission you to act as our _________ agent in Japan.

5. 我們希望成為貴公司在法國的獨家代理商。

We hope to become your _________ agent in France.

6. 很抱歉，我們已經找到代理商了。

I _________ but we have already found an agent.

7. 我們指定貴公司為我方在巴西為期三年的代理商。

We have _________ you as our agent in Brazil for a period of 3 years.

8. 敝公司在業界有多年經驗，足以為貴公司提供在台灣的代理服務。

We have been in this line of business for many years, so we can ________ our services as your agent in Taiwan.

9. 請考慮一下我的提案。

Please ________ my proposal.

10. 本公司決定接受貴公司的提案。

We have decided to ________ your proposal.

• 答案 •

Ⓐ 單字填空

① A	⑥ F
② E	⑦ B
③ J	⑧ I
④ D	⑨ H
⑤ G	⑩ C

Ⓐ 單字填空

① I'm here to	⑥ apologize
② establish	⑦ appointed
③ agent	⑧ offer
④ general	⑨ consider
⑤ exclusive	⑩ accpet

做足功課，保持良好的態度

任何的合作與買賣關係都是互相的，你挑選對方，對方也挑選你。因此，事先做好功課再出擊，讓對方感受到誠意，了解彼此講的是一樣的語言，才有機會展開更深入的討論，進而放心展開後續的交流與合作。另外，商場上沒有永遠的敵人或朋友，無論是陌生開發、初次拜訪客戶，或是長期合作的熟客，洽談生意時除了基本的禮貌，請隨時保持良好、誠懇的態度，千萬別因為短期內沒有合作機會，臉就整個垮下來或者態度轉變，一個不小心可是會影響到將來雙方的發展。

商業往來

相關名詞

代理權	agency	市場	market
代理商	agent	分公司	branch
總代理商	general agent	品牌	brand
獨家代理商	exclusive agent	產品	product
銷售代理	sales representative	商品	goods
經銷商	distributor	品質	quality
零售商	retailer	數量	quantity
批發商	wholesaler	合作關係	partnership
採購	buyer	競爭者	competitor
採購	purchasing agent	競爭優勢	competitive edge

相關動詞

建立	establish	做為…	act as
討論	discuss	出口	export
協商	negotiate	進口	import
獲得	acquire	採購	buy
委任	commission	採購	purchase

Part 6

合約事宜

Contracts

合約事宜

CONTRACTS

MP3 006

情境會話

辦公室 同事 簽約前夕

Jennifer	We're going signing a contract tomorrow. I am so nervous.
Peter	Why are you nervous?
Jennifer	This is the first time I've signed a contract that is worth so much money.
Peter	Calm down. If you read carefully and make sure about all the details, everything will be fine.
Jennifer	I am still worried about it. Can you read the contract for me?
Peter	I do want to give you a hand, but I am kind of busy. Maybe Wendy can help you.
Jennifer	OK. Thanks a lot.

Jennifer：明天就要簽約了，好緊張。
Peter：有什麼好緊張？
Jennifer：這是我第一次簽這麼大筆的合約。
Peter：冷靜點，只要你仔細閱讀並確認過所有細節，一切會很順利。
Jennifer：我還是不太放心…可以請你幫我看一下合約嗎？
Peter：我也想幫你，但我在忙。也許溫蒂能幫你。
Jennifer：好，謝啦！

與客戶簽約

你有合約範本嗎？	Do you have any sample agreements?
我們可以先草擬一份合約。	We can first draft a contract. ◎ draft (v.) = 打草稿。draft a contract = 草擬合約。
這份草約煩請過目。	Please look over this draft contract.
我們有足夠時間來協商。	We have plenty of time to negotiate. ◎ negotiate (v.) = 協商、談判。
關於這份草約，我有幾點看法。	I have a few concerns about the draft contract.
日期方面有問題。	There is a problem with the dates.
合約的生效日要在成立以後。	The effective date should be after we agree on the contract.
出貨量要再斟酌。	The quantity of shipments must be reconsidered carefully. ◎ reconsider (v.) = 重新思考。
違約金的部分我們要再商量。	We will have to discuss the breach penalty. ◎ penalty (n.) = 罰款。
違約會有什麼處罰嗎？	Are there any penalties for breaking the contract? ◎ break the contract = 違約。 💬 會有 [違約金 / 罰款]。 There's a [penalty charge / fine / forfeit.]

這份合約並不合理。

This contract is unreasonable.

◎ unreasonable (a.) = 不合理的。

這份合約是有效的。

This contract is valid.

◎ valid (a.) = 有效的。

請簽訂這份合約。

Please sign the contract.

合約內容有任何問題或不合理的地方，務必在簽約之前確認清楚，以免權益受損。

注意事項

合約不一定要書面的。

The contract doesn't have to be in written form.

◎ written form = 書面形式。

口頭契約也有效力。

A verbal contract is also in effect.

◎ verbal (a.) = 口頭的。

◎ in effect = 有（法律）效力。

合約通常是一式兩份。

Contracts are usually in duplicate.

◎ in duplicate = 一式兩份。

合約簽訂日即為合約生效日。

The date we sign the contract is the effective date.

◎ offective (a.) =（法律、合約等）生效的。

合約期限通常是一年。

Usually contracts are valid for one year.

◎ be valid for + 時間 = 有效期限為⋯。

簽約時要注意什麼？

What should I be careful of when signing the contract?

一定要仔細閱讀合約內容。
You have to read the content of the contract carefully.
◎ carefully (ad.) = 仔細地。

反覆確認合約上的日期。
Double check the dates of the contract.
◎ double check = 反覆確認。

看清楚頭期款。
You have to make sure of the down payment.
◎ down payment (n.) = 頭期款。

注意賠償金的條款部分。
Note the penalty clauses.

確認已經簽名蓋章。
Make sure it's signed and stamped with the chops.

仔細地確認過合約內容無誤後，就可以簽約了。

"Successful people are always looking for opportunities to help others. Unsuccessful people are always asking, 'What's in it for me?'"

– Brian Tracy, Motivational Coach

「成功的人總是在找幫忙別人的機會，失敗的人總是在問：『對我有什麼好處？』」
～ 布萊恩 · 崔西 (勵志教練)

練習問題

選擇題　請選出正確的答案。

A)	breach penalty	F)	unreasonable
B)	look over	G)	sign the agreement
C)	penalty clauses	H)	quantity of shipments
D)	plenty of time	I)	a problem with
E)	sample agreements	J)	a few concerns

1. 違約金的部分我們要再商量。

   We will have to discuss the ________ .

2. 你有合約範本嗎？

   Do you have any ________ ?

3. 我們有足夠時間來協商。

   We have ________ to negotiate.

4. 要注意賠償金的條款部分。

   Note the ________ .

5. 這份合約煩請過目。

   Please ________ this contract.

6. 請簽訂這份合約。

   Please ________ .

7. 出貨量要再斟酌。

   The ________ must be reconsidered carefully.

8. 這份合約並不合理。

This agreement is ________ .

9. 關於合約，我有幾點看法。

I have ________ about the agreement.

10. 日期方面有問題。

There is ________ the dates.

單字填空 請填入適當的單字。

1. 合約期限通常是一年。

Usually contracts are ________ for one year.

2. 合約內容一定要仔細閱讀。

You have to read the content of the contract ________ .

3. 合約不一定要書面的。

The contract doesn't have to be in ________ form.

4. 合約簽訂日即為合約生效日。

The date we sign the contract is the ________ date.

5. 簽約時要注意什麼？

What should I be careful of when signing the ________ ?

6. 要反覆確認合約書上的日期。

________ check the dates of the contract.

7. 要看清楚頭期款。

You have to make sure of the ________ .

8. 違約會有什麼罰款嗎？

Are there any penalties for ________ the contract?

9. 口頭契約也有效力。

A ________ contract is also in effect.

10. 合約通常是一式兩份。

Contracts are usually in ________ .

• 答案 •

A 單字填空

① A　⑥ G

② E　⑦ H

③ D　⑧ F

④ C　⑨ J

⑤ B　⑩ I

A 單字填空

① valid　⑥ Double

② carefully　⑦ down payment

③ written　⑧ breaking

④ effective　⑨ verbal

⑤ contract　⑩ duplicate

騎縫章

騎縫章指的是蓋在文件騎縫處的印章，通常用於合約書、政府機關的公文等重要文件，目的是防止內容造假或被任意竄改。

騎縫章怎麼蓋呢？基本上沒有硬性規定。文件頁數不多的話，整份攤開蓋一個跨過每頁邊縫的章即可；若文件很厚，則每隔幾頁蓋個騎縫章，直到蓋完整本為止。雖然沒有明文規定，但為了謹慎起見，在重要的公文或契約上加蓋鋼印或騎縫章也算是多一層保障。

合約事宜

合約常見單字

協議書	agreetment
合約	contract
日期	date
姓名	name
簽訂	sign
有效的	valid
頭期款	down payment
違約	breach
罰款	penalty
一式兩份	in duplicate
一式三份	in triplicate
一式四份	in quadruplicate
署名欄	signature
附件	exhibit / appendix
定義條款	Definition Clauses
保密條款	Confidentiality Clauses
不可抗力	Force Majeure
契約效期	Term
契約期滿前之終止	Termination Before Expiration
契約終止之影響	Effects of Termination
契約存續條款	Survival Provisions
契約讓渡	Assignment
完全合意	Entire Agreement
準據法	Governing Law
權利放棄	Waiver
紛爭及仲裁	Dispute and Arbitration
裁判管轄	Jurisdiction
可分離性	Severability

memo

Part 7

管理與行銷

Management & Marketing

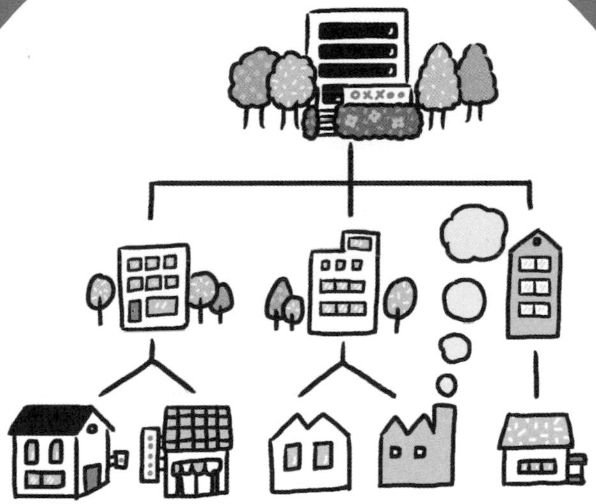

管理與行銷

MANAGEMENT & MARKETING

MP3 007

情境會話

辦公室　上司　與上司對話

Abby	What do you think of management?
Ken	Management is a specialized field.
Abby	How is it possible to be a qualified manager?
Ken	Managers should be in charge of cost control and have good problem solving skills.
Abby	Anything else?
Ken	Managers need to work hard to keep their employees happy enough to stay with the company.
Abby	Exactly! By the way, I have a good news for you. You will be promoted next month.

Abby：你認為管理是什麼？
Ken：管理是一門學問。
Abby：好的管理者需要具備何種條件？
Ken：管理者應該要控制成本和具備良好的問題解決能力。
Abby：還有呢？
Ken：想要留住員工，管理者要用心。
Abby：沒錯。對了，告訴你一個好消息。你下個月將升職了。

經營與管理

經理在公司的管理經驗已經超過十年了。	The manager has over 10 years of management experience here. 文 *數字 + year (s) + of + … + experience = 有…年…的經驗。*
你覺得經理的管理技巧如何？	What do you think of the manager's management skills? ◎What do you think of … = 你對…的看法是？ 他管理得很好。 He's a good manager. 他不太會管理。 He's not good at managing people. 太古板了。 Too outdated. ◎ outdated (a.) = 古板的、過時的。 管理方面太鬆散。 Management is too lax. ◎ lax (a.) = 鬆散的。
管理是一門學問。	Management is a specialized field.
如果管理不好，公司運作會出問題。	If the management is bad, it will create problems for the company.
管理者應該要控制成本。	Managers should be in charge of cost control. ◎ cost control = 控制成本。
管理者應具備良好的問題解決能力。	Managers should have good problem solving skills. ◎ skill (n.) = 技巧。

主管級要多用心在管理方面。	Directors need to spend more energy on management.
主管級要多閱讀管理方面的書籍。	Directors should read more books on management.
想要留住員工，管理者要用心。	Managers need to work hard to keep their employees happy to stay with the company.
事業策略會影響公司績效。	Business strategy will affect the company's performance. ◎ affect (v.) = 影響。 ◎ performance (n.) = 表現、成果。
管理有很多種類。	There are many forms of management.
人力資源必須有效管理。	Human resources must be effective in management. ◎ human resources = 人力資源，簡稱 RH。
人力資源管理包括協調部分。	Human resource management includes coordination.
人資管理可以將人力加以組織運用。	Human resources management can arrange manpower and utilize it well.
不能忽視顧客關係管理。	Customer relationship management should not be overlooked. ◎ overlook (v.) = 忽略；眺望。
顧客關係管理可以讓客人們覺得受到重視。	Customer relationship management can make clients feel important.

知識管理有助於員工減少失誤。	Knowledge management can help employees reduce errors.
流程管理可以減少的員工疑惑。	Process management can reduce employees' confusion.
時間管理有助於提高員工效率。	Time management helps improve employee's efficiency. ◎ improve (v.) = 提高。
成本管理能夠減少不必要的支出。	Cost management can reduce unnecessary expenditures.
永續經營是很好的理念。	Sustainable management is a good concept. ◎ sustainable (a.) = 永續的。
好的想法才能使公司進步成長。	Good concepts lead to the growth of the company. ◎ concept (n.) = 想法、概念。
多角化經營可以讓企業蓬勃發展。	Running a business means needing to innovate constantly. ◎ innovate (v.) = 改革、創新。
在經營方面，重視人才很重要。	It's important to value employees' talents when it comes to managing. ◎ when it comes to... = 談論到…。
老闆應該要了解誰是關鍵性人才。	The boss should understand who the key personnel are.
本公司的理念是強調價格低廉。	Our principle is to keep prices low.

請想出本公司的口號。	Please come up with a slogan for our company. ◎ slogan (n.) = 口號。 ◎ come up with… = 想出…；跟上。
本公司的經營理念是：責任和態度。	Our philosophy of business is duty and attitude. ◎ philosophy = 哲學、理念。Our philosophy of business is…= 我們的經營理念是…。My philosophy of life is… = 我的人生觀是…。

經營理念很重要，通常會影響企業的發展方向。

行銷策略

行銷有最重要的 4P。	In marketing, there are four Ps that are the most important elements. ★ 4P 指的是 Product（產品）、Price（價格）、Place（通路）和 Promotion（促銷）。
我們的廣告和行銷很成功。	Our advertising and marketing are really successful.
明天請把行銷企劃書給我看。	Please give me the marketing proposal tomorrow.
你覺得哪種行銷方式最有效？	What kind of marketing methods do you think are the most effective?
我覺得傳統行銷方式已經落伍了。	I think traditional marketing methods are already outdated.

行銷策略有哪幾種？	What kinds of marketing strategies are there in practice? ◎ What kinds of …? =…有哪幾種？ 網路行銷。 Internet marketing. ★也可以說 E-marketing 或 Online marketing。 電視行銷。 TV marketing. 報紙行銷。 Newspaper marketing. 置入性行銷。 Product placement.
最近很流行網路行銷。	Lately Internet marketing is really popular. ◎ lately (ad.) = 最近。
網路行銷的方式很多元。	Internet marketing methods are really diverse. ◎ diverse (a.) = 多樣化的。
我認為你的行銷企劃書不適合。	I don't think your marketing proposal is appropriate.
你的產品定位不明。	The orientation of your product is not clear enough. ◎ orientation (n.) = 定位。

告訴我行銷企劃書分為哪些重點。	Tell me what points is the marketing proposal split into. ◎ spill into = 分成…。 整體環境。 Overall environment. 競爭優劣勢。 Competitive advantages and disadvantages. ◎ advantage (n.) = 優勢 。 反 disadvantage = 劣勢。 產品特色。 The products features. 產品策略。 Product strategies. 目標市場。 Target market. 市場區隔。 Market segmentation. 通路策略。 Distribution channels. 行銷計劃。 Marketing plan.
請把銷售統計表寄給我。	Please e-mail me the sales data.
下星期一之前把價格策略擬好。	Get your pricing strategy ready by next Monday.
跟我報告你的行銷策略。	Report to me regarding your marketing strategies. ◎ regarding (prep.) = 關於。
想一些企業公關活動。	Plan some public relations activities. ◎ plan (v.) = 計畫。

記得發布新聞稿。	Remember to issue the press release. ◎ issue (v.) = 發佈、發行。
誰負責籌劃活動？	Who's in charge of the activity arrangement?

有人說行銷已經從 4P 變成 5P，而第五 P 指的正是消費者，可見消費者是行銷方面非常重要的一環。

Good management consists in showing average people how to do the work of superior people"

– John D. Rockefeller, industrialist

「好的管理主要在於展現一般人如何做傑出人所做的事。」
～ 約翰 · 洛克斐勒（工業家）

練習問題

選擇題 請選出正確的答案。

A) Customer relationship	F) press release
B) specialized field	G) innovate constantly
C) marketing proposal	H) features of products
D) company's performance	I) problem solving skills
E) cost control	J) orientation of your product

1. 經營事業要不斷革新。
   Running a business means needing to ________ .

2. 你的產品定位不明。
   The ________ is not clear enough.

3. 記得發布新聞稿。
   Remember to issue the ________ .

4. 經營管理是一門學問。
   Management is a ________ .

5. 他不瞭解產品特色。
   He doesn't understand the ________ .

6. 管理者應該要控制成本。
   Managers should be in charge of ________ .

7. 管理者應具備良好的問題解決能力。
   Managers should have good ________ .

8. 事業策略會影響公司績效。

Business strategy will affect the ________ .

9. 顧客關係管理也不能忽視。

________ management should not be overlooked.

10. 明天請把行銷企劃書給我看。

Please give me the ________ tomorrow.

單字填空 請填入適當的單字。

1. 在經營方面，重視員工的才能很重要。

It's important to ________ employees' talents when it comes to managing.

2. 經理在公司的管理經驗已經超過十年了。

The manager has over 10 years of management ________ here.

3. 流程管理可以讓員工減少疑惑。

Process management reduces employees' ________ .

4. 我覺得傳統行銷方式已經落伍了。

I think ________ marketing methods are already outdated.

5. 最近很流行網路行銷。

Lately Internet marketing is really ________ .

6. 關係管理可以讓顧客覺得受到重視。

Customer ________ management can make clients feel important.

7. 好的理念才能使公司進步成長。

Good ________ lead to the growth of the company.

8. 請提出本公司理念的口號。

Please come up with a ________ for our company.

9. 成本管理可以減少不必要的支出。

Cost management can reduce ________ expenditures.

10. 時間管理可以提高員工效率。

Time management helps ________ employee's efficiency.

• 答案 •

Ⓐ 單字填空

① G ⑥ E

② J ⑦ I

③ F ⑧ D

④ B ⑨ A

⑤ H ⑩ C

Ⓐ 單字填空

① value ⑥ relationship

② experience ⑦ concepts

③ confusion ⑧ slogan

④ traditional ⑨ unnecessary

⑤ popular ⑩ improve

知人善任

管理者不用樣樣通，但一定要懂得知人善任。一個好的管理者平常應該多觀察員工，了解每個人的價值，並適時給予導正或鼓勵。許多管理者習慣把所有事都交給心腹去做，拒絕聽取不同意見。這種風氣除了造成公司內部派系鬥爭，還會導致案子無法推動或停滯不前。時間久了，原本滿懷抱負的員工也會失去熱情，不敢再提出反對意見。唯有拋開個人好惡，依照各人能力分配工作，才能激發出不同火花，讓公司不斷成長。

管理與行銷

企業組織

集團	group
公司	company
小公司、事務所	firm
有限公司	corporation
控股公司	holding company
中小企業	small and medium-sized company
民營公司	private company
新創公司	startup company
關係企業	associated company
關係企業	affiliated company
合資公司	joint venture company
總公司、總店	headquarter / head office / main office
分公司、分店	branch
母公司	parent company
子公司	subsidiary
地方辦事處	regional office
分處辦公室	satellite office
聯絡處	liaison office
工廠	factory
工廠	plant
實驗室	laboratory

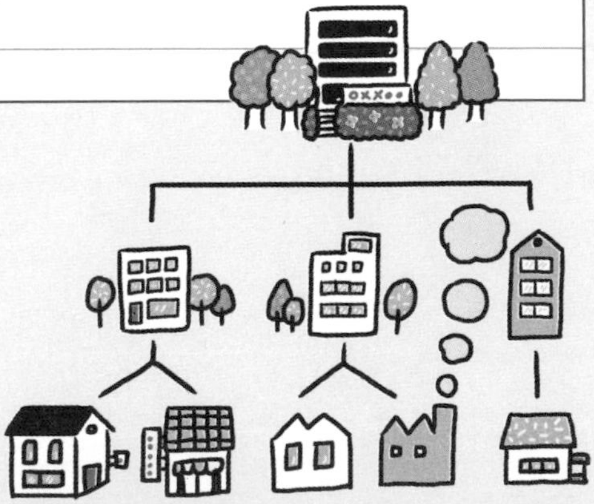

memo

Part 8

電話禮儀

Phone Etiquette

電話禮儀

PHONE ETIQUETTE

MP3 008

情境會話

客服中心　顧客　客訴電話

Staff	Thank you for calling the Customer Service Department. How may I help you?
Customer	Where are those books that you promised to send to me? You said those books would arrive within three days, but now it has been over two weeks. I don't want to wait anymore. Please refund my money.
Staff	I apologize for the inconvenience. We will deal with the problem immediately. What is your order number, please?
Customer	My order number is AB3333.
Staff	AB3333… OK, We will refund you the money in 24 hours. In addition, we will send you a preferential serial number to your email for compensation.

Staff：	客服部您好，請問需要什麼服務呢？
Customer：	你們說好要幫我補寄的書呢？當初跟我說 3 天內會送達，現在已經過 2 個禮拜了，我還沒收到。我不想等了，請退錢給我。
Staff：	很抱歉造成您的不便，我們立刻為您處理。方便請問您的訂單編號嗎？
Customer：	我的訂單編號是 AB3333。
Staff：	AB3333……好的，我們會在 24 小時內退款。為了補償您，我們會寄一組優惠序號至您的 Email，衷心期待您下次的購買。

接電話（1）

早安，這裡是 DT 公司。	Good morning. This is DT Company.
DT 公司您好，感謝您的來電。	Thank you for calling DT Company. ◎ Thank you for calling = 感謝您的來電。
有什麼可以為您服務的嗎？	How may I help you?
請問今天需要什麼服務呢？	How may I serve you today?
請問來電有什麼事？	May I ask what this call is regarding, please?
請問要找哪位？	Who would you like to speak to?
請問您貴姓大名？	May I have your name, please? May I ask who's calling, please? Who am I speaking to, please? I'm sorry, you're…?
請問您姓名的拼法嗎？	How do you spell your name, please?
可以請教貴公司的名稱嗎？	Could I have your company's name?
請問貴公司名字的拼法是？	Could you spell your company's name, please?
我再重複一次，是 C-O-M-E-T 嗎？	Let me repeat that. C-O-M-E-T. Is that right? ◎ Is that right? = 對嗎？

這裡有兩個馬克。請問他貴姓？	There are two Mark here. What's his last name? ◎ first name = given name= 名字。 ◎ last name = family name = surname = 姓氏。 💬 他姓史密斯。 His last name is Smith. 💬 我不清楚。 I'm not sure.
可以告訴我他的分機嗎？	Can you tell me his extension? ◎ extension (n.) = 分機。
請稍等，我看看她在不在。	Hold on. Let me see if he's here. ★ hold on 也有堅持的意思。
請稍等。我幫您把電話轉給他。	Please hold a moment. I'll put you through to him. ◎ put through = 轉接。
幫您轉接到分機 602。	I'll transfer your call to extension 602. ◎ transfer = 轉移。
請稍等。我幫您查一下經辦的部門。	Just one moment, please. I'll help you find out which department handles this sort of thing.
請稍等，幫您轉接給業務承辦人。	Hold on, please. Let me put you through to the person in charge.

某些公司行號會要求總機或接電話者在電話鈴響的三聲內接電話，才不會讓對方等太久。最好也避免電話一響就馬上接起，會太過倉促的感覺。

接電話（2）

我就是。	This is [she / he] speaking.
這裡是銷售部。我是溫蒂。	Sales Department. This is Wendy.
您好，我是這件事的負責人。	Hello. I'm in charge of that.
抱歉，讓您久等了。	I'm sorry for keeping you waiting.
很抱歉，一直沒有接到您的電話。	I'm very sorry that I keep missing your call. ◎ I'm very sorry that⋯ = 我很抱歉⋯。
請問今天有什麼事呢？	What can I do for you today?
很抱歉，我現在不方便講電話。	I'm very sorry, but I can't talk now.
我 10 分鐘後再回電好嗎？	Can I call you back in 10 minutes? 好，我等你的回電。 Fine. I'll be waiting. 沒問題，等等再談吧。 Sure. Talk to you later. ★ 熟人間傳訊息時，常會將 Talk to you later 縮寫成 TTYL。

電話接通後，要有禮貌地主動問好，接著再詢問對方需要什麼服務。

對方要找的人不在位子上

抱歉，他目前不在位子上。	I'm sorry, but he's not available at the moment.

他一分鐘後就回來，您要稍候嗎？	He'll be back in a minute. Do you want to hold? ◎ S + will be back in + 時間 = 某人…內會回來。
我想他快回來了，可以請您半小時後再來電嗎？	I think she'll be back soon. Could you call back in half an hour?
請問是急事嗎？	Is it urgent? ◎ urgent (a.) = 緊急的。
可以請您明天再打來嗎？	Would you mind calling again tomorrow?
他目前不方便接聽電話。	He can't come to the phone right now.
他現在電話中。	He's on the other line.
他正在開會。	He's in a meeting now.
他正在會客。	He has a visitor right now.
他出去吃午餐了。	He's out to lunch now.
他下班了。	He's already left for the day. He's already left the office for today.
他今天休假。	He's off today.
他今天請假。	He took the day off today.
他今天生病沒進公司。	He's sick today and not in the office.

王先生去出差，五天後才會回來。	Mr. Wang's on a business trip. He'll be back after 5 days. ◎ on a business trip = 出差。
他已經轉調其他部門。	He has been transferred to another department.
他已經離職了。	He's no longer with us.
王小姐接了他的職位。我幫您把電話轉給她。	Miss Wang took over his job; I'll transfer you to her.

對方要找的人不在時，應避免草草說聲「他不在喔。」就把電話掛斷，應該進一步詢問是否需要留言或回電，並留下對方的聯絡方式。

詢問是否需要留言或回電

請問您要留言嗎？	Would you like to leave a message?
請問需要他回電嗎？	Would you like him to call you back? ★ call you back 也可以換成 return your call。
他知道如何與您聯繫嗎？	Does he know how to get in touch with you? ◎ get in touch with … = 和…聯絡。
可以請您留下姓名與電話號碼嗎？	May I have your name and phone number?
很抱歉，我沒聽清楚您的電話號碼。	I'm sorry; I didn't catch your phone number.

我再確認一下您的電話號碼。	Let me confirm your phone number again. ◎ confirm (v.) = 確認。 ★請注意 confirm 的發音，很多人都會唸成 conform。
是 2012-3456 嗎？	It's 2012-3456, is that correct? ★ Is that correct? 是商用英語的常用句，若想更客氣，可以用 Would that be right?
我一定會轉告他。	I'll be sure to let him know.
我會告知他您打過電話。	I'll let him know you called.
我會請他盡速回電。	I'll have him call you back as soon as possible. ◎ as soon as possible = 盡速。

請對方留下聯絡方式後，務必再次確認，以免傳達錯誤。很多人都會犯一個錯誤，就是只寫下對方來意，卻忘了記下對方的姓名與聯絡方式。

聽不懂或聽不清楚時

抱歉，我不會說法文。	I'm sorry. I can't speak French.
請容我轉接給其他人。	Please allow me to transfer your call to someone else.
請稍等，我找位會說法文的同事來。	Please hold on a minute, I'll get someone who speaks French.

我不懂您的意思。	I don't understand that. ◎ understand (v.) = 理解。
抱歉，我沒聽懂您說的。	Sorry, I don't get what you said.
不好意思，我聽不清楚。	I'm sorry, but I can't hear you very well. I'm sorry, but I'm having trouble hearing. ◎ I'm having trouble Ving = 做…有困難。
您聽得見嗎？您還在嗎？	Are you still there?
請您大聲一點好嗎？	Could you speak a little louder, please? Could you speak up a little, please?
請您說慢一點好嗎？	Could you speak a little slower, please?
電話有雜音，可以再說一次嗎？	There's some noise on the line. Could you repeat that again? ◎ repeat (v.) = 重複。
電話收訊不佳，可以請您再打一次嗎？	I think we have a bad connection. Could you please call again?
這隻電話有點問題，可以請您撥打另一個號碼嗎？	Something's wrong with this phone. Could you call the other number please?

此部分都是關於聽不清楚時的反應，非常實用，請務必熟背幾句。

告知同事有來電

溫蒂，5 線有你的電話。	Wendy, there is a call for you on line five. ◎ on line + 數字 = 分機…線。
我開會時有人打電話找我嗎？	Did someone call me while I was in a meeting?
K 公司的林先生打電話給你。	Yes, Mr. Lin from K Company is calling.
他請你盡速回電。	He wants you to call him back as soon as possible.
他說三點左右會再打來。	He said he'll call back around 3 o'clock.
他什麼話也沒說就掛電話了。	He hung up the phone without a word. ◎ hang up = 掛斷。
又是那個奧客。	It's the difficult customer again. ◎ difficult customer = 奧客。

打電話

您好，我是亨利。	Good morning, this is Henry calling. 文 *電話用語：This is + 人名 = 我是…。請注意不是 I am + 人名。*
早安，我是 DT 公司的亨利。	Hello, this is Henry from DT Company.

請問溫蒂在嗎？	May I speak to Wendy, please? May I have Wendy, please? ◎ May I speak to + 人名 = May I have + 人名？ = 我可以和…說話嗎？
我要找分機號碼 223 的溫蒂。	Please connect me to Wendy , extension number 223.
請幫我轉分機 123。	Could you transfer me to 123? Extension 123, please.
我要找業務承辦人。	May I speak to the person in charge, please?
瑕疵商品退貨的事要和誰聯絡？	Who should I talk to about returning defective products? ◎ defective (a.) = 有瑕疵的。

請讓我幫您確認一下，稍後回電給您。可以請您留下電話號碼嗎？
Let me check and call you back later. May I have your phone number?

請稍等。幫您查一下經辦的部門。
Just one moment, please. I'll help you find out which department handles this sort of thing.

您應該聯繫客服中心。
You need to contact our customer service center.

請稍等，幫您轉接給業務承辦人。
Hold on, please. Let me transfer your call to the person in charge.

打電話前先把要說的事情列成清單，就能避免漏掉重要的事，也不會因為過度緊張而腦袋空白。

說明目的

我為了［ E-MAIL / 傳真 ］的事情打電話來。	I'm calling about my [e-mail / fax].
我打電話來查看我的訂單。	I am calling to check the status of my order. ◎ status (n.) = 狀態、情況。
我打電話來詢問貴公司的職缺。	I'm calling to see if there are any openings in your company at this time. ◎ I'm calling to/about… = 我為了…打電話。
王小姐要我兩點後打給她。	Miss Wang asked me to call her after 2 o'clock.
我回電給王小姐。	I'm returning a call from Miss Wang. ◎ I'm returning a call from… = 我回電給…。

電話接通後，除了說明身分與要找的對象，還可以簡單說明去電目的，避免讓對方摸不著頭緒。

要找的人不在

沒關係。我稍後再撥。	It's fine. I'll call back later.
請問她何時回來？	When do you expect her back?
你知道她幾點會回來嗎？	Do you know what time she might be available?
請問她什麼時候［出差 / 休假］回來？	When will she be coming back from her [business trip / vacation] ?

我有急事，必須馬上和她談。	It's urgent. I need to talk to her right away. ◎ It's urgent. = 很緊急。 ★ right away 可以換成 right now。
請問我可以和其他知情的人談嗎？	Could I talk to anyone who knows about the situation?
我可以留言嗎？	Could you take a message for me?
可以告訴他我打過電話嗎？	Could you tell him that I called?
請他別忘了明天的派對。	Please tell him don't forget about tomorrow's party.
請他回來時打電話給我。	Please tell him to call me when he gets back.
我的電話是 0910234567，請他回電。	My cell phone number is 0910234567. Please let him call me back.
我手機快沒電了，請撥辦公室電話。	My cell phone is out of batteries. Please call the office.
請問他有公司用的手機嗎？	Does he have a company cell phone?
可以給我她的手機號碼嗎？	Could you give me her cell phone number? 抱歉，我們不提供私人電話號碼。但我可以幫您聯絡她。 Sorry. We don't give out private numbers. But I can call her for you. ★公司通常不會輕易透露員工的私人號碼，若對方堅持要索取，可以這樣回覆。

Part 8
電話禮儀

抱歉，我好像抄錯號碼了。	I'm sorry, but I think I wrote down the wrong number. ◎ write down … = 寫下…。
可以請您再給我一次嗎？	Could you give it to me again?
我打好幾通了，但她沒有接電話。	I called a bunch of times, but she didn't pick up. ◎ pick up = 接電話 同 answer。

與要找的對象通話

不好意思打擾您了。	I'm sorry to have bothered you. ◎ bother (v.) = 打擾。
抱歉，常常打電話給您。	I'm sorry to call you so often.
抱歉，這麼晚還打電話給您。	I'm sorry for calling so late.
您現在有時間嗎？	Is this a good time for you?
您現在方便說話嗎？	Can you talk now?
前陣子謝謝您。	Thank you for the other day. ◎ the other day = 前幾天。
一切還好嗎？	How's everything? 一切順利。 Everything is going well. 還是老樣子囉。 Everything is the same.

不好意思，我不得不掛電話了。	I'm afraid I need to hang up now. ◎ hang up = 掛電話。
好的，我們下次再談。	OK. Talk to you later.
佔用您的時間了。	Thanks for your time.
很高興與您談話。	Nice talking to you.
代我向陳先生問好。	Please give my best regards to Mr. Chen.

詢問辦公時間

請問你們的辦公時間是？	What are your business hours? ★ business 可換成 office。
我們的辦公時間從早上 9 點到下午 5 點，中午 12 點至 1 點休息 1 小時。	We are open from 9a.m to 5p.m, with one hour lunch break from 12 p.m. to 1p.m.
周末也有上班嗎？	Are you open on weekends? 沒有，我們星期六、日和國定假日都休息。 No. We're closed on Saturdays, Sundays, and national holidays. 有，我們全年無休。 Yes, we never close.

打錯電話・詐騙電話

抱歉，您打錯電話了。	I'm sorry, but you got the wrong number.
不好意思，我們這裡沒有這個人喔。	I'm afraid there's no one here by that name.
請問這裡是 2123-4567 嗎？	Is this 2123-4567?
電話號碼沒錯，但我們不是 ABC 書局。	The number is correct, but this is not ABC bookstore.
抱歉，我打錯電話了。	Sorry, I've dialed the wrong number.
要小心詐騙電話。	Beware of phone scams.
不要回電，這一定是詐騙電話！	Don't call back. It must be a phone scam!
別再惡作劇了！	Don't trick me anymore!
我現在很忙，上班時間不要打來。	I'm busy now; never call me at work.

打錯電話時不該失去耐心而隨便掛電話，仍要客氣的應對，這是很基本的禮貌。

"The telephone is a good way to talk to people without having to offer them a drink."

—Fran Lebowitz (author)

「講電話是很棒的溝通方式，不用請人們喝酒就能和他們談話。」

～ 芙蘭 ・ 雷伯維茲（作家）

練習問題

選擇題　請選出正確的答案。

A) I'm sorry for	F) May I speak
B) got the wrong number	G) help you
C) extension	H) call you back
D) put you through	I) is not available
E) at work	J) place an order

1. 有什麼可以為您服務的嗎？
   How may I ________ ?

2. 你打錯了。
   You ________ .

3. 我現在很忙，上班時間不要打來。
   I'm busy now; never call me ________ .

4. 請問需要他回電嗎？
   Would you like him to ________ ?

5. 請幫我轉接分機 88。
   Please transfer me to ________ 88.

6. 你好，我是 Zoe，請問 Amy 在嗎？
   Hello, this is Zoe. ________ to Amy?

7. 抱歉，讓您久等了。
   ________ keeping you waiting.

8. 他現在無法接聽您的電話。

No, he ________ .

9. 請稍等。我幫您轉接給她。

Please hold a moment. I'll ________ to her.

10. 我想要訂購商品。

I'd like to ________ .

單字填空 請填入適當的單字。

1. 他一分鐘後就回來，您要稍候嗎？

He'll be back in a minute. Do you want to ________ ?

2. 請問您要留言嗎？

Would you like to ________ a message ?

3. 我再確認一下您的電話號碼。

Let me ________ your phone number again.

4. 不好意思打擾您了。

I'm sorry to have ________ you.

5. 別再惡作劇了！

Don't ________ me anymore!

6. 他知道如何與您聯繫嗎？

Does he know how to ________ you?

7. 這一定是詐騙電話！

It must be a phone ________ !

8. 王先生去出差，五天後才會回來。

Mr. Wang's on a ________ . He'll be back after 5 days.

9. 請您大聲一點好嗎？

Can you speak a little ________ , please?

10. 我無法馬上回答你。

I'm ________ to give you an answer right away.

• 答案 •

Ⓐ 單字填空

①G ⑥F

②B ⑦A

③E ⑧I

④H ⑨D

⑤C ⑩J

Ⓐ 單字填空

① hold ⑥ get in touch with

② leave ⑦ scam

③ confirm ⑧ business trip

④ bothered ⑨ louder

⑤ trick ⑩ unable

電話禮儀

電話禮儀很重要也很實用。上班族每天都會接電話與打電話，因此對答之間千萬要小心，不能太隨心所欲的回答，或是輕率的掛電話。試著想想，當接到打錯的電話時，對方連道歉都沒有就掛掉電話，或是不說明身份與來意，沒頭沒尾就要找上司或老闆談生意，此時想必是一頭霧水，感覺也很差。沒有禮貌絕對是電話的大忌。對外會讓人對公司印象不好，對內也讓同事感到不悅，千萬不能小看電話禮儀喔。

英語補給站

First name 和 Last name?

first name = givename= 名字

last name = family name = surname = 姓氏

雖然對這兩個字不陌生，卻常常會分不清哪個是姓，哪個是名。這是因為歐美國家通常是 first name + (middle name) + last name 的順序，而這點正好跟台灣、韓國等亞洲國家相反，所以在填資料的時候要注意別填反了。舉例來說，如果您叫王美麗，那麼 first name = 美麗，而 last name = 王。

詐騙電話

隨著通訊的普及，詐騙手法也越來越多了。您是否也接過詐騙電話（phone scam），或是收到過可疑的未接來電和簡訊呢？千萬要多加留心，別輕易照對方的指示行動，也不要隨便回電，才不會中了詐騙集團的圈套。

國際無線電通話拼寫字母

國際無線電通話拼寫字母(International Radiotelephony Spelling Alphabet)又稱為北約音標字母(NATO phonetic alphabet)，是最常用的拼寫字母。原本是戰爭時為了確保無線電傳達正確而使用，現在也被運用在航空及通訊領域。

與外國人談到某個字母時，要避免聽錯混淆，當然可以說 D as in Dog 或是 D for Dog，但若能記下或使用國際通用的說法，不但溝通會更流暢，對方報字母時也能更快反應過來。

字母	代碼	字母	代碼
A	Alpha	N	November
B	Bravo	O	Oscar
C	Charlie	P	Papa
D	Delta	Q	Quebec
E	Echo	R	Romeo
F	Foxtrot	S	Sierra
G	Golf	T	Tango
H	Hotel	U	Uniform
I	India	V	Victor
J	Juliet	W	Whiskey
K	Kilo	X	X-ray
L	Lima	Y	Yankee
M	Mike	Z	Zulu

電話禮儀

公司各部門的說法

總公司	headquarters / head office
分公司	branch office
秘書室	Secretary's Office
～部	～ department
營業部	Business Department
銷售部	Sales Department
海外銷售部	Overseas / International sales department
企劃部	Planning Department
行銷部	Marketing Department
公關部	Public Relations Department
總務部	General Affairs Department
會計部	Accounting Department
財務部	Financial Department
廣告部	Advertising Department
工程部	Engineering Department
研發部	Research and Development Department (=RD)
人資部 / 人事部	Human Resource Department (=HRD)
產品開發部	Product Development Department
營運管理部	Operation Management Department
國際部	International Department
出口部	Export Department
進口部	Import Department
客服部	Customer Service Department

Part 9

E-mail 處理公事

E-mail

E-mail 處理公事

E-MAIL

MP3 009

情境會話

辦公室　同事　漏接 E-mail

Abigail	Have you replied to B&B Company's email already?
Bill	email?
Abigail	The email about the next conference was sent at four yesterday afternoon.
Bill	I didn't get it. I have problems receiving emails with this current email address. Can you forward it to me?
Abigail	Sure. I will forward it to you right away.
Bill	Let's chat later then. I have to reply the email now.
Abigail	Remember to CC it to the supervisor.
Bill	I see. Thank you very much.

Abigail：B&B 公司的信你回了嗎？
Bill：　信？
Abigail：就是昨天下午 4 點左右寄來，有關下禮拜研討會的信。
Bill：　我沒收到，我的信箱會漏信。你可以轉寄給我嗎？
Abigail：好，我馬上轉給你。
Bill：　那晚點聊，我得趕快回信。
Abigail：記得 CC 給主任。
Bill：　我知道，謝啦。

一般公事

你有收到 DMC 公司寄來的信嗎？	Have you received any email from DMC Company?
你收到我的信了嗎？	Did you get my email?
你沒收到我的信嗎？	Didn't you get my email?
郵件的主旨是『合作提案』。	The subject of the email is "proposal for cooperation."
你檢查過垃圾信件夾了嗎？	Did you check the junk folder? ◎ junk folder = 垃圾信件夾
會不會跑到垃圾信件夾裡？	Did the mail go to the junk folder?
請問貴公司有別的信箱嗎？	Do you have any other email addresses?
我寄給貴公司的信被退信了。	The email I sent to you was returned to me.
我已經寄兩封信了。	I've already sent two emails.
請查明原因。	Can you please check and see what the problem is?
您寄給我的信是亂碼。	The email you sent me was garbled. ◎ garbled (a.) = 混亂不清的，亂碼。
您寄來的檔案有誤。	There is an error in the file you sent. 請問是哪方面的問題？ What is the problem you are referring to?

抱歉。我會再重寄一次。
I apologize. Let me try and send it again.

我會再作確認。
I will reconfirm.
◎ reconfirm (v.) = 再確認。
I will make sure it is all right.

沒有附加檔。	There was no attachment.
您可以再寄一次嗎？	Could you send it again?

寄了重要信件，對方卻遲遲沒回覆時，務必打電話或 E-mail 確認，以防沒有傳達到。

寫信索取資料

您好，初次寫信給您，我是奧利佛。	Hello, my name is Oliver, and I'm writing for the first time. ◎ for the first time = 第一次、初次。
我是 KTP 公司的採購人員。	I'm the purchasing agent of KTP company.
我在看過貴公司的廣告後，寫了這封信給您。	I'm writing to you after reading your advertisement. ◎ write to someone = 寄信給某人。 ◎ advertisement (n.)= 廣告。
我們對貴公司的新產品很有興趣。	We are interested in your new products. ◎ be interested in … = 對…有興趣。

可以請貴公司寄一份包含最新價目表的產品型錄給我們嗎？	Would you please send us a catalog with the latest price list? ◎ catalog (n.) = 目錄；illustrated catalog 則是有圖片的目錄。
我們希望您用電子郵件寄送貴公司的產品資訊。	We'd like you to send us your product information by email. ◎ We'd like to ⋯ = 我們想要⋯。 ◎ information (n.) = 資訊、訊息。 ◎ by email = 用電子郵件的方式。
可以請您提供型錄中部份產品的樣品嗎？	Would you please provide us some samples on your catalog?
希望能進一步瞭解貴公司的產品。	We'd like to have more information about your products.

對於初次寫信的對象，應先報上自己的身分，並簡短說明寫信的理由。切記不要亂裝熟，省得無法拉近關係，還讓對方感到不愉快。

詢問價格

我們想要詢價。	We'd like to inquire about prices. ◎ inquire (v.) = 詢問。
請告訴我貴公司的手錶不含稅的價格。	Please tell me how much your watches are, not including tax. ◎ tax (n.) = 稅金。
我們想知道貴公司身體乳的最低報價。	We'd like to know the lowest price you can offer us on your body lotion. ◎ highest (a.) = 最高的。 反 lowest (a.) = 最低的。 ◎ offer (v.) = 提供、給予。

我的客戶有意詢問兩百盒筆的報價。	My client is interested in getting a quotation for 200 boxes of pens. ◎ a quotation for + 物品 = 詢問…報價。
請提供以上產品報價。	Please provide an estimate for the above listed products. ◎ estimate (n.) = 估價 。
價格請直接標示在產品名右側。	Please mark the price on the right side of the product name.
請給我們最 [優惠 / 最具競爭力] 的價格。	Please quote your [best / most competitive] price. ◎ competitive (a.) = 有競爭力的。
貴公司報價時，請註明是否含稅。	When you give us the quote, please note that if it includes tax.
報價時記得註明付款條件。	Remember to include the terms of payment with the estimate. 文 *remember + Ving = 記得做過某事；remember +to Vr= 記得要做某事。兩者意思完全相反，請特別注意。*
請將貴公司的報價寄到以下電子郵件地址。	Please send your estimate to the email address below. ◎ below (ad.) = 在下面。
我們於八月一號詢價。	We requested a quote on August 1st.
我們尚未收到貴公司的答覆。	We haven't heard from you yet.

請在這個星期二以前報價給我們。	Please give us the quotation by this Tuesday.
請儘早報價。	Please tell us the quote as soon as possible.
大量訂購有打折嗎？	Could we get a better price for a large order?
一次最少要購買五百份嗎？	Is your minimum order 500 pieces? ◎ minimum (a.) = 最小值的。 反 maximum (a.) = 最大值的。
此商品價錢含稅嗎？	Does this product price include taxes?
這家的報價比較高。	This company's quote is higher.
我們對貴公司的報價感到滿意。	We are satisfied with your quotation. ◎ be satisfied with = 對…感到滿意。
貴公司的報價似乎過高。	Your quotation seems to be too high.
這個商品的報價有問題。	There is something wrong with the quotation of this product. ◎ There is something wrong with… = …有問題。

詢價時應將產品名稱、購買數量等資訊，用白紙黑字寫清楚，免得哪天出問題時找不到證據，一切死無對證。

收到詢價＆報價

我們今天收到很多詢價單。	We received many requests for quotes today.
感謝貴公司對我們的產品有興趣。	We appreciate your interest in our products.
感謝貴公司詢價。	We appreciate your request for a quote.
我們很樂意提供咖啡壺的報價。	We are pleased to quote for the coffee pots. ◎ We are pleased to quote … = 我們很樂意提供…的報價。
煩請告知數量，以便為您報價。	Please tell me your desired numbers so I can help you prepare a quote.
我們將提供一百台耳機的報價。	We would like to provide an estimate for 100 headphones.
請問報價時要註明什麼？	What should be included in the quote?

交貨時間。
Time of delivery.
◎ delivery (n.) = 送貨。

付款條件。
Terms of payment.
◎ term (n.) = 條件。
◎ payment (n.) = 付款。

付款方式。
Methods of payment.
◎ method (n.) = 方法。

最低購買量。
Minimum order.

聯絡人姓名電話。
Contact person's name and telephone number.

此為聯合報價。	This is a combined offer. ◎ combined (adj.) = 聯合的。 ◎ offer (n.) = 報價。
我們隨信附上一份價目表。	We have attached a price list to the email. ◎ price list (n.) = 價目表。
我們附上樣品一份。	We are including a sample here.
價格皆含稅。	All prices include tax.
運費另計。	All prices exclude delivery. ◎ exclude (v.) = 排除、不包含。 反 include (v.) = 包括、包含 。
價格包含空運及包裝費用。	Air freight and packing charges are included in the price.
價格不包含運費及保費。	Delivery and insurance are not included in the price.
我們的價格為 CIF 報價。	Our prices are CIF prices. ◎ CIF = Cost , Insurance and Freight = 含保費及運費。

所有報價有可能更動，恕不通知。	All prices are subject to change, without notice. ◎ without ＝沒有，without notice = 不通知。 文 *without + N/Ving。如 : without thinking = 未經思考。*
運費如果上漲，由買方負擔。	Buyers are responsible for the delivery surcharges. ◎ surcharge (n.) = 附加費用、額外費用。
我們已於上星期寄出報價，請問是否有收到？	We sent a quote out to you last week, and I'm not sure if you have received it yet.
十月十日前收到貴公司答覆，此報價才生效。	This quote is not valid until we get your response before October 10th.
我們將在一星期後更改報價。	We will revise the quote in a week. ◎ revise (v.) = 修改。
我們將於兩天後漲價。	We are going to increase our rates in two days. ◎ increase (v.) = 增加。 ◎ rate (n.) = 價格；比率。
我們建議貴公司馬上接受報價。	We suggest that you accept our quote immediately. 文 *S+suggest+that+S+Vr = 建議某人⋯。請注意子句裡的動詞，一定要用原形動詞，這是很容易犯錯的地方。*
希望貴公司對我們的報價感到滿意。	I hope you find our estimate satisfactory. ◎ satisfactory (a.) = 滿意的。

若有任何問題，請立刻與我們聯繫。	If you have any questions, please don't hesitate to contact us. ◎ don't hesitate +to +Vr= 不要猶豫⋯
我們不勝感激。	We appreciate it a lot. We are greatly obliged.

> 詢價和報價務必謹慎思考其中的細節，譬如是否含稅，或是有什麼特別的要求，都要附註清楚，才不會差之毫釐，失之千釐。

確認庫存

我們想要下大量訂單。	We'd like to place a substantial order. ◎ place an order = 下訂單。 ◎ substantial (a.) = 大量的。
關於庫存量的事應該和誰聯絡？	Who should we contact to about the inventory level? ◎ inventory (n.) = 庫存。
請問貴公司的 300-BK 咖啡機是否還有庫存？	Do you have the 330-BK coffee machine in [inventory / stock] ?
請問貴公司有足夠的庫存嗎？	Do you have enough inventories?
請問貴公司有多少庫存？	How much inventory do you have?
請問確認庫存需要多久的時間呢？	How long will it take for you to check the inventory?

如果暫時缺貨，請問什麼時候會有貨呢？	If the product is temporarily out of stock, when will it be in stock? ◎ temporarily (ad.) = 暫時地。 ◎ out of stock = 缺貨。
貴公司會再進貨嗎？	Will you be getting more?
請問要多久才能供貨呢？	How long will it take to fill our order?

若無庫存是否會再進貨？何時會到貨？若已停產是否有類似產品？等問題都要確認清楚。

回覆有無庫存

我們的庫存量很充足。	We have plenty of that in inventory. ◎ plenty of⋯ = 大量的。
我們還有該型號的庫存。	We still have the model in stock.
此商品還有庫存，但已經有改良過的新機種。	Though we still have the model in stock, there's a new model which is an improved version of this model.
我們庫存所剩不多。	We're almost out of stock.
如果沒有庫存，我們需要 2 週的時間才能交貨。	If the product is out of stock, it will take 2 weeks to deliver it to you.
很抱歉，貴公司要的商品目前沒有庫存。	We're sorry. The goods you require are temporarily out of stock.

我們預計 2 個星期之內進貨。	We expect to get more within 2 weeks. ◎ We expect to … = 我們預計…。
很遺憾，貴公司要的商品已經賣完了。	We regret the products you require are sold out. ◎ be sold out = 售罄。
很抱歉，330-BK 咖啡機已經停產了。	We're very sorry, but we no longer manufacture the 330-BK coffee machine. We're very sorry, the 330-BK coffee machine has been discontinued. ◎ be discontinued = no longer manufacture = 停產。
我們可以提供造型、顏色和尺寸相近的替代品。	We can offer a substitute which is similar in style, color and size. ◎ substitute (n.) = 替代品。

顧客詢問的商品不見得最符合對方所需，若有條件相似、更值得推薦的商品，不妨主動建議對方，顯示出積極的態度。不過，推薦商品時務必提出具體的理由，才不會給人誇大不實、沒誠意的感覺。

下訂單

感謝貴公司 1 月 3 日的報價。	Thanks for your quotation of January 3 .
我們想要訂購 100 個咖啡壺。	We'd like to order 100 coffee pots.
隨信附上本公司的訂單。	We're enclosing our order form.

我們想要追加訂單。	We'd like to place an additional order. ◎ additional(a.) = 額外的。
我們想要更改訂單，由 100 個變成 150 個。	We'd like to change the order from 100 pcs to 150 pcs.
因為不景氣，我們想要減少訂單。	Due to the economic depression, we would like to reduce our order. ◎ Due to… = 由於…。
非常抱歉，我們決定取消訂單。	We are very sorry, but we've decided to cancel our order.
請以 [空運 / 海運] 方式寄出。	Please send by [air / sea] freight. ◎ freight (n.) = 貨運。 ◎ air/sea freight = 空運 / 海運。
請以貨到付款方式寄出。	Please send by POD. ◎ POD= payment on delivery = 貨到付款。
請告訴我們最快的交貨日期。	Please let us know your earliest date of delivery.
請於 3 月 11 號中午前到貨。	Please deliver the goods before noon on March 11.
一旦延誤要賠償十倍。	You have to pay 10 times the price if it's delayed. ★ 如果是單純假設，if 接的句子都會用現在式代替未來式。譬如本句，因為延誤是有可能發現，所以是單純假設。

請隨貨附上收據。	Please attach the receipt for the goods. ◎ receipt (n.) = 收據。
支付條件如訂單所示。	The terms of payment are as our order form.
我們會在收到發票後付款。	We will pay as soon as we receive your invoice.
收到訂單後請告知。	Please confirm receipt of the order.
請在訂單上簽名，並傳真一份至本公司。	Please sign and fax one copy of the order form to us.

下訂單前請務必再次確認訂單內容是否正確。

回覆訂單

感謝貴公司的訂單。	Thank you for your order.
所有商品皆有庫存，我們將於近期內安排出貨。	All products are in stock. We will arrange shipment as soon as possible. ◎ arrange (v.) = 安排。
交貨日期是本月三十日。	The delivery date is the 30th of this month. ◎ delivery date = 交貨日期。

收到貴公司的款項後立即出貨。	We will begin shipment immediately once we receive your payment.
隨信附上本公司的發票。	We're enclosing our invoice.
訂單一旦成立概不接受取消。	Once your order is confirmed, you cannot cancel your order.
很抱歉，我們無法接受貴公司的訂單。	We are sorry that we cannot accept your order.
造成貴公司的不便我們深感抱歉。	We apologize for any inconvenience we have caused to your company. ★ We apolpgize for any inconvenience … 也可以改成 We are sorry for any inconvenience…，是很常見的用法。
再次感謝貴公司給我們機會。	Thank you again for giving us the opportunity. ◎ opportunity (n.) = 機會。
希望很快有機會為貴公司服務。	We hope we will have the opportunity to serve your company in the near future. ◎ in the near future = 不久的將來。
希望未來還有後續的合作機會。	We hope we have more chance to cooperate in the future.
我們很遺憾地通知您，因為颱風的關係，交貨日期將延後 2 個星期。	We are sorry to inform you the date of the delivery will be postponed for two weeks due to typhoon. ◎ We are sorry to inform … = 我們很遺憾地通知…。

請問貴公司要取消訂單嗎？	Would you like to cancel your order?
請盡速告知貴公司的決定。	Please inform us of your decision as soon as possible.
商品送達後煩請告知。	Please inform us after receiving the goods.

回覆訂單時，務必要注意商品付款條件、運送方式、出貨日期等資訊。要是忽略任何環節而出了差錯，絕對會一個頭兩個大喔。

付款、催款與延遲付款

這是我們第一次交易。	This is our first transaction. ◎ transaction (n.) = 交易。
我們會先預付三分之一的貨款。	We'll pay 1/3 of the payment in advance.
本公司已於 3 月 10 日付款。	The payment took place on March 10th.
若貴公司三天內仍未收到款項，請盡快通知我們。	If you haven't received our payment within three days, please notify us as soon as possible. ◎ notify (v.) = 通知。
貴公司的付款方式為何？	How will you be paying? 我們付現。 We'll pay by cash.

我們以轉帳方式付款。
We'll transfer the money to you.
◎ transfer (v.) = 轉帳。

我們使用支票。
We'll use checks.

我們尚未收到貴公司的付款。

We haven't received your payment yet.

文 *S+ have/has + not received ... = …尚未收到…。*

如果貴公司已付款，請與我們聯絡。

Please contact us if your payment is completed.

◎ complete (v.) = 完成。

◎ Please contact us if ... = 如果…請與我們聯絡。

如果貴公司尚未付款，請立即付款。

If your payment hasn't been completed, please pay immediately.

◎ immediately (ad.) = 立刻。

若貴公司無法於 3 月 15 日中午前完成付款，請於今天打電話給我。

If you cannot complete your payment before noon March 15, please call me today.

我們已收到貴公司的預付金。

We have received advance payments of the company.

◎ advance payment (n.) = 預付款。

尾款請於收到商品 15 天內付清。

After you receive the goods, please pay the balance in 15 days.

◎ balance (n.) = 尾款、餘額。

我們已收到貴公司的款項。

We have received your payment.

感謝貴公司迅速付款。	Thank you for your prompt payment. ◎ prompt (a.) = 迅速的。
懇請貴公司寬限 3 個月的償付期限。	Please grant us a three-month grace period. ◎ grant (v.) = 同意。 ◎ grace(n.) = 寬限。

> 催繳付款或延遲付款都是讓人很尷尬的事，不論是催繳者或希望延期者，用字上都必須小心。因此，請注意禮貌用字，切勿給人一種輕率的感覺。

Email 疑難雜症

我的 outlook 好像怪怪的。	My outlook seems to act funny.
為什麼我的密碼不能用？	Why isn't my password working? ◎ work (v.) = 運作。 你是不是按錯順序？ Did you type it in the wrong order? ◎ order (n.) = 順序。 你是不是按到大寫鍵？ Did you type it in all caps? 你是不是改過密碼？ Did you change your password?
糟糕，我忘記密碼了。	Damn, I forgot the password. 別著急，可以問問 IT 人員。 Don't worry! You can ask the IT staff. 用你的生日試看看。 Try using your birth date.

會不會是你的幸運號碼？
Could it be your lucky number?

再仔細想一下。
Think about it carefully.
★ think 的常用片語；think of = 考慮，想起。think on = 考慮。think through = 徹底地想清楚。 think out = 仔細考慮。

收件匣全都是垃圾信。	It's all spam in my inbox. ◎ inbox (n.) = 收件匣。
要怎麼防止垃圾信呢？	How do I stop getting all this junk mail? 文 *stop+Ving = 停止做某事；stop+toV = 停下來，去做某事。兩者意思完全相反，請特別注意。*
我剛剛不小心開了病毒信件。	I just accidentally opened an email with a virus. ◎ accidentally (ad.) = 意外地。
艾咪的信件夾帶病毒。	Amy's email contained a virus. ◎ virus (n.) = 病毒。
要怎麼轉寄附加檔案呢？	How do you forward this attachment? ◎ attachment (n.) = 附件。
記得不要隨便開啟附加檔案。	Remember to be careful when opening attachments.
我忘記夾帶檔案了。	I forgot to attach the file. ◎ attach (v.) = 附加。

糟糕，我把寫到一半的信寄出了。	Oops! I sent off a half-written email. ◎ send off = 寄出、送出。
這封信沒有換行，真難閱讀。	This mail without line breaks is really hard to read. ◎ line break (n.) = 斷行。
檔案太大了無法附加。	The file is too large to attach. ◎ attach(v.) = 附加。 ◎ too…to… = 太…而不能…。
你可以把資料轉成壓縮檔。	You can transfer your data to a zip file.
附加檔案要下載好久。	It takes much time to download the attachment. ◎ download (v.) = 下載。 ◎ It takes much time to …= 做…很花時間。

等待重要信件時收到一堆垃圾信真的很討厭。

"We all have possibilities we don't know about. We can do things we don't even dream we can do."

— Dale Carnegie, Motivational Expert

「我們擁有未知的可能性。我們能辦到做夢也沒想過的事。」

~ *戴爾 · 卡內基（勵志專家）*

練習問題

單字填空（初階）

A)	email addresses	F)	attachments
B)	estimate	G)	the wrong order
C)	in the file	H)	subject of the email
D)	accidentally	I)	from DMC company
E)	returned to	J)	Think about

1. 請貴公司報價，寄到以下電子郵件地址給我。

   Please send your ________ to the email address below.

2. 您寄來的檔案有誤。

   There is an error ________ you sent.

3. 記得不要隨便開啟附加檔案。

   Remember to be careful when opening ________ .

4. 郵件的主旨是『合作提案』。

   The ________ is “proposal for cooperation”.

5. 你是不是按錯順序？

   Did you type it in ________ ?

6. 請問貴公司有別的電子郵件地址嗎？

   Does your company have any other ________ ?

7. 我的郵件被貴公司退回。

   The email I sent to your company was ________ me.

8. 再仔細想一下。

_________ it carefully.

9. 有沒有收到 DMC 公司寄來的信啊？

Have you received any email _________ ?

10. 我剛剛不小心開了病毒信件。

I just _________ opened an email with a virus.

單字填空 請填入適當的單字。

1. 請檢查你的收件匣。

Please _________ your inbox.

2. 要怎麼轉寄附加檔案呢？

How do you _________ this attachment?

3. 為什麼我的密碼不能用？

Why isn't my _________ working?

4. 我的 outlook 好像怪怪的。

My outlook _________ act funny.

5. 你是不是按到大寫鍵？

Did you type it in _________ ?

6. 你是不是修改過密碼？

Did you _________ your password?

7. 檔案太大無法附加。

The file is _________ large _________ attach.

8. 您好，初次寫信給您，我是 Oliver。

Hi, my name is Oliver, and I'm writing ________ .

9. 我會再作確認。

I will ________ .

10. 要怎麼防止垃圾信呢？

How do I stop getting all this ________ ?

• 答案 •

Ⓐ 單字填空

①B ⑥A

②C ⑦E

③F ⑧J

④H ⑨I

⑤G ⑩D

Ⓐ 單字填空

① check ⑥ change

② forward ⑦ too ; to

③ password ⑧ for the first time

④ seems to ⑨ reconfirm

⑤ caps ⑩ junk mail

商業書信

關於商業書信，有幾點要特別注意。

1. **主旨 (Subject)**：簡潔扼要寫重點。譬如訂單、報價、詢價等。
2. **稱謂 (Opening)**：不確定收件者時可以寫 To whom it may concern 或 Dear Sir or Madam。
3. **正文 (Body)**：應寫明來意，譬如道歉信先寫 "We are sorry…" 之後再接信件重點。
4. **結尾**："We look forward to your reply. (期待回覆)" 或 "Thank you again for your attention. (再次謝謝您的重視)" 等。

E-mail 處理公事

電子郵件

帳號	account	回覆	reply (Re :)
密碼	password	轉寄	forward (Fw :)
資料夾	folder	副本	carbon copy (CC)
收件匣	inbox	密件副本	blind carbon copy (BCC)
草稿	drafts	主旨	subject
寄件備份	sent mail	附檔	attachment
未讀信件	unread mail	資源回收桶	trash
待處理	follow up	垃圾郵件	junk / spam mail

國際商業用語 (International Commercial Terms，簡稱 Incoterms)

工廠交貨	EXW (Ex Works)
運送人交貨	FCA (Free Carrier)
船邊交貨	FAS (Free Alongside Ship)
船上交貨	FOB (Free on Board)
含運費	CFR (Cost and Freight)
到岸價格，含運費及保險費	CIF (Cost, Insurance and Freight)
含運費	CPT (Carriage Paid to)
含運費及保費	CIP (Carriage and Insurance Paid to)
國境交貨	DAF (Delivered at Frontier)
目的港船上交貨	DES (Delivered Ex Ship)
目的港碼頭交貨	DEQ (Delivered Ex Quay)
買主指定地交貨(不含關稅)	DDU (Delivered Duty Unpaid)
買主指定地交貨(含關稅)	DDP (Delivered Duty Paid)

memo

Part 10

電腦與網路

Computer & Internet

電腦與網路

COMPUTER & INTERNET

MP3 010

情境會話

辦公室 同事 電腦故障

Abigail	I can't turn on my computer.
Bill	How about calling a computer technician to check it?
Abigail	OK. I hope my project hasn't been deleted. I've spent a lot of time in it.
Bill	Are you not used to backing up your files?
Abigail	Nope. I never think my computer will crash.
Bill	You are too ridiculous!

Abigail：我的電腦無法開機。
Bill： 要不要找電腦工程師來檢查？
Abigail：好。希望我做的專題簡報不會消失。我為此花了很多心血。
Bill： 你平常沒有備份的習慣嗎？
Abigail：沒有。我從沒想過電腦會故障。
Bill： 你太誇張了。

每天都少不了電腦

這台電腦怎麼開機？	How do you turn on this computer? ◎ turn on⋯ = 打開⋯。 按下這邊的電源鍵就行了。 Just push the power button down here.
這台電腦是用什麼作業系統？	Which operating system is this computer on? 辦公室的電腦作業系統都是 Windows。 All of the office computers use Windows as the operating system. ◎ operating system = 作業系統，簡稱 OS。
電腦有設螢幕保護程式嗎？	Is the computer's screensaver set up? ★ set up 除了設置，還有「建造」與「設計陷害某人」的意思。
電腦有連接到印表機嗎？	Is this computer connected to the printer?
這台電腦可以燒錄 DVD。	This computer can burn DVDs. ◎ burn (v.) = 燒錄。
這台電腦有夠爛。	This computer sucks.
電腦跑得好慢。	The computer is so slow.
這台電腦安裝更新很花時間。	This computer takes a long time to install updates. ◎ install (v.) = 安裝。

電腦螢幕好小。	The computer screen is so small.
電腦外殼溫度好高。	The computer case is really hot.
這台電腦沒有灌 Photoshop。	This computer doesn't have Photoshop installed.
記得要用正版軟體。	Remember to use authenticated software.
預防硬碟故障，請定期備份重要文件。	In case of hard disk failure, please back up your important data regularly. ◎ regularly (ad.) = 定期地。
這台筆記型電腦是最新型的。	This laptop is the latest model.
這台筆記型電腦很輕薄。	This laptop is really light and thin.
你的桌面圖案好可愛喔。	Your desktop wallpaper is so cute.
下班記得關機哦。	Don't forget to shut down the computer before you leave work. ◎ shut down…= 關閉…。

電腦已經成為大多數上班族的一部份了，請記得每隔一段時間起來動一動，順便讓眼睛適度休息，以免出現乾眼症、烏龜頸等電腦症候群。

使用電腦問題多

也許我們該請電腦維修人員來看看。	Maybe we should call a computer repair technician.
我無法安裝這套防毒軟體，因為它和 Windows 不相容。	I can't install the antivirus software because it's not compatible with Windows. ◎ be compatible with… = 和…相容。
為什麼我的電腦不斷發出嗡嗡聲？	Why is my computer constantly making a humming noise? ◎ constantly (ad.) = 不斷地。
這台電腦的密碼是多少？	What is the password to this computer?
這台電腦有灌防毒軟體嗎？	Does this computer have anti-virus software installed?
要怎麼把檔案儲存到隨身碟？	How do I save this file to a USB flash drive? ◎ How do I + Vr…? 我該如何…？
我打不開這個檔案。	I can't open this file. 這是加密的檔案，要有密碼才能開啟檔案。 This is a password protected file. You can't open it unless you have the password. ◎ unless (conj.) = 除非…。
要怎麼把這個網頁加入我的最愛？	How do I add this webpage to my favorites?

奇怪，怎麼突然跑出這麼多視窗？	That's weird! How come all of a sudden all these windows came up? ◎ How come ? = 為什麼？、怎麼會？
筆電過熱該怎麼辦？	What should I do if my laptop gets overheated? ◎ overheated (a.) = 過熱的。 💬 可以買筆電散熱墊。 You can buy a laptop cooling pad. ◎ cooling pad (n.) = 散熱墊。
電腦好像中毒了。	I think the computer has a virus. ◎ virus (n.) = 病毒。
我的電腦中了木馬程式，請幫我解決。	My computer has a Trojan virus, so please help me get rid of it. ◎ get rid of = 解決，除掉。
電腦會自動關機。	The computer will automatically turn itself off. ◎ automatically (ad.) = 自動地。 ★ turn off 可換成 shut down。
電腦記憶體不足。	There's not enough of memory on the computer. ◎ There is not enough of …= 沒有足夠的…。
電腦記憶體損壞了。	The computer's memory crashed. ◎ crash (v.) = 電腦當機。
我的電腦無法顯示圖片，請幫我解決。	My computer won't display images. Please help me get it running.
我的電腦有問題，請幫忙檢查一下。	There's something wrong with my computer. Please take a look at it.

要怎麼查 IP 位置呢？	How do I find the IP address?
請教我怎麼格式化電腦。	Please tell me how to format the computer.

使用電腦最怕硬碟壞掉或是重灌後資料毀損或消失，為了避免這個情況，應該養成定期備份的好習慣。短短幾分鐘的步驟就能拯救長久以來的心血。

上網跟世界接軌

你們公司是用無線網路嗎？	Do you use wireless Internet at company? ◎ wireless(a.) = 無線的。 對啊，速度很快喔。 Yes, it's really fast. 不是，我們是用 ADSL。 No, we have ADSL.
我沒辦法上網。	I can't get online. 我幫你檢查。 I'll check it out for you. 重新開機試看看。 Try to restart the computer.
網頁跳出錯誤訊息。	There is an error message on the webpage.
網路拍賣有很多詐騙的賣家。	There are a lot of people defrauding on the online auction platforms. ◎ defraud (v.) = 詐取，欺騙。

不要在網路上隨便給人個人資料。	You should be careful not to give out your personal information online indiscreetly. ◎ give out = 公佈；分發；用盡。 ◎ indiscreetly (ad.) = 輕率地。
很多人利用 Facebook 交友。	A lot of people meet people through Facebook.
Facebook 讓我和老同學保持聯繫。	I can keep track of my old classmates through Facebook. ◎ track (v.) = 追蹤。 ◎ through (prep.)= 藉由。 ★ track 的相關單字：track events = 徑賽。track meet = 田徑運動會。
真不想加老闆 Facebook。	I really don't want my boss to be my Facebook friend.
我的 Facebook 被駭了。	My Facebook account has been hacked.
Skype 是很方便的討論工具。	Skype is a convenient discussion platform. ◎ discussion (n.) = 討論。 ◎ platform (n.) = 平台；月台。
你可以加我 Skype 嗎？	Can you add me on Skype? 當然好啊。你的 SKYPE 是？ Sure. What's your Skype name? 可以阿，但我很少用喔。 Yes, but I rarely use it.

你有 Skype 的帳號嗎？

Do you have Skype account?

★ Skype 字尾的 e 不發音，千萬別唸成 p。

我沒有耶。可以教我申請帳號嗎？
No, I don't have. Can you teach me how to create an account?

有啊。我的 SKYPE 是⋯。
Yes. My Skype is ....

網路發達固然方便，還是要注意個人的隱私，千萬別隨意把地址、電話、信用卡卡號等個人資料告訴網友。

"Be not forward, but friendly and courteous; the first to salute, hear and answer; and be not pensive when it is time to converse."

— George Washington

「別太主動，但要友善有禮貌；做第一個打招呼、傾聽與回應的人；該說話時別沉思太久。」

～ 喬治 · 華盛頓（美國第一任總統）

練習問題

選擇題　請選出正確的答案。

A)	get online	F)	restart
B)	operating system	G)	wireless Internet
C)	shut down	H)	connected to
D)	add	I)	anti-virus software
E)	crashed	J)	get rid of it

1. 這台電腦是用什麼作業系統？

   Which ________ is this computer on?

2. 電腦記憶體損壞了。

   The computer's memory ________ .

3. 沒辦法上網！

   I can't ________ !

4. 重新開機試看看。

   Try to ________ the computer.

5. 下班記得關機哦。

   Don't forget to ________ the computer before you leave work.

6. 你可以加我 Skype 嗎？

   Can you ________ me on Skype?

7. 你們公司是用無線網路嗎？

   Do you use ________ at company?

8. 電腦有連接到印表機嗎？

Is this computer ________ the printer?

9. 我的電腦中了木馬，請幫我解決。

My computer has a Trojan virus, so please help me ________ .

10. 台電腦有灌防毒軟體嗎？

Does this computer have ________ installed?

單字填空 請填入適當的單字。

1. Amy 忘記登出。

Amy forgot to ________ .

2. 這台電腦的密碼是多少？

What is the ________ to this computer?

3. 網路拍賣有很多詐騙的賣家。

There are a lot of people ________ on the online auction platforms.

4. 電腦會自動關機。

The computer will ________ shut itself down.

5. 網頁跳出錯誤訊息。

There is an error message on the ________ .

6. 要怎麼把檔案儲存到隨身碟？

How do I ________ this file to a USB flash drive?

7. 請教我怎麼格式化電腦。

Please tell me how to ________ the computer.

8. 我無法安裝這套防毒軟體，因為它和 Windows 不相容。
I can't install the antivirus software because it's not ________ with Windows.

9. 我的電腦無法顯示網頁圖片。
My computer won't ________ images.

10. 要有密碼才能開啟檔案。
You can't open it ________ you have the password.

• 答案 •

Ⓐ 單字填空

①B ⑥D
②E ⑦G
③A ⑧H
④F ⑨J
⑤C ⑩I

Ⓐ 單字填空

① log out
② password
③ defrauding
④ automatically
⑤ webpage
⑥ save
⑦ format
⑧ compatible
⑨ display
⑩ unless

個資值千金

隨著網路的發達，上班族幾乎都繞著網路轉。請假不再需要打電話，可以用電郵或者其他通訊軟體。要開會，只要寄封email，全部的人都能收到，省下非常多的時間。

網路確實帶來方便，但也暗藏了許多危機。之前就有人遇到朋友請他幫忙買點數，最後才發現是友人的帳號被盜用了。使用網路千萬要謹慎，不要隨便將個人資料透露給任何人。

電腦與網路

電腦按鍵

暫停	Pause
插入	Insert
刪除鍵	Delete
退位鍵	Backspace
跳出目前所執行的功能	Esc
跳欄鍵	Tab
輸入鍵，換行鍵。	Enter
結束鍵	End
大小寫轉換鍵	Caps Lock / Caps LK
移位鍵	Shift
數字鎖定鍵	Num lock

社群網站相關單字

上線	online
離線	offline
註冊	sign up
登入	log in
登出	log out
更新	update
狀態	status
打卡	check-in
標籤	tag

即時動態	ticker
塗鴉牆	wall
傳送檔案	attach a document
交友邀請	friend request
封鎖聯絡人	block user
隱私設定	privacy settings
通知	notification
訂閱	subscriptions
社群網站	social network

memo

Part 11

辦公室用品

Office Supplies

辦公室用品

OFFICE SUPPLIES

MP3 011

情境會話

辦公室 同事 閒聊

Jane: This [multifunctional printer / all-in-one printer] that the company just bought is outstanding.

Allen: Yes. We don't have to deal with any paper jams anymore.

Chris: I think there is no difference between the new one and the used one.

Jane: Are you kidding? OK. Perhaps you didn't use it often.

Chris: Maybe. I will go shopping at the stationery store. Do you need anything?

Allen: Please buy a roll of double-sided tape and a folder for me.

Chris: OK.

Jane：公司新買的多功能事務機就是不一樣。

Allen：真的，卡紙總算結束了。

Chris：我覺得和上一台差不多。

Jane：你開玩笑吧？好吧，也許是你不常使用的關係。

Chris：大概吧。我要去文具店買些用品，你們需要買什麼嗎？

Allen：幫我買雙面膠和資料夾。

Chris：好。

影印機

這台影印機怎麼操作？	How do you use this copier? ◎ How do you use…? = 你如何使用…？
可以告訴我這些按鈕的功能嗎？	Can you tell me what the functions of these buttons are? ◎ function (n.) = 功能、作用。 當然可以。首先… Of course, first… 你可以看看操作手冊說明。 You can look at the manual. ◎ manual (n.) = 說明書。
可以讓我先印一頁嗎？	Can you let me copy one page?
影印機的碳粉快用完了。	The copier is almost out of toner. ◎ toner (n.) = 碳粉。
要怎麼更換碳粉匣？	How do I change the toner cartridge?
慘了，又卡紙了。	Damn, there is another paper jam. ◎ paper jam = 卡紙。
卡紙要怎麼處理呢？	How do I handle this paper jam? ◎ handle (v.) = 處理。
這台影印機的印稿太 [淡 / 深] 了。	This copier's copies are too [light / dark]. ◎ light (a.) = 淺的。 反 dark 深的。

這台影印機的影印速度如何？	**What's the speed for this copier?** ◎ speed (n.) = 速度。 💬 每分鐘 30 張。 　　30 pages per minute.
這台影印機可以印彩色嗎？	**Can this copier make color copies?** 💬 當然可以。 　　Of course. 　　★其他類似用語：Sure!、Definitely!、 　　Certainly!、No doubt!、Absolutely! 💬 沒辦法，只能印黑白。 　　No, only black and white.
這台影印機最大可印到 A3 尺寸。	**This copier can make copies up to A3 size.**
這台影印機是分期付款購買的。	**This copy machine was paid by installments.** ◎ installment (n.) = 分期付款。
耗材一定要向原廠購買嗎？	**Do we have to buy the consumables from the original equipment manufacturer?** ◎ original equipment manufacturer = 原廠， 簡稱 OEM。 💬 不一定，但是原廠相對有保障。 　　Not necessary. However, buying from 　　the original equipment manufacturer 　　is relatively secure. 　　◎ relatively (ad.) = 相對地。

> 影印機最令人頭痛的就是卡紙，紙太潮濕、破損、訂書針殘留等情況都會造成卡紙，加紙前一定要仔細檢查。

印表機

印表機的彩色墨水沒了。	The printer has run out of colored ink.
印表機的紙張要選哪一種？	Which kind of paper should I choose for the printer?
這台是彩色印表機還是黑白印表機呢？	Is this a color printer or a black and white one?
這台多功能事務機看起來很貴。	This [multifunction printer / all-in-one printer] looks expensive.
這台的確很貴，因為功能很多。	This one is really expensive because it has many functions.
這台是用月租方式。	This one is rented monthly.
印表機一直發出奇怪的聲音。	This printer keeps making a weird noise.
印表機要如何清潔呢？	How do you clean the printer?
維護印表機是很重要的事情。	It's important to perform maintenance on your printer. ◎ It's important …= …是很重要的。
無法列印怎麼辦？	What do I do if I can't print?
列印出來有奇怪的數字。	There are weird numbers on the page.
為什麼列印出來有部分是空白的？	Why is there a blank space in the printout?

這台印表機好像壞了。	This printer seems like it doesn't work anymore.
這台印表機保固期限是一年。	This printer has a one year warranty. ◎ warranty (n.) = 保固、保證書。
你知道這台印表機的型號嗎？	Do you know the model number for this printer? ◎ the model number = 產品型號。 知道阿，印表機前側有標。 Yes. It's marked on the printer's front cover.

為了環保，越來越多公司提倡影印及列印文件時使用雙面列印了。

傳真機

請問貴公司的傳真號碼？

What is the fax number for your office?

幫我檢查傳真機為什麼不能用？

Help me figure out why the fax isn't working.

因為卡紙了。
There's a paper jam.

你沒有切換到傳真功能。
You didn't switch it over to fax mode.
◎ switch (v.) = 改變、轉移。

對方的傳真號碼忙碌中。
The recipient's fax has a busy signal.

我已經將資料傳到貴公司。

I already faxed over the materials to your company.

對方傳真機一直忙線中。	The recipient's fax machine always has a busy signal.
您傳來的資料不清楚，請重傳。	The fax is all blurry. Please send it again. ◎ blurry (a.) = 模糊不清的。
傳真少了一頁。	I'm missing a page in the fax.
這台傳真機有什麼功能？	What functions does this fax machine have? ◎ function (n.) = 功能。
它有傳真、影印和掃描的功能。	It has fax, copy, and scan functions.
大量傳真要怎麼操作？	How do I send a high-volume fax?
傳真機的紙用完了。	The fax is out of paper.
要怎麼幫傳真機加紙？	How do I add paper to the fax? ◎ add paper = 加紙。
記憶傳送可以節省很多時間。	A memory fax can save a lot of time.
原來這台傳真機可以接上電腦當印表機用喔。	I never knew that the fax can be connected to the computer and be used as a printer.

發送傳真後，最好於 3 ～ 5 分鐘後打通電話，確認對方有無收到傳真。

文書用品

公司的辦公用品應有盡有。	The company has all sorts of office supplies. ◎ all sorts of … = 各式各樣的…。
所有文具用品的申請必須由經理批准。	All stationery supply orders must be approved by the manager. ◎ approve (v.) = 批准、贊成。
要申請用品請填單子。	If you want to order supplies, please fill out the form. ◎ fill out = 填寫。 同 fill in。 ★ fill 的相關片語：fill with = 充滿；fill of = 填滿；fill up = 裝滿；fill the bill = 符合要求。
你要申請什麼辦公用品？	What kind of office supplies do you want to order? 我需要兩個檔案夾。 I need two file folders. 我需要收納盒。 I need a desk organizer. 我要五份便利貼。 I'd like five pads of post-it notes. 可以申請筆記本嗎？ Can I order notebooks?
你申請用品的次數太頻繁。	You order supplies too often.
我的筆沒水了。	My pen is out of ink.
用完膠水後請歸位。	Bring back the glue when you are done using it. ◎ glue (n.) = 膠水、黏著劑。

有人看見我的尺嗎？	Does anyone see my ruler?
請問釘書機在哪裡？	Excuse me, where are the staplers? ◎ stapler (n.) = 釘書機。
訂書機就在你眼前。	The stapler is in front of you.
空白光碟片要沒了。	We are running out of blank discs.
請不要沒有經過允許就拿走我桌上的東西。	Please don't take anything from my desk without my permission. ◎ permission (n.) = 許可、同意。

隨時隨地都能學英文，看到各種辦公用品的時候，不妨腦力激盪一下，想想它們的英文怎麼說吧。

"Our minds can shape the way a thing will be because we act according to our expectations."

— Federico Fellini, Director

「我們的思維將會影響一件事情的發展，因為我們是依據我們的預期來做事。」

～ *費德里柯・ 費里尼（導演）*

練習問題

選擇題　請選出正確的答案。

A)	paper jam	F)	copy
B)	all blurry	G)	It's important
C)	fill out	H)	without my permission
D)	high-volume	I)	functions of
E)	Bring back	J)	all sorts of

1. 卡紙要怎麼處理呢？

   How do I handle this _________ ?

2. 大量傳真要怎麼操作啊？

   How do I send a _________ fax?

3. 維護印表機是很重要的事情。

   _________ to perform maintenance on your printer.

4. 要申請用品請填單子。

   If you want to order supplies, please _________ the form.

5. 可以告訴我這些按鈕的功能嗎？

   Can you tell me what the _________ these buttons are?

6. 公司的辦公用品應有盡有。

   The company has _________ office supplies.

7. 用完膠水後請歸位。

   _________ the glue when you are done using it.

8. 請不要沒有經過允許就拿走我桌上文具。

Please don't take anything from my desk ________ .

9. 可以讓我先影印一頁嗎？

Can you let me ________ one page?

10. 您傳真的資料不清楚，請重傳。

The fax is ________ . Please send it again.

單字填空 請填入適當的單字。

1. 沒有切換到傳真功能。

You didn't ________ it over to fax mode.

2. 這台的確很貴，因為功能很多。

This one is really ________ because it has many functions.

3. 這台影印機的印稿太淡了。

This copier's copies are too ________ .

4. 記憶傳送可以節省很多時間。

A memory fax can ________ a lot of time.

5. 印表機紙張要選哪一種？

Which kind of paper should I ________ for the printer?

6. 我需要兩個檔案夾。

I need two file ________ .

7. 為什麼列印出來有部分是空白的？

Why is there a ________ space in the printout?

8. 你要申請什麼辦公用品？

What kind of office ________ do you want to order?

9. 這台印表機保固期限是一年。

This printer has a one year ________ .

10. 傳真機的紙用完了。

The fax is ________ of paper.

• 答案 •

Ⓐ 單字填空

① A	⑥ J
② D	⑦ E
③ G	⑧ H
④ C	⑨ F
⑤ I	⑩ B

Ⓐ 單字填空

① switch	⑥ folders
② expensive	⑦ blank
③ light	⑧ supplies
④ save	⑨ warranty
⑤ choose	⑩ out

有借有還，再借不難

和別人借東西要有禮貌，等對方同意後再使用。還有，用完後一定要記得歸還。想和別人借東西可以這麼問：

Can I borrow your~?（可以借我你的～嗎？）

要是有人向你借東西，你可以這麼回答：

Sure. But you should return it to me before you leave office.

（可以呀。但要在下班前還我。）

Sorry, I'm using it.

（對不起，我正在使用。）

辦公室用品

辦公室硬體設備

打卡鐘	time clock
電話	telephone
影印機	(photo)copier
傳真機	fax

印表機	printer
掃描機	scanner
飲水機	water dispenser

印表機種類

雷射印表機	laser printer
噴墨式印表機	inkjet printer
感熱式印表機	thermal printer
點陣式印表機	dot matrix printer
網路印表機	network printer
多功能印表機	multifunction printer [all-in-one printer]

辦公室文具用品

計算機	calculator
打洞機	paper punch
釘書機	stapler
釘書針	staple
迴紋針	paper clip
圖釘	thumbtack
信封	envelope
檔案夾	file folder
便條紙	notepad
便利貼	Post-it
螢光筆	highlighter

麥克筆	marker
白板筆	(whiteboard) marker
中性筆	medium point pen
自動鉛筆	automatic pencil
橡皮擦	eraser
墨水匣	ink cartridge
膠水	glue
膠台	tape dispenser
雙面膠	double sided tape
立可白	white out
立可帶	correction tape

memo

Part 12

面對上司

Getting along with Supervisors

面對上司

GETTING ALONG WITH SUPERVISORS MP3 012

情境會話

公司 同事 討論上司

Audrey	I respect my supervisor. He has good leadership skills.
Candice	I envy you so much. My supervisor is annoyed. He not only has bad temper, but also refuses to listen to other's opinions.
Will	I can tell. My department manager does nothing but kiss the boss's ass.
Candice	It is not easy to have a good supervisor.
Will	I totally agree with you.
Audrey	Let's stop the topic. Today is Friday. Do you fancy a drink?

Audrey： 我很尊敬我的上司，他很有領導能力。
Candice： 真羨慕你，我的主管很煩。不但脾氣差，又拒絕聽別人的意見。
Will： 我懂你的感受。我們部門的經理只會老闆拍馬屁，什麼都不會。
Candice： 要遇到好的上司真的不容易。
Will 我也覺得。
Audrey： 我們別再聊這個了。今天是星期五耶，我們去喝一杯吧？

和老闆談話

你覺得這份工作怎麼樣？	What do you think about your job? ◎ What do you think about…? = 你認為…?
老實說很累，但可以學到很多。	Frankly, it is pretty tiring, but I can learn much from this job. ◎ learn from… = 從…學習。
非常充實。	It enriches my life.
你對這次的企劃案有什麼看法？	What do you think about this proposal?
我覺得還有討論的必要。	I think there is a need to discuss it.
如果你是我，你會怎麼做？	If you were me, what would you do? 文 *本句是和現在事實相反的假設句。句型為 If + S+ were +…, S + would + Vr*

不爽在心內

老闆的記憶力真差。	The boss's memory is so bad.
主任每天都遲到。	The director is late every day.
我上司是個急性子。	My direct supervisor is a hasty person. ◎ hasty (a.) = 匆忙的、草率的。
組長動作慢吞吞的。	Our group leader is a slowpoke. ◎ slowpoke (n.) = 動作慢的人。

我上司很小心眼。	My direct supervisor is really narrow-minded. ◎ narrow-minded (a.) = 心胸狹窄。
我上司是全世界最難相處的人。	My direct supervisor is the world's hardest person to get along with.
其他部門的主管似乎比較好相處。	The managers in other departments seem to be easier to get along with. ◎ get along with = 和…相處。hard to get along with = 難相處。easy to get along with = 好相處。
經理真的很愛挑人毛病。	The manager really likes to nitpick. ◎ nitpick (v.) = 吹毛求疵。
總經理看起來很兇。	The president looks really mean.
董事長從來不笑的。	The chairman never smiles.
我的上司脾氣真是暴躁。	My direct supervisor has a really short temper. ◎ short temper (n.) = 脾氣暴躁。
我的上司是個龜毛的人。	My direct supervisor is a fussy person. ◎ fussy (a.) = 挑剔的、難以取悅的。
我的上司一點邏輯也沒有。	My direct supervisor doesn't use any logic. ◎ logic (n.) = 邏輯。

我的上司常常朝令夕改。	My direct supervisor changes his mind all the time. ◎ change one's mind = 某人改變主意。 ◎ all the time = 隨時。
看到主任就讓人厭煩。	I get so annoyed when I see the director.
我們經理真的很無能。	Our manager is so incompetent. ◎ incompetent (a.) = 無能的、不稱職的。
我們經理很喜歡吹牛。	Our manager likes to brag.
主任很會推卸責任。	The director always shirks his responsibilities. ◎ shirk (v.) = 逃避責任（或義務）。
我的上司很愛擺架子。	My direct supervisor loves to put on airs. ◎ put on airs = 擺架子。
我上司覺得自己永遠是對的。	My direct supervisor thinks he is always right.
副理光說不練。	The assistant manager can talk, but won't act on it.
我的上司每天都在上網。	My direct supervisor is always surfing the Internet every day. ◎ surf the Internet = 上網。
我的上司廢話連篇。	My direct supervisor is full of bullshit.

我的上司有夠囉嗦。	My direct supervisor is a real nag. ◎ nag (n.) = 嘮叨的人。

有時上司比較嚴苛，是希望員工把事情做好，並期待員工能有所突破與成長，也許會從中學到更多待人處事的道理。心中怨言再多，仍然要避免在公司講壞話，若被有心人轉述或剛好被聽見就慘了。

上司很好相處

老闆真的很有能力。	Our boss is very capable. ◎ capable (a.) = 有能力的。
老闆每天都充滿活力。	Our boss has a lot of energy every day.
老闆對我們很慷慨。	Our boss is really generous with us. ◎ be generous with + 人 = 對某人很慷慨。
老闆對我們很體恤。	Our boss is really considerate towards us. ◎ be considerate towards + 人 = 很體恤某人。
老闆很會替我們著想。	Our boss always considers where we are coming from.
老闆很好溝通。	It's really easy to communicate with our boss. ◎ It is easy⋯= 做⋯很容易。
老闆常常誇獎我們。	Our boss often gives us compliments. ◎ compliment (n.) = 讚美。

老闆常常請我們吃飯。	Our boss treats us to a meal very often.
老闆是很積極的人。	Our boss is a really aggressive person.
我們老闆事必躬親。	Our boss likes to do things himself.
我們老闆做事很果斷。	Our boss is very clear out. ◎ clear out = 果斷。 類 *decisive*；*firm*；*determined*；*purposeful*。
我們老闆講話很精簡。	Our boss speaks clearly and concisely. ◎ concisely (ad.) = 簡潔地。
我們老闆是很坦率的人。	Our boss is really straightforward. ◎ straightforward (a.) = 坦率的、老實的。
我們老闆脾氣很好。	Our boss is even-tempered. ◎ even-tempered (a.) = 脾氣平和的。
我上司是很活潑的人。	My direct supervisor is really energetic.
我上司真是個善良的人。	My direct supervisor is a good person.
我們上司永遠懂我們的需求。	Our direct supervisor always knows what we need.
我上司是個幽默的人。	My direct supervisor is a funny guy.

主管很好相處。	The manager is easy to get along with.
江主任常正面思考。	Miss Jiang, the director, often has a positive attitude. ◎ positive (a.) = 正面的。
我們組長動作很快、效率很好。	Our group leader is really fast and efficient. ◎ efficient (a.) = 有效率的。
總經理看起來很和藹可親。	The president looks benevolent. ◎ benevolent (a.) = 和藹可親的。
楊經理個性很溫和。	Mr. Yang, the manager, is really a gentle person.
葉課長很熱心。	Section manager Yeh is really enthusiastic. ◎ enthusiastic (a.) = 熱心的。
董事長很有領導能力。	The chairman has good leadership skills.
董事長每天都笑嘻嘻。	The chairman is always in a good mood.

好上司可遇不可求，對你而言，怎樣才算是一個好上司呢？

練習問題

選擇題 請選出正確的答案。

A) hasty person	F) communicate with
B) generous with	G) act on it
C) nitpick	H) narrow-minded
D) get along with	I) changes his mind
E) clearly and concisely	J) use any logic

1. 主管人很好相處。

   The manager is easy to ________ .

2. 我們老闆講話很精簡。

   Our boss speaks ________ .

3. 我上司真是個急性子。

   My direct supervisor is a really ________ .

4. 副理只會講不會做。

   The assistant manager can talk, but won't ________ .

5. 我上司很小心眼。

   My direct supervisor is really ________ .

6. 經理真的很愛挑人毛病。

   The manager really likes to ________ .

7. 我們老闆很好溝通。

   It's really easy to ________ our boss.

8. 老闆對我們很慷慨。

Our boss is really ________ us.

9. 我的上司毫無邏輯觀念。

My direct supervisor doesn't ________ .

10. 我的上司常常朝令夕改。

My direct supervisor ________ all the time.

單字填空 請填入適當的單字。

1. 老闆真的很有能力。

Our boss is very ________ .

2. 我們老闆做事很果斷。

Our boss is very ________ cut.

3. 主任很會推卸責任。

The chief always shirks his ________ .

4. 我們經理真的很無能。

Our manager is so ________ .

5. 我們組長動作很快、效率很好。

Our group leader is really fast and ________ .

6. 我們老闆常常請我們吃飯。

Our boss ________ us to meals often.

7. 老闆常常誇獎我們。

Our boss often gives us ________ .

8. 總經理看起來很兇。

The president looks really ________ .

9. 老闆對我們很體恤。

Our boss is really ________ towards us.

10. 老闆是很積極的人。

Our boss is a really ________ person.

• 答案 •

Ⓐ 單字填空

① D	⑥ C
② E	⑦ F
③ A	⑧ B
④ G	⑨ J
⑤ H	⑩ I

Ⓐ 單字填空

① capable	⑥ treats
② clear	⑦ compliments
③ responsibilities	⑧ mean
④ incompetent	⑨ considerate
⑤ efficient	⑩ aggressive

性騷擾（sexual harassment）

性騷擾指的是用帶有性暗示的言語或行動造成他人不快，是很常見的職場霸凌，無論男女皆有可能被性騷擾。不過，許多人會礙於上司與下屬關係忍氣吞聲，或是把錯歸咎到自己身上。默默承受或自我責備都是不對的，感覺被性騷擾時，可以試著這麼做：①記錄：性騷擾常變成雙方各說各話，請盡可能記錄事發經過。②蒐證：蒐集相關人證，例如事發當時有無目擊者。可以拍照或錄音存證更好。請確保證據不被別人銷毀。③溝通：請別人間接轉達你的感受，或請人陪同與加害人溝通。請務必找人同行，以免發生危險。④公司內部申訴：如果溝通無用，請透過公司內部申訴管道處理。⑤主管機關申訴：若沒有申訴管道或雇主未採取適當的措施，請直接向當地勞工行政主管機關申訴。勇敢說出口才能讓職場更建全。

面對上司

職位稱呼

董事長	chairman of the board
副董事長	vice chairman
常務董事	managing director
董事	director
首席執行官	CEO (Chief Executive Officer)
首席行政官	CAO (Chief Administrative Officer)
總裁	president
副總裁	vice president
執行總裁	executive president
特別助理	special assistant
總經理	general manager
經理	manager
副理	assistant manager
襄理	junior manager
部長	department head
課長	section chief
專員	specialist
秘書	secretary
職員	staff
助理	assistant
工程師	engineer
技術員	technician

人格特質

顧人怨的特質

讓人厭煩的	annoyed
無趣的	boring
不誠實的	dishonest
講話刻薄的	harsh / mean
易怒的	irritated
失禮的	impolite
無能的	incompetent
優柔寡斷的	indecisive
不懷好意的	malicious

心胸狹窄的	narrow-minded
挑剔的	nitpicking
悲觀	pessimistic
自私的	selfish
奇怪的	strange
吝嗇的	stingy
嚴格的	strict
多疑的	suspicious
不開心的	unhappy

好逗陣的特質

積極的	aggressive
和藹可親的	benevolent
有能力的	capable
體貼的	considerate
果斷的	decisive
熱心的	enthusiastic
效率好的	efficient
活潑的	energetic / outgoing
友善的	friendly

慷慨的	generous
認真的	hardworking
幽默的	humorous
親切的	kind
樂觀的	optimistic
開朗的	open-minded
有耐心的	patient
正面的	positive
特別的	special

Part 13

與同事交流

Getting along with Coworkers

與同事交流

GETTING ALONG WITH COWORKERS　MP3　013

情境會話

茶水間　同事　抱怨同事

Claire	I don't like Tom.
Frank	For what reason?
Claire	He always thinks he is humorous. Actually, he is very unctuous.
Frank	Really? I think he is very funny.
Claire	We don't see eye to eye.
Frank	Don't say that. Maybe you should let him know you don't like what he has done.
Claire	I doubt that it would work.
Frank	Never know until you try.

Claire：我不喜歡湯姆。
Frank：怎麼說？
Claire：他總是自以為幽默，實際上他很油腔滑調。
Frank：會嗎？我覺得他很有趣。
Claire　那就是我和他個性不合了。
Frank：別這麼說，也許你該讓他知道你不喜歡他做的事。
Claire　我很懷疑說了是否有用。
Frank：沒試過怎麼會知道呢。

待人應對進退

人際關係很複雜。	Human relations are complicated. ◎ complicated (a.) = 複雜的。
職場霸凌是普遍現象。	Bullying in the workplace is a universal phenomenon. ◎ bullying (n.) = 霸凌。
職場上必須小心翼翼的。	You have to be very cautious in the workplace.
別人說話時請勿打斷。	Don't interrupt others when they are talking.
你應該聽完別人的話。	You should hear out what others have to say. 文 *You should +Vr⋯= 你應該⋯，建議某人做某事。*
和別人講話時要看對方眼神。	You should make eye contact when talking to others.
和長輩說話，眼神勿飄忽不定。	Don't let your eyes wander when speaking with elders. ◎ wander (v.)=（目光）游移，游蕩，閒逛。
客人來訪時要和對方打招呼。	When you have guests, make sure you make appropriate greetings. ◎ appropriate (a.) = 恰當的。
進門前要先敲門。	You should knock before entering. 文 *前後主詞一樣，before 的子句可省略主詞，變成 before + Ving。*

開會時要注意聽。	Listen carefully during meetings.
上班前先把早餐吃完。	You should have breakfast before you start to work.
下班時要和同事道別。	You should say "bye" before you leave work.
批評別人時，試著保持溫和的態度。	When you criticize others, try to maintain a warm attitude. ◎ criticize (v.) = 批評。 ◎ maintain (v.) = 保持。
犯了錯要道歉。	Apologize when you are wrong.
不要得罪上司。	Don't offend your boss. ◎ offend (v.) = 得罪。
不要和上司大小聲。	Don't argue with your boss. ◎ argue (v.) = 爭論、爭吵。aregue with + 人 = 和某人爭論。
討論事情時不要吃東西。	Don't eat anything when you are having a discussion.
上班不要一直聊天。	Don't chat and talk all day while you are at work.
不要打擾其他同事。	Don't bother your coworkers. ◎ bother (v.) = 打擾。
走路時步伐要輕點。	Don't stomp around; tread lightly.
講電話要輕聲細語。	Speak softly when you are on the phone.

抽菸請到吸菸區。	Smoking is only allowed in the smoking areas.

待人應對進退有許多眉角，例如和人說話時眼睛要看著對方，態度要謙遜有禮，謹記這些技巧，才能在職場上如魚得水。

讚美與祝福

你同事艾倫個性如何？	What's Ellen like? 她是公司的開心果。 She is the one who makes everyone happy. 她總是笑容滿面。 She always has wide and happy smiles. 她是開朗的女孩。 She is an open-minded girl. ◎ open-minded (a.) = 開朗的。 她很樂觀。 She is very optimistic.
你很有時間觀念。	You are very punctual. ◎ punctual (a.) = 準時的。
你做事很有效率。	You're very efficient.
你工作很認真。	You are very earnest in your work. ◎ earnest (a.) = 認真的。
你是個努力的好員工。	You are a hard worker.
你的口風很緊。	You're tight-lipped. ◎ tight-lipped (a.) = 守口如瓶的。

你的細心值得稱讚。	Your carefulness deserves praise. ◎ deserve (v.) = 值得。praise (n.) = 讚美。 ★英文有句 You deserve it. 這句話有褒貶兩意，用在正面情況為「這是你應得的。」；用在負面情況時，就有「活該、自作自受」的意思。
你常常幫助其他同事。	You often help your coworkers out. ◎ help someone out = 幫助某人。
我喜歡你的幽默感。	I like your sense of humor. ★ sense of …= …感。例：sense of humor = 幽默感。sense of responsibility = 責任感。sense of direction = 方向感。sense of smell = 嗅覺。sense of occasion = 預感。
我喜歡你的笑話。	I like your jokes. ◎ joke (n.) = 笑話。
你看起來很有氣質。	You look elegant. ◎ elegant (a.) = 優雅的，端莊的。
你的聲音很甜美。	Your voice is really sweet.
你的穿著很有品味。	You have great taste in clothes. ◎ have great taste in = 某方面品味很好。
我覺得你很有教養。	I think you have a good upbringing. ◎ upbringing (n.) = 教養。
你身材真好，怎麼保持的呢？	You have a great body. How do you keep in shape? ◎ keep in shape = 維持身材。

你家的 [貓咪 / 狗狗] 好可愛，真想跟牠一起玩！	Your [cat / dog] is so cute; I'd love to play with it!
業務部的人都很活潑。	Everyone in the sales department is energetic.
莫妮卡對什麼都很感興趣。	Monica has a lot of interests.
莉塔喜歡幫助人。	Rita likes to help people.
威利很友善。	Willy is friendly.
他沒有心機。	He's not calculating. ◎ calculating (a.) = 心機重的。
艾美對人很親切。	Amy is kind to others.
恭喜你升為經理。	Congratulations on your promotion to manager.
聽說你要結婚囉，恭喜！	I heard you're getting married. Congratulations!
恭喜你當 [爸爸 / 媽媽] 囉！	Congratulations on becoming a [father / mother] ! ◎ Congratulations on + V-ing…= 恭喜…。

應該沒有人會討厭被讚美，但也別誇獎過了頭，反而讓人覺得是拍馬屁。

抱怨同事

你跟新同事處得如何？	How do you get along with your new coworker? 我跟他合不來。 I can't get along well with him. 我沒辦法和他溝通。他太主觀了。 I don't know how to communicate with him. His opinions are too strong. ◎ communicate (v.) = 溝通。
我受夠你了。	I've had enough of you.
我再也受不了了。	I can't take it anymore.
你常常請人幫忙打卡。	You often ask others to punch your card.
你上班常常打瞌睡。	You often doze off at work. ★ doze off = 打瞌睡；fall asleep = 睡著；feel sleepy = 想睡的，三者是有差別的哦。
你精神很差。	You don't have much energy.
你工作太散漫。	You don't take work seriously enough.
你工作態度不佳，需要改進。	You don't have a good attitude at work. You need to improve that.
你常常利用上班時間吃早餐。	You often eat breakfast at work.
你常在上班時間講手機。	You often talk on cell phone at work.

你手機講太久了。	You've been on your cell phone too long.
我討厭用公司電話打給朋友的人。	I hate people who use the company phone to call their own friends.
你自私的行為讓人討厭。	Your selfish behavior is annoying. ◎ selfish (a.) = 自私的。 ◎ behavior (n.) = 行為舉止。 ◎ annoying (a.) = 惱人的。
你不會替別人著想。	You don't think about others.
你很沒禮貌。	You're so impolite. ◎ impolite (a.) = 無禮的。
王秘書濫用職權。	Secretary Wang abuses his power. ◎ abuse (v.) = 濫用。 ◎ power (n.) = 權力。
莎莉是馬屁精。	Sally is a brown-noser. ◎ brown-noser (n.) = 馬屁精。
她常常拍老闆馬屁。	She often kisses the boss's ass. ◎ kiss one's ass = 拍馬屁。
她的手段很高明。	She is good at jockeying. ◎ be good at + Ving/N = 擅長⋯。 ◎ jockeying (v.) = 耍手段。
她很做作。	She is so fake. ◎ fake (a.) = 虛偽的。
她的心機很重。	She is calculating.

凱莉常常感到徬徨。	Kelly often feels at a loss.
她太悲觀了。	She's too pessimistic. ◎ pessimistic (a.) = 悲觀的。
她很愛哭。	She cries easily.
她常常懷疑別人。	She is often suspicious of others. ◎ suspicious (a.) = 多疑的。
她永遠都在抱怨。	She is always complaining.
她喜歡講別人壞話。	She likes to bad-mouth others. ◎ bad-mouth (v.) = 說人壞話。
我討厭長舌的女人。	I hate nagging women. ◎ nagging (a.) = 嘮叨的。
喜歡搞小團體是不受人歡迎的。	People who are into cliques aren't welcome.
王經理脾氣很差。	Mr. Wang, the manager, has a bad temper.
他很易怒。	He gets irritated easily.
他常常和人吵架。	He often gets into arguments with others.
他喜歡指揮別人。	He likes to manage others. He is bossy.
亞當講話喜歡挖苦別人。	Adam often speaks sarcastically.

安得魯喜歡扯別人後腿。	Andrew likes to get others in trouble. ◎ get others in trouble = 扯別人後腿。
大衛不老實，他從不說實話。	David is not honest. He never tells the truth.
他做事虎頭蛇尾。	He has a fine start and a poor finish.
他做事常常拖延。	He often procrastinates.
都是他害的！這個企劃案的進度嚴重落後。	All his fault! This project is seriously far behind schedule. ◎ behind schedule =（進度）落後。
你不要推卸責任給他人。	Don't push your responsibilities onto others. ◎ push one's responsibility onto = 推卸責任。

> 再討厭同事也要避免在茶水間抱怨，如果因此得罪人就不妙了，嚴重的話說不定還會被開除，得不償失！真有滿腹苦水，不妨等到了家裡或公司以外的地方再說。

八卦閒聊

我這星期已經加班二十小時了。	I've already worked 20 hours of overtime this week.
我已經累到無法說話了。	I'm so tired that I can't talk. ◎ so…that = 如此…以致於…。 ◎ tired (a.) = 疲倦的。be tired of + N/Ving = 對…感到厭倦。
上班讓我覺得很煩。	I'm really irritated by work. ◎ be irritated by… = …使煩躁。

我想要換工作。	I want to fly the coop. ★ fly the coop 也可以用 jump ship。
最近想要換工作。	Lately I've been meaning to change jobs.
你為何想辭職？	Why do you want to quit? 因為職業倦怠。 It's due to professional burnout. ◎ professional burnout (n.) = 職業倦怠。 ◎ It's due to…= 因為…，由於…。 我覺得太常加班了。 I think there is too much overtime. 薪水太少。 The salary is too low. 其他公司挖角。 Other companies have made better offers. 我想要去留學。 I want to study abroad. ◎ abroad (ad.) = 在國外。 我想要環遊世界。 I want to travel around the world. ◎ travel around the world = 環遊世界。 我爸希望我繼承家業。 My father hopes that I can inherit the family business. ◎ inherit (v.) = 繼承。
你可以等領完年終再走。	You can wait after receiving the [year-end / annual] bonus. ◎ year-end bonus (n.) = 年終獎金。

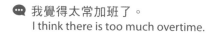

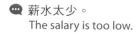

你們能想像他花了多少錢買那台車嗎？	Can you guys imagine how much he spent on that car? ◎ imagine (v.) = 想像。
告訴你一個秘密，你千萬要保密。	I have a secret to tell you, but you must keep it to yourself. ◎ keep sth to oneself = 保守秘密。
老闆和他的秘書結婚了。	Our boss married his own secretary.
你知道艾倫有外遇嗎？	Did you know that Ethan is having an affair? ★ have an affair = 和他人有緋聞，通常指負面的關係。因此在此可翻譯成外遇。
你知道艾倫和女同事傳緋聞嗎？	Did you know that there is a scandal between Allen and a female colleague? ◎ scandal (n.) = 醜聞。 不會吧？我不信！ Really? I can't believe it! 你消息也太不靈通，我早就知道了。 Your message is very ill-informed, and I know it already.
有人是走後門進公司的。	Someone got the job through the back door. ◎ through the back door = 走後門。
聽說我們部門有個空降部隊？	Did you hear that someone was parachuted into our department? ◎ parachute into = 空降至（某職位），常用來形容從外部調來公司的人。 ◎ Did you hear that …? = 你有聽說…嗎？

原來新來的經理是董事長的兒子。	So the new manager is the chairman's son.
新來的助理是總經理的姪女。	The new assistant is the president's niece.
新來的主任是被高薪挖角的。	The new director was brought here by the higher salary.
新來的副理長得很帥。	The new assistant manager is really handsome.
我聽說有人在背後說你是非。	I heard someone bad mouthing you behind your back.
你從哪裡聽來的小道消息？	Where did you hear that gossip? ◎ gossip (n.) = 流言蜚語。 我從人事部那裡聽來的。 I heard it from the human resources department.
你確定這個消息是真的嗎？	Are you sure that information is correct?
你不要隨便造謠。	Don't spread rumors. ◎ spread (v.) = 散播。 ◎ rumor (n.) = 謠言。
人際溝通是我的罩門。	Human relations and communication are my weaknesses. ◎ weakness (n.) = 弱點。
我講話常不小心得罪同事。	I often offend my colleagues by accident with my words. ◎ by accident = 意外地。

討論報稅

5 月又要申報個人所得稅了。	It's May. It's time to file the individual income tax again.
你今年已經報稅了嗎？	Have you filed your taxes this year?
我什麼時候要報稅？	When do I have to file my income taxes? 5月31日前。 Before May 31. 截止日是5月31日。 The deadline is May 31. ◎ deadine (n.) = 最後期限。
我用自然人憑證報稅。	I use the MOICA to file my taxes.
我根本不想繳稅。	I don't want to pay the income taxes at all. ◎ not…at all = 一點也不。
如果不繳稅會怎麼樣？	What are the consequences if I don't pay the taxes? ◎ consequence (n.) = 後果、結果。 你將要付罰金。 You will have to pay a penalty. ★ penalty 可以改成 fine 。
繳完稅後錢包大失血。	After paying the taxes, my wallet is almost empty. ◎ empty (a.) = 空的。

再怎麼不情願也要準時完成報稅，逾繳或逃漏稅被抓到都會被罰錢。

討論員工旅遊

我們公司今年有員工旅遊嗎？	Does our company have staff travel this year ?
去年我們是全額補助去日本，不曉得今年有沒有這項預算。	Last year we went on an all-expenses-paid trip to Japan, but I wonder if we have the budget for it this year. ◎ budget (n.) = 預算、經費。
下個月要去員工旅遊。好興奮哦！	We'll go on a staff travel next month. I'm so excited!
我們要去哪？去國外還是在台灣旅行呢？	Where will we go? Will we travel abroad or in Taiwan?
大家投票表決吧。	Let's take a vote.
我們要去香港 3 天 2 夜。	We're going to Hong Kong for three days (two nights).
員工旅遊的行程聽起來不太有趣。	The plans for the staff travel don't sound too interesting.
我們的行程規劃要加入哪些資訊？	What information do we need to put on our travel plan?
飯店訂好了嗎？	Did you reserve the hotel?
車票買了嗎？	Did you buy the train tickets?
公司會補助多少旅費？	How much will the company compensate for travel expenses? ◎ compensate (v.) = 補償。

由於業績不佳，今年的員工旅遊取消。	Due to the poor performance, this year's staff travel is cancelled.
公司的財務狀況不容許員工旅遊。	Our company's financial situation doesn't permit a staff travel.

員工旅遊能夠促進彼此間的情誼，好好出去玩吧。

"Don't let someone else's opinion of you become your reality."

– Les Brown

「不要讓別人對你的評論變成事實。」

～ 萊斯・布朗

練習問題

選擇題 請選出正確的答案。

A) tells the truth	F) abuses his power
B) far behind schedule	G) having an affair
C) spread rumors	H) punch
D) doze off	I) imagine
E) good at jockeying	J) gossip

1. 這個企劃案的進度嚴重落後。

   This project is seriously _________ .

2. 你上班常常打瞌睡。

   You often _________ at work.

3. 你知道伊森有外遇嗎？

   Did you know that Ethan is _________ ?

4. 她的手段很高明。

   She is _________ .

5. 大衛不老實，他從不說實話。

   David is not honest. He never _________ .

6. 你常常請人幫忙打卡。

   You often ask others to _________ your card.

7. 你能想像他買那台車花了多少錢嗎？

   Can you guys _________ how much he spent on that car?

8. 你不要隨便造謠。

Don't ________ .

9. 王秘書濫用職權。

Secretary Wang ________ .

10. 你從哪裡聽來的八卦？

Where did you hear that ________ ?

單字填空 請填入適當的單字。

1. 我想要跳槽。

I want to ________ .

2. 新來的主任是被高薪挖角的。

The new director was brought here by the higher ________ .

3. 你做事很有效率。

You're very ________ .

4. 安德魯喜歡扯別人後腿。

Andrew likes to get others in ________ .

5. 她永遠都在抱怨。

she is always ________ .

6. 你工作很認真。

You work very ________ .

7. 你上班時常常講手機。

You often talk ________ cell phone at work.

8. 你的穿著很有品味。

You have great ________ in clothes.

9. 你做事態度不好，要改進。

You don't have a good ________ at work. You need to improve that.

10. 你的細心值得稱讚。

Your carefulness ________ praise.

• 答案 •

Ⓐ 單字填空

① B	⑥ H
② D	⑦ I
③ G	⑧ C
④ E	⑨ F
⑤ A	⑩ J

Ⓐ 單字填空

① fly the coop	⑥ hard
② salary	⑦ on
③ efficient	⑧ taste
④ trouble	⑨ attitude
⑤ complaining	⑩ deserves

Part 14

新同事

New Employees

新同事

NEW EMPLOYEES

MP3 014

情境會話

員工餐廳 同事 新同事

Henry I heard that there is a new employee joining your department.

Grace Yes. She is an outgoing girl.

Henry Oh. What about her job capability?

Grace She has only worked here for two weeks and put all of our messy files in order. What do you think?

Henry It seems you've found a suitable one.

Henry： 聽說你們部門來了新同事。

Grace： 對啊，是個開朗的女生。

Henry： 是喔，那工作能力怎麼樣？

Grace： 她才來兩個禮拜，就把亂七八糟的資料整理好了。你說呢？

Henry 看來你們找到合適的人選了。

歡迎新同事

今天會有新同事報到。	There are new employees joining us today.
歡迎會六點開始，請準時出席	The welcome party is at 6. Please be on time.
歡迎會預計三個小時。	The welcome party will last about three hours.
歡迎會上會有表演。	There will be a performance at the welcome party. ◎ performance (n.) = 表演。
新人要在歡迎會上致詞。	All the new staff members should make a speech at the welcome party. ◎ make a speech = 致詞、演講。
歡迎會的地點在哪裡？	Where is the welcome party?
這次的新進人員都很優秀。	The newcomers this time are really talented. ◎ newcomer (n.) = 新進人員。
讓我們歡迎新來的同事。	Let us welcome our new coworkers. ◎ coworker (n.) = 同事。
不要緊張，我們這裡就像個大家庭。	Don't worry! Everyone here is like a family.
昨天歡迎會你怎麼沒來？	Why didn't you come to the welcome party yesterday?
有任何問題都可以問我們。	If you have any questions, you can ask us.

好奇新同事背景

你畢業多久了？

How long has it been since you graduated from school?

◎ graduate (v.) = 畢業。

大概三、四年。
Around 3 or 4 years.

你是哪間學校畢業的？

Which school did you graduate from?

我是 DT 大學研究所畢業的。
I graduated from the graduate school at DT university.

我是 DT 大學畢業的。
I graduated from DT University.

你讀什麼科系？

What is your major?
What did you major in?

我主修財務金融。
My major is finance. / I majored in finance.
◎ major in + 學科 = 主修…。

你家有幾個人呢？

How many people are there in your family?

你老家在哪裡？

Where's your hometown?

你和家人一起住嗎，還是自己住？

Do you live alone or with your family?

我和爸媽一起住。
I live with my parents.

我和朋友一起租公寓。
I rent an apartment with my friends.

你多久回家一次？	**How often do you go home?** ★ How often 用來詢問某人做某事的頻率，可以回答 once a week 或 twice a month 等。 我每個月搭高鐵回家一次。 I take the high speed rail home once a month. 我每兩週搭火車回家一次。 I take the train home every two weeks. 我半年回家一次。 I go home once every six months.
你有［男 / 女］朋友嗎？	**Do you have a [boyfriend / girlfriend]?** **Are you in a relationship?**
你結婚了嗎？	**Are you married?**
你有兄弟姊妹嗎？	**Do you have any brothers or sisters?** 有啊。我有一個哥哥和一個妹妹。 Yeah, I have an older brother and a younger sister. 沒有。我是獨生子〔女〕。 No, I'm an only child.

> 公司的新人多半看起來很緊張，老鳥主動上前搭話或許能讓對方放鬆。但也別太著急，一開口就問太多個人隱私問題。

"The only way to have a friend is to be one."

— Ralph Waldo Emerson, Poet

「交到朋友的唯一方法是先成為一個朋友。」

～ 拉爾夫· 沃爾多· 愛默生（詩人）

練習問題

選擇題　請選出正確的答案。

A)	questions	F)	make a speech
B)	live alone	G)	graduate from
C)	talented	H)	Why didn't
D)	majored in	I)	in a relationship
E)	Don't worry	J)	How many people

1. 你家有幾個人呢？

   ________ are there in your family?

2. 你和家人一起住嗎？還是自己住？

   Do you ________ or with your family?

3. 我主修財務金融。

   I ________ finance.

4. 你是哪間學校畢業的？

   Which school did you ________ ?

5. 你有女朋友嗎？

   Are you ________ ?

6. 有任何問題都可以問我們。

   If you have any ________ , you can ask us.

7. 歡迎會上新進人員要致詞。

   All the new staff should ________ at the welcome party.

8. 這次的新進人員都很優秀。

The newcomers this time are really ________ .

9. 我們這裡像個大家庭，不要緊張。

________ ! Everyone here is like family.

10. 昨天歡迎會你怎麼沒來？

________ you come to the welcome party yesterday?

單字填空 請填入適當的單字。

1. 你讀什麼科系？

What is your ________ ?

2. 我是 DT 大學畢業的。

I graduated ________ DT university.

3. 你老家在哪裡？

Where's your ________ ?

4. 你多久回家一次？

How ________ do you go home?

5. 讓我們歡迎新來的同事。

Let us welcome our new ________ .

6. 你結婚了嗎？

Are you ________ ?

7. 我每個月搭高鐵回家一次。

I ________ the high speed rail home once a month.

8. 我在台北租套房。

I rent a ________ in Taipei.

9. 你畢業多久了？

________ has it been since you graduated?

10. 每兩星期搭火車回家一次。

I take the train home ________ two weeks.

• 答案 •

Ⓐ 單字填空

① J ⑥ A

② B ⑦ F

③ D ⑧ C

④ G ⑨ E

⑤ I ⑩ H

Ⓐ 單字填空

① major ⑥ married

② from ⑦ take

③ hometown ⑧ studio

④ often ⑨ How long

⑤ coworkers ⑩ every

職場人際關係

與人相處真是門大學問。有人認為和同事能夠成為交心的朋友，有些人則主張同事就是同事，公私分明。也常見許多人離職的原因，不是因為工作能力，而是遭到職場霸凌，無法融入同儕。學習如何與同事和平共處，也是上班族重要的課程，如果發現有人被霸凌，請適時伸出援手，千萬別跟著加害者一起欺負人。

新同事

各種情緒

喜

喜悅的	cheerful
高興的	delighted
高興的	glad
快樂的	happy
喜悅的	joyous
輕鬆愉快的	lighthearted
開心的	pleased

怒、哀

生氣的	angry
惱怒的	annoyed
惱火的	mad
沮喪的	depressed
沮喪的	upset
傷心的	sorrowful
不快樂的	unhappy
難過的	sad

其他

焦慮的	anxious
冷靜的	calm
難堪的	embarrassed
緊張的	nervous
驕傲的	pride
平靜的	peaceful
擔心的	worried

形容外貌的單字

漂亮的	beautiful
漂亮的	pretty
好看的	good-looking
帥氣的	handsome
優雅的	elegant
迷人的	charming
強壯的	strong
矮壯的	stocky
健美的	well-built
豐滿的	plump
苗條的	slim
瘦的	thin
過瘦的	skinny
過重的	overweight
胖的	fat
年輕的	young
中年的	middle-aged
年長的	elderly
蒼白的	pale
高的	tall
矮的	small
嬌小的	petite

memo

Part 15

吃吃喝喝

Eating & Drinking

吃吃喝喝

EATING & DRINKING

MP3 015

情境會話

辦公室　同事　決定午餐

Emma	Wow! It's Friday! Let's go out for lunch.
Rebecca	Sounds great. What do you prefer?
Emma	It's pretty hot today. I'd like to have sour and spicy Thai food.
Tony	Vietnamese food is good, too.
Rebecca	There is a new Indian Restaurant across from the building. Everything is 50 % off during their opening .
Emma	Sounds good. Let's have Indian food.
Tony	OK.
Rebecca	Great!

Emma：　哇，今天星期五！我們中午去外面吃。
Rebecca：好阿。要吃什麼？
Emma：　今天超熱，好想吃酸酸辣辣的泰式料理。
Tony：　越南料理也不錯。
Rebecca：公司對面最近新開了一間印度餐廳，開幕期間所有餐點都半價。
Emma：　聽起來很棒，就吃印度料理吧。
Tony：　好啊。
Rebecca：太棒了！

午餐吃什麼

你今天有帶午餐嗎？	Did you bring your lunch today?
我也沒帶午餐，要一起出去吃嗎？	I didn't bring my lunch either; do you want to go out for lunch with me?
我們午餐要吃什麼？	What should we eat for lunch?
每天都吃一樣的好膩喔。	I'm fed up with the same lunch every day. ◎ be fed up with… = 對…感到厭煩。
可以換個口味嗎？	Can we try something different? ◎ different (a.) = 不同的。
有清淡一點的選擇嗎？	Is there something light? ◎ light (a.) = 清淡的。
今天換一家不同的餐廳。	Let's try a different restaurant today.
上禮拜新開的越南小吃店看起來很棒，菜單的選擇很多。	The Vietnamese eatery that opened last week looks great, and the menu has a very diverse choices. ◎ diverse (a.) = 各式各樣的。
今天兩人同行，一人免費。	There is a special today. 2 people eat for the price of one.
我有一張折價券。	I have a discount coupon.
要訂午餐的同事請填單子。	Please fill out the order form if you want to order lunch.

請在十一點前訂餐。	Please place your meal orders before 11.
請在十一點半之前把錢交給凱莉。	Please give the money you owe for lunch to Kelly before 11:30.
我想訂涼麵，你呢？	I'd like to order cold noodles. What about you? ◎ I'd like to … = 我想要 …。 ◎ What about you? = 那你呢？
這家便當料多又便宜。	This place's bentos are cheap and the portions are big. ◎ portion (n.) = 一份。
這家便當每份只要五十元。	This place's bentos are only NT$50.
這家便當店買便當附贈飲料。	This place gives you a free drink with your bento.
這家餐廳至少要訂十個才會外送。	This restaurant requires a minimum order of 10 for them to deliver. ◎ a minimum order = 最低訂量。
這家便當店外送要加五十元。	This place charges NT$ 50 for delivery. ◎ charge…for… = 收取…費用。
我今天不餓。	I'm not hungry today.

天氣太熱或外面人太多時真不想外出用餐，這時候訂便當最方便了。每天更換不同家的便當有時也是種期待。

吃到地雷了

這家餐廳的肉不入味。	The meat at this restaurant has no taste.
牛肉煮得太老太硬了。	The beef is overcooked and tough. ◎ overcooked (a.) = 過熟的。tough (a.) = 咬不動的；堅韌的 。
豬排麵粉沾太厚，裡面都沒熟。	The breading on the pork cutlet is too thick, and the inside remains raw. ◎ remain (v.) = 保持。raw (a.) = 生的。
蝦子不新鮮。	The shrimp is not fresh. ◎ fresh (a.) = 新鮮的。
飯永遠是冷的。	The rice is always cold.
菜色每天都一樣。	It's the same dishes every day.
口味選擇不夠多。	There aren't enough choices.
青菜很難吃。	The vegetables taste horrible.
青菜炒太久了。	The vegetables are overcooked.
湯太鹹了。	The soup is too salty. ★其他形容食物的單字：sweet（甜的）。sour（酸的）。bitter（苦的）。spicy（辣的）。overcooked（過熟的）。rawish（有點生的）。delicious（美味的）。yummy（美味的）等。

天哪，我的午餐裡面有蟑螂。	Oh my god! There's a cockroach in my lunch. ◎ cockroach (n.) = 蟑螂，複數為 cockroaches。
我在湯裡發現一根頭髮。	I found a hair in my soup.
這個便當讓我倒胃口。	This bento made me lose my appetite. ◎ lose one's appetite = 某人沒胃口。
一個便當三百元貴得太誇張了。	NT$300 for a bento is ridiculously expensive. ◎ ridiculously (ad.) = 荒謬地。
送餐每次都遲到。	They always deliver late.
這是這個月第五次送錯午餐了。	This is the fifth time this month they got the order wrong.
這家餐廳的地板很髒。	The floor of this restaurant is dirty. ◎ dirty = 骯髒的。

> 嚐試新口味的時候最容易踩到雷了……。

大家來團購吧

幾乎所有東西都能團購。	Almost anything can be group purchased.
團購商品的種類五花八門。	There are so many different kinds of commodities for you to group buy. ◎ commodity (n.) = 商品。

團購可以省運費。	Group buying can get buyers free shipping. ◎ free shipping = 免運費。
團購可以拿到便宜的價格。	Group buying allows buyers to get a cheaper price. ★和金錢相關的單字：price = 價格。cost = 某物值多少錢，主詞是物。spend = 花費（金錢或時間），主詞是人。take = 花費（時間）。pay = 付錢，主詞是人。
最近什麼團購商品最熱門？	What are the hottest items in group buying recently?
這是最近大家最愛的團購商品。	This is what people like most to group buy recently.
要不要一起團購捲心酥？	Will you group buy some wafer rolls?
你要和我們一起團購牛肉乾嗎？	Do you want to group buy some beef jerky with us?
要滿多少才有團購優惠？	What's the minimum number to get a group discount?
最少 15 包。	The minimum is 15 pieces.
如果一次團購三十包，最多可以打八五折。	We can save up to 15% if we group buy 30 packages at a time. ◎ up to = 最多。

多久會送來？	How many days will it take to deliver? 付款完成後三個工作天內。 It will be delivered in three days after you complete the payment. 大概半個月。 About half a month.
當主購很辛苦。	It's painstaking to be a group buying initiator. ◎ initiator (n.) = 發起人、創始人。
你有團購的經驗嗎？	Do you have any experience in group buying? ◎ Do you have any experience in +Ving/N…? = 你有…的經驗嗎？ 這是我第一次團購，很好玩。 No.This is my first time group buying, and it's fun. 當然，我什麼都買過哦。 Sure. I've bought everything.

團購商品不僅能分攤運費，量多還有折扣，真是經濟又實惠。不過瘋團購之餘，還是要好好上班喔。

討論聚餐

公司聚餐可以促進同事間的感情。	Company dinners can improve relations among coworkers. ★ among 用於三者以上，between 則用於兩者之間。

大家想吃什麼料理？

What kind of food are you in the mood for?

- 日本料理如何？
  What about Japanese food?
- 韓式料理不錯。
  Korean food sounds good.
- 今天好熱！我想吃泰式料理。
  It's so hot today! I feel like eating Thai food.
  ◎ I feel like + Ving/N... = 我想要⋯。
- 天氣冷吃火鍋啦！
  Since it's cold, let's eat hot pot!
- 歐式自助餐不錯。
  European buffet isn't bad.
- 我們很久沒吃義大利菜了。
  We haven't had Italian food in a long time.
- 我們可以試試看西班牙菜。
  We could try Spanish food.

我對海鮮過敏。

I'm allergic to seafood.

◎ be allergic to... = 對⋯過敏。

我不敢吃生魚片。

I can't eat sashimi.

有人吃素嗎？

Is anyone vegetarian?

◎ vegetarian (n.) = 素食主義者。

我們乾脆去吃吃到飽？

Why don't we just go to an all you can eat buffet?

大家來投票表決吧。

Let's take a vote.

◎ Let's + 原形動詞 = 讓我們⋯吧。

我們聚餐要先收費。	We pay before we eat.
每人平均分攤三百元。	If we split it, everyone owes NT$300 each. ★各付各的是 go Dutch。
這次聚餐可以攜伴參加。	You can bring a companion to our dinner. ◎ companion (n.) = 同伴。
聚餐時間定於星期五下午六點。	Our dinner reservation is for Friday at 6 pm.
五點五十分在餐廳門口集合。	Please meet us at the entrance of the Restaurant at 5:50.
聚餐時間和地點有問題嗎？	Do you have any problems with the dinner's time or place?

在餐廳

請問有訂位嗎？	Do you have a reservation? ◎ reservation (n.) = 預約。 我們有預約今晚六點。 Yes. We have a reservation for six o'clock tonight.
請問有低消嗎？	Is there a minimum charge? ◎ a minimum charge = 最低消費。
我們要點餐。	Excuse me, we are ready to order.

請問要點什麼呢？	What would you like to order? ◎ What would you like to + Vr…? = 請問你想要…？這是禮貌的用法。 我要牛排五分熟。 I'd like the steak, cooked medium. 我要咖哩豬排和綠茶去冰無糖。 I want the the pork cutlet curry, and a green tea, no ice and sugar. 給我一份燻雞義大利麵套餐。 I'll have the smoked chicken pasta set meal.
請問餐點有附飲料嗎？	Does the meal include a drink? ◎ include (v.) = 包含。
附餐要先上還是後上？	Do you want the side dishes before or after the main course?
我點的菜還沒來。	My order hasn't come yet.
這不是我點的東西。	This is not what I ordered.
請幫我打包。	Can I have a doggy bag, please?
我要結帳。	May I have the check, please? Check, please.
可以分開結帳嗎？	Can we pay separately? ◎ separately (ad.) = 分開地。
服務費是多少呢？	How much is the service charge? ◎ service charge = 服務費。

請問刷這張卡有打折嗎？	Are there any discounts available if I use this credit card?

每間餐廳都有各自的規定，建議用餐前先了解一下，譬如有沒有服務費，最低消費多少等，就能減少很多認知不同而造成的糾紛。

下午茶

下午茶要吃什麼點心？

What kind of dessert would you like for afternoon tea?

- 起司蛋糕怎麼樣？那家咖啡店有蛋糕買一送一。
  What about cheesecake? That coffee shop's cakes are buy one get one free.
  ◎ What about / How about + Ving /N …?
  = …怎麼樣？

- 我想吃手工餅乾。
  I want to have the homemade cookies.

- 甜甜圈不錯。
  Donuts sound good.

回辦公室時順便幫我買杯珍奶。	Get me a cup of bubble milk tea on your way back to the office.
要來杯咖啡嗎？這個品牌的咖啡是最頂級的喔。	Would you like some coffee? This brand of coffee is the top of the line.
來訂飲料吧。	Let's order something to drink.

你要喝什麼？	What kind of drink do you want? 我有點累，我需要咖啡提神。 I'm a little tired, so I need some coffee to perk me up. ◎ perk up = 振作起來。 我要一杯黑糖紅茶。 I'd have a cup of brown sugar black tea.
你的咖啡要加奶精還是鮮奶？	Do you want to add instant creamer or milk to your coffee? 鮮奶。 Milk. 我習慣加奶精。 I am used to using instant creamer. 都可以。 Either will do. It doesn't matter. 都不加。 Neither. ◎ neither = 都不是。
我比較喜歡喝茶。	I prefer tea. I like tea better.
你喜歡哪種茶？	What kind of tea do you like? 我喜歡烏龍茶。 I like oolong tea.
你都喝什麼口味的奶茶？	What flavor milk tea do you usually drink? 伯爵奶茶是我的最愛。 Earl grey milk tea is my favorite. ◎ earl (n.) = 伯爵。

喝白開水既省錢又健康。 | Drinking water saves money and is good for your health.

只有水才能夠解渴，含糖飲料會使人發胖、加速老化，甚至會提高罹患糖尿病的機率，若能少喝就盡量少喝。

年末尾牙

今年尾牙要辦得更盛大。 | This year's annual party is going to be bigger.

尾牙的地點在希爾頓飯店。 | The annual party is at Hilton hotel.

尾牙將在一月二十日舉行。 | Our annual year-end party will take place on January 20.

◎ take place = 舉行。
★ take 的相關單字： take a chance = 冒險。take a look at = 看看。take a note of = 把…記下。take a risk = 冒險。take a walk = 散步。take after = 相似。take account of = 考慮到…。

抽獎活動獎品豐富。 | There are plenty of prizes for the lottery.

尾牙人人有獎。 | Everyone gets a prize at the party.

頭獎為現金五萬元。 | The first prize is NT$50,000 in cash.

抽到特別獎可獲得小折一台。 | The one who wins special prize will get a folding bicycle.

安慰獎是五百元禮券。	The booby prize is NT$500 gift vouchers. ◎ booby prize (n.) = 安慰獎。 ◎ gift voucher (n.) = 禮券 。
如果人不在場，獎項就會取消。	Your prize is invalid if you are not there at the time of drawing. ◎ invalid (a.) = 無效的 。
不知道能不能抽中股票。	I'm not sure if we can win some stocks in the lottery. 文 *S + be + not sure if = 某人不確定是否⋯。if 在此處的意思為「是否」。*
如果抽中頭獎，我請大家去唱歌。	If I win first prize, I'll treat you to karaoke. ◎ treat = 請客。It's my treat. = 我請客。
我抽中第五獎。	I picked 5th place in the lottery.
今年尾牙還邀請到歌手。	We even invited singers to this year's party.
尾牙的餐點很好吃。	The food at the party is really good.
不過，地點實在很遠很不方便。	However, the location is really far and inconvenient. ◎ however (ad.) = 然而。 ◎ inconvenient (a.) = 不方便的 。
公司規定每個人都要參加尾牙。	Our company requires everyone to attend the annual party. Everyone is required to attend the annual party.

我要趕回家，不能參加尾牙。	I have to hurry home and can't attend the party.
每年的尾牙都很無聊。	The party is boring every year.
公司今年取消尾牙。	The company has cancelled the annual party this year.
我們公司從來沒辦過尾牙。	Our company never holds an annual party.

尾牙時氣氛最熱烈的莫過於抽獎了！你抽中過什麼獎品呢？

"One cannot think well, love well, sleep well, if one has not dined well."

– Virginia Woolf

「一個人若吃得不好，便無法好好思考、好好去愛、好好睡著。」

～ 吳爾芙

練習問題

選擇題　請選出正確的答案。

A)	perk me up	F)	What about
B)	prefer	G)	reservation
C)	something different	H)	run out of
D)	am used to	I)	favorite
E)	all you can eat	J)	What kind of

1. 我有點累，我需要咖啡提神。

   I'm a little tired, so I need some coffee to ________ .

2. 我習慣加奶精。

   I ________ using instant creamer.

3. 你喜歡哪種茶？

   ________ tea do you like?

4. 起司蛋糕如何？

   ________ cheesecake?

5. 我比較喜歡喝茶。

   I ________ tea.

6. 伯爵奶茶是我的最愛。

   Earl grey milk tea is my ________ .

7. 咖啡豆已經用完了。

   We've ________ coffee beans.

8. 可以換個口味嗎？
Can we try ________ ?

9. 我們怎麼不去吃吃到飽？
Why don't we just go to an ________ buffet?

10. 請問你有訂位嗎？
Do you have a ________ ?

單字填空 請填入適當的單字。

1. 下午茶要吃什麼點心？
What kind of ________ would you like for afternoon tea?

2. 今天三人同行，一人免費。
There is a special today. 3 people eat for the ________ .

3. 我想吃手工餅乾。
I want to have the ________ cookies.

4. 請問餐點有附飲料嗎？
Does the meal ________ a drink?

5. 我對海鮮過敏。
I'm ________ to seafood.

6. 每天都吃一樣的好膩喔。
I'm ________ the same lunch every day.

7. 青菜炒太久了。
The vegetables are ________ .

8. 這個便當讓我倒胃口。

This bento made me ________ .

9. 我點的菜還沒來。

My ________ hasn't come yet.

10. 要來杯咖啡嗎？

________ some coffee?

• 答案 •

Ⓐ 單字填空

① A	⑥ I
② D	⑦ H
③ J	⑧ C
④ F	⑨ E
⑤ B	⑩ G

Ⓐ 單字填空

① dessert	⑥ fed up with
② price of two	⑦ overcooked
③ homemade	⑧ lose my appetite
④ include	⑨ order
⑤ allergic	⑩ Would you like

餐桌禮儀

餐桌禮儀非常重要，千萬別讓小細節毀了別人對你的印象。通常坐圓桌時，地位最高的人要坐在最裡面，很多人以為先來先搶，殊不知這是沒禮貌的行為。用餐時，請勿邊吃東西邊講話，或發出咀嚼的聲音，這也是常犯的錯誤。如果餐桌禮儀真的令你頭痛不已，或是臨時到了高級餐廳讓你手足無措，不妨先觀察其他同事怎麼做，然後照著做就對了。

上班族常用單字匯總

吃吃喝喝

團購相關單字

團購	group buying ; group purchase ; team buying
主購	team buying initiator
團購者	team buyer
團購優惠	group discount
運費	shipping
免運費	free shipping
交貨	delivery
贈品	freebie

餐廳相關單字

服務生	waiter（男）/ waitress（女）
服務費	service charge
小費	tip
帳單	bill
餐前酒	aperitif
開胃菜	appetizer
冷盤	cold dishes
沙拉	salad
湯品	soup
主菜	main course
甜點	dessert
飲料	drink
酒	wine

Part 16

請假

Taking the Day Off

請假

TAKING THE DAY OFF

MP3 016

情境會話

咖啡廳 朋友 討論旅遊

Grace	I'm taking some time off to visit France from July sixth to July twelfth.
Bella	Where are you visiting in France?
Grace	I plan to visit the lavender fields in Provence.
Bella	Wow, great! I heard the sea of flowers there is beautiful.
Grace	Right. I look forward to it. Anyway, I will pick up a postcard and send it to you. Can you give me your address again?
Bella	You can send the postcard to the company directly! I can share the postcard with my colleagues.

Grace：我 7 月 6 號到 12 號要請特休假去法國。

Bella：你打算去法國哪？

Grace：我要去普羅旺斯看薰衣草。

Bella：真好。聽說那裡的花海很美耶。

Grace：對，我非常期待。總之我會在當地挑張明信片寄給你。可以再給我一次你家的地址嗎？

Bella：直接寄到公司吧！我可以和同事分享。

病假

我［今天／早上／下午］可以請假去看醫生嗎？	Can I take the [day / morning / afternoon] off to go see a doctor?
我今天要請病假。	I have to take a sick leave today.
你為什麼請假？怎麼了？	Why are you taking the day off? What's wrong? ◎ take the day off = 請假；脫下；起飛。

我覺得身體不舒服。
I'm not feeling well today.

我感冒了。
I have a bad cold.

我生理期不舒服。
My period is really bothering me today.

我咳嗽咳不停。
I can't stop coughing.

我喉嚨痛。
I've got a sore throat.
◎ sore throat = 喉嚨痛。
My throat hurts.

我頭很痛。
I have a terrible headache.

我發燒了。
I have a fever.

我眼睛受到感染。
I have an eye infection.

我長針眼。
I have a sty.

我牙痛得很厲害。
My teeth hurt a lot.

我胃痛。
My stomach aches.

我胃脹氣。
I have bad flatulence.

我食物中毒。
I have food poisoning.

我拉肚子。
I have diarrhea.

我要在家休息一天。

I'm going to take a rest at home.

◎ take a rest = 休息。

請病假要附醫生證明。

If you take a sick day, you will have to get proof of your sickness, like a doctor's note.

糟糕，我沒有醫生證明。
Shoot, I don't have a doctor's note or anything.

健保記錄也可以。
Your medical insurance record will do as well.
◎ medical insurance (n.) = 健保 。

如果沒有證明，要扣當日薪水。

If you don't have proof, then the day will be deducted from your pay.

◎ deduct (v.) = 扣除。

這並不合理啊。
That's not reasonable.
◎ reasonable (a.) = 合理的。

根據規定，生理假不扣薪。

According to the regulations, taking a day off due to periods is allowed, and does not incur a penalty.

◎ according to … = 根據…。

病假請超過三天要給經理核准。	If you take more than three sick days, you will need to get the manager's approval.
你這個月病假請了超過七天！	You've taken more than 7 sick days this month! ◎ more than … = 超過…。 文 *S + has/have + p.p. 是現在完成式的句型。*
你必須多調養身體。	You have to take care of yourself. ◎ take care of + 人 = 照顧某人。take care = 保重。

工作雖然重要，健康卻是一輩子的事，千萬不要以為自己是鋼鐵人。稍有感冒前兆或身體不舒服時，務必及早就醫，否則小病拖成大病就麻煩囉。

各種請假狀況

我明天可以請假嗎？	Can I take the day off tomorrow?
你為什麼要請假？	Why are you taking the day off? 明天要去繳稅。 I have to pay my taxes tomorrow. 明天要考汽車路考。 I have a driver's license road test tomorrow. 我要去換身分證。 I have to renew my ID card. ◎ renew (v.) = 換新 。 臨時有事。 Something came up. 個人私事。 It's a personal matter.

我想要好好休個假。	I'd like to take time off for vacation.
我想請三天特休假。	I'd like to take three annual leave days. ◎ annual leave = 特休假。 公司最近業務繁忙，你恐怕不能連請三天。 The company's really busy right now, so I'm afraid you can't take three days off in a row. ◎ in a row = 連續。
車子在路上熄火，要請半天假。	The car broke down, so I need to take a half day off. ◎ break down = 拋錨。 ★ break 的相關片語：break off = 斷交。break up = 分手；結業。break into = 闖入。break out = 爆發。
請假要填假單。	You have to fill out the absence form to take the day off. ◎ fill out = 填寫。
請事假要提前一天告知。	You have to tell us one day in advance if you want to take a personal day. ◎ in advance = 預先。
主管批示後才能成立。	It will be established after the manager's approval. ◎ It will be +Ved =…將被…。
請假請以電話告知。	Please call if you are going to take the day off.

用電子郵件可以嗎？	Can I just send an email?
沒有理由的話，我沒辦法批准。	Without a reason, I can't give you permission.
這是你這月第三次請事假。	This is your third time this month taking a personal day. ★ take a personal day = 請事假；take an annual leave day = 請特休；take a sick day = 請病假。
三天沒到公司又沒請假，要扣薪水。	You haven't been at work for three days, and you didn't call in, so we are docking your pay. ◎ dock one's pay = 扣除某人薪水。
我這個月請事假被扣薪三千元。	They took NT$3000 off this month's paycheck because I took personal days this month. 文 *because + 子句，表示原因。* ◎ paycheck = 薪水支票。

請假是門學問，要有充分的理由主管才會批准。請假時也要尊重主管，不要讓對方感到不愉快。

"Your mind will answer most questions if you learn to relax and wait for the answer."

– *William S. Burroughs*

「如果你學會放鬆並等待答案，你的心會回答大部分的問題。」

～ *威廉· S· 巴勒斯（小說家）*

練習問題

選擇題　請選出正確的答案。

A)	manager's approval	F)	have a fever
B)	sore throat	G)	take care of
C)	feeling well	H)	I'm afraid
D)	eye infection	I)	came up
E)	get proof of	J)	Without a reason

1. 病假請超過三天要給經理核准。
   If you take more than three sick days, you will need to get the ________ .

2. 公司最近業務繁忙，你恐怕不能連請三天。
   The company's really busy right now, so ________ you can't take three days off in a row.

3. 我發燒了。
   I ________ .

4. 我覺得身體不舒服。
   I'm not ________ today.

5. 沒有理由的話，我沒辦法批准。
   ________ , I can't give you permission.

6. 我眼睛受到感染。
   I have an ________ .

7. 我喉嚨痛。
   I've got a ________ .

8. 你必須要多調養身體。

You have to __________ yourself.

9. 請病假要附醫生證明。

If you take a sick day, you will have to __________ your sickness, like a doctor's note.

10. 臨時有事。

Something __________ .

單字填空 請填入適當的單字。

1. 我這個月請事假被扣薪三千元。

They took 3000 dollars off this month's paycheck because I took ________ days this month.

2. 我想請三天特休。

I'd like to take three __________ leave days.

3. 這個月你已經請第三次事假。

This is your __________ time this month taking a personal day.

4. 如果沒有看病記錄，要扣當日薪水。

If you don't have proof, then the day will be __________ from your pay.

5. 個人私事。

It's a personal __________ .

6. 我沒有醫生證明。

I don't have a doctor's __________ or anything.

7. 這並不合理啊。

That's not __________ .

8. 請事假要提前一天告知。

You have to tell us one day in ________ if you want to take a personal day.

9. 請假要填寫請假單。

You have to fill out the ________ form to take the day off.

10. 根據規定，生理假不扣薪。

According to the ________ , taking a day off due to periods is allowed, and does not incur a penalty.

• 答案 •

Ⓐ 單字填空

① A	⑥ D
② H	⑦ B
③ F	⑧ G
④ C	⑨ E
⑤ J	⑩ I

Ⓐ 單字填空

① personal	⑥ note / proof
② annual	⑦ reasonable
③ third	⑧ advance
④ deducted	⑨ absence
⑤ matter	⑩ regulations

特休假

根據勞基法規定，勞工在同一間公司工作滿一定期間者，應照比例給予特別休假：六個月以上一年未滿者，三天。一年以上二年未滿者，七日。二年以上三年未滿者，十日。三年以上五年未滿者，每年十四日。五年以上十年未滿者，每年十五日。十年以上者，每一年加給一日，加至三十日為止。勞工之特別休假，因年度終結或契約終止而未休之日數，雇主應發給工資。

請假

請假相關單字

特休假	annual leave
公假	official leave
病假	sick leave
事假	personal leave
婚假	marital leave
生理假	menstrual leave
產假	maternity leave

陪產假	paternity leave
家庭照顧假	family care leave
喪假	funeral leave / bereavement leave
生日假	birthday leave
有薪假	paid leave
無薪假	unpaid leave

各類身體不適

感冒	cold
流行性感冒	flu
發燒	fever
宿醉	hangover
頭痛	headache
偏頭痛	migraine
針眼	sty
牙痛	toothache

食物中毒	food poisoning
肚子痛	stomachache
拉肚子	have the runs
火燒心	heartburn
消化不良	indigestion
抽筋、經痛	cramps
過敏	allergy
貧血	anemia

看醫生

去看～	see a/an~
醫生	doctor
牙醫	dentist
眼科醫生	eye doctor
皮膚科醫生	skin doctor
耳鼻喉科醫生	ENT doctor

婦產科醫生	ob-gyn
整形醫生	plastic surgeon
精神科醫生	psychiatrist
外科醫生	surgeon
內科醫生	physician
中醫	traditional Chinese physician

memo

Part 17

出差旅行：在機場

At the Airport

出差旅行：在機場

AT THE AIRPORT

MP3 017

情境會話

失物招領處 機場人員 遺失行李

Clerk	How may I help you?
Christina	What should I do if I lose my baggage?
Clerk	Please fill out the form.
Christina	OK.
Clerk	How long will you be staying in Seattle?
Christina	Ten days.
Clerk	When we find your luggage, we will send it to the hotel you are staying at. Please leave us your hotel information.
Christina	No problem.

Clerk： 我能為您服務嗎？
Christina：請問行李遺失該怎麼辦？
Clerk： 請填寫這份表格。
Christina：好。
Clerk： 你會在西雅圖待多久？
Christina：十天。
Clerk： 我們找到行李後，會將它寄到您的旅館。所以請詳填旅館資訊。
Christina：沒問題。

購買機票

我想訂三張 ABC 航空到洛杉磯的來回機票。	I'd like to book 3 round-trip tickets to Los Angeles on ABC Air. ◎ book (v.) = 訂購。
到首爾的單程機票票價多少？	How much is a one-way ticket to Seoul? ◎ round-trip ticket (n.) = 來回票。 反 one-way ticket 單程票。
到溫哥華的經濟艙票價多少？	How much does an economy ticket to Vancouver cost?
這個價格有含機場稅跟燃料費嗎？	Does this price include airport tax and fuel surcharge? ◎ include (v.) = 包括。 ◎ airport tax (n.) = 機場稅。 ◎ fuel surcharge(n.) = 燃料費。
我要訂機票加酒店的套裝行程。	I'd like to book a flight and hotel package.
你的搭機日期是幾月幾號？	What dates would you like to fly?
我預定12月6日出發，12月11日回來。	I'm scheduled to leave on December 6 and come back on December 11. ◎ schedule (v.) = 排定行程。
你要搭哪一種艙等？	What class would you like to fly? 我要搭經濟艙。 I'm flying economy class.

我想把經濟艙機票改成商務艙的。	I want to exchange the economy class ticket for a business class ticket. ★ first class 頭等艙；business class 商務艙；economy class 經濟艙。
我要確認台北到東京的班機。	I want to confirm my flight from Taipei to Tokyo.
我要取消機票並退款。	I'd like to cancel my booking and refund my ticket. ◎ refund (v.) = 退款。
我的機票要改期。	I'd like to change my flight date.

機票不可轉讓他人，也不能擅自修改內容，所以購買機票時請仔細確認所有資料都正確，尤其是姓名拼音的部分。

機場 & 報到櫃檯

最晚請於起飛前一小時辦理劃位。	Please check in at least an hour before departure. ◎ departure (v.) = 起飛。
您的機票和護照，謝謝。	May I have your tickets and passport?
您要靠窗還是走道？	Would you like the window seat or aisle seat ? ◎ aisle (n.) = 走道。請注意 s 不發音。 我要靠窗的座位。 I want a window seat.

可以把我們的座位排在一起嗎？	Can we get our seats together?
我要確認機位。	I want to confirm my seat.
你的座位是靠走道的。	Your seat is an aisle seat.
請問您有幾件行李呢？	How many pieces of baggage do you have?
每人只能攜帶一件隨身行李。	Everyone is allowed one carry-on baggage. ◎ allow (v.)= 允許。
我要託運這兩件行李。	I'd like to check these two pieces of baggage.
我的行李 [沒超重 / 超重了]。	My baggage is [under the weight limit / overweight] . ◎ overweight (a.) = 超重的。
行李超重的費用是多少？	How much is the excess baggage charge? ◎ excess (a.) = 超重的、額外的。
幾點要到登機門？	What time should I be at the boarding gate? ◎ What time should + S + Vr + …? 幾點要…？
登機時間是八點半。	Your boarding time is 20:30.
登機門是八號。	The boarding gate is No. 8.
請準時前往登機門。	Please go to the boarding gate on time.

這是您的登機證和行李收據。	Here is your boarding pass and baggage receipt.
飛機會準時起飛嗎？	Is the plane going to leave on time?
本航班會延誤多久？	How long will this flight be delayed? 會延誤一個小時。 This flight will be delayed an hour.
本航班因為濃霧取消。	This flight is cancelled because of heavy fog.

刷卡購買機票，在辦理登機手續時通常要出示信用卡，若是用他人信用卡購買，對方又沒有同行的話，請務必準備好相關證明（航空公司可能會要求填寫授權書），以免無法劃位登機。

搭飛機

請問有會講中文的空服員嗎？	Are there any flight attendants who speak Mandarin Chinese?
請問座位 18B 在哪裡？	Could you please show me where the seat 18B is? ◎ Could you please show me where + 地點…? = 可以請您告訴我…在哪裡嗎？
請幫我放行李，謝謝。	Please help me with my baggage, thank you.
請給我一份海關申報表。	Please give me a customs declaration form.

請教我怎麼填寫入境卡。	Please tell me how to fill out this arrival card.
請給我一個嘔吐袋。	Please give me a barf bag.
我想要一個枕頭和毛毯。	I'd like a pillow and a blanket.
不好意思，請給我暈機藥。	Excuse me, can you give me some medicine for airsickness?
別忘記把手錶調整成當地時間。	Don't forget to adjust your watch to the local time. ◎ adjust (v.) = 調整。

飛機起飛和降落時，記得先將電子產品關機，等安全警示燈熄滅後再使用。

辦理入境

請出示你的護照。	Please show your passport.
你此行的目的是什麼？	What's the purpose of your visit? ◎ purpose (n.) = 目的。 出差 / 觀光。 [Business / Sightseeing]. 拜訪朋友 / 親戚。 I'm visiting [friends / relatives]. 我來讀書。 I'm going to study.
你要停留多久？	How long are you staying? 我會在這裡待六天。 I'll be here 6 days.

你要住在哪裡？	Where are you staying? 旅館。 At a hotel. 我會待在［朋友 / 親戚］家。 I'm staying at [my friend's / relative's house]. 我姊姊的公寓。 I'm staying at my sister's apartment.
你曾經來過美國嗎？	Have you been to the United States before? ◎ Have you (ever) been to + 地點？＝你到過…嗎？ 我一年前來過美國。 I came to the U.S. a year ago.
這次旅行有人和你同行嗎？	Is anyone accompanying you on this trip? ◎ accompany (v.) = 陪伴、陪同。
你有幫別人帶行李嗎？	Did you bring any baggage for other people?
你有什麼物品要申報嗎？	Do you have anything to declare? ◎ declare (v.) = 申報。 沒有，完全沒有。 No, nothing at all.

辦理入境時，海關人員會詢問幾個問題，若能將上面的句子先記下來，過海關時也能更自在，不至於太緊張而結結巴巴。

練習問題

選擇題　請選出正確的答案。

A) round-trip tickets	F) fill out
B) economy ticket	G) purpose of
C) fasten	H) package
D) because of	I) on this trip
E) will be delayed	J) How long

1. 到溫哥華的經濟艙票價多少？
   How much does an ________ to Vancouver cost?

2. 這班機會延誤多久？
   ________ will this flight be delayed?

3. 會延誤一個小時。
   This flight ________ an hour.

4. 請教我怎麼填寫入境卡。
   Please tell me how to ________ this arrival card.

5. 這班機因為濃霧取消。
   This flight is cancelled ________ heavy fog.

6. 我想訂三張長榮航空到洛杉磯的來回機票。
   I'd like to book 3 ________ to Los Angeles on Eva Air.

7. 我要訂機加酒／機票加酒店的套裝行程。
   I'd like to book a flight and hotel ________ .

8. 請繫緊安全帶。

Please ________ your seatbelt.

9. 你此行的目的是什麼？

What's the ________ your visit?

10. 這次旅行有人和你同行嗎？

Is anyone accompanying you ________ ?

單字填空 請填入適當的單字。

1. 行李手推車在哪裡？

Where are the ________ ?

2. 別忘記妳的登機證。

Don't forget your ________ .

3. 我要搭經濟艙。

I'm flying ________ class.

4. 我們將在西雅圖轉機。

We will ________ in Seattle.

5. 我想把經濟艙機票改成商務艙。

I want to exchange the economy class ticket for a ________ class ticket.

6. 出發時間是何時？

When is the ________ time?

7. 你的座位是靠走道。

Your seat is an ________ seat.

8. 我的旅行支票忘了簽名。

I forgot to ________ my traveler's checks.

9. 每人只能攜帶一件隨身行李。

Everyone is allowed one ________ baggage.

10. 我的行李超重了。

My baggage is ________ .

• 答案 •

Ⓐ 單字填空

① B	⑥ A
② J	⑦ H
③ E	⑧ C
④ F	⑨ G
⑤ D	⑩ I

Ⓐ 單字填空

① baggage carts	⑥ departure
② boarding pass	⑦ aisle
③ economy	⑧ sign
④ transfer	⑨ carry-on
⑤ business	⑩ overweight

緊急出口座位

你是否有坐在緊急出口座位，碰到空服員前來確認能否用英語溝通的經驗呢？根據民航相關法規，發生緊急狀況時，緊急出口座位乘客必須協助執行以下事項：坐在緊急出口位置。辨識打開緊急出口之裝置、瞭解如何開啟並打開緊急出口。遵守組員指引，協助機上旅客完成撤離準備。確認逃生滑梯可正常使用，協助旅客以逃生滑梯撤離。評估並選擇一條安全逃生路徑，儘速遠離飛機。如果真的無法順利溝通，或是沒把握能在急難時幫上忙的話，空服員會為你更換位置，別以為他們是沒事找碴喔。

出差旅行：在機場

機場相關單字

旅客	tourist / traveler
地勤人員	ground staff
安檢人員	security staff
機票	ticket
護照	passport
簽證	visa
服務台	information counter
報到櫃檯	check-in counter
行李手推車	baggage cart
行李磅秤	luggage scale
行李輸送帶	baggage carousel
託運行李	checked baggage
手提行李	carry-on baggage
時刻表	timetable
航班顯示看板	flight information board
接駁公車	shuttle bus
免稅商店	duty-free shop
登機門	boarding gate
登機證	boarding pass
安全檢查	security check
金屬探測儀	metal detector
X 光機	X-ray machine
出境／出發	departure
入境／到達	arrival
出境大廳	departure hall
入境大廳	arrival hall
出境卡	departure card / card / outgoing passenger card
入境卡	arrival card / landing card / incoming passenger card

海關申報表	customs declaration form
入境檢查	immigration inspection
行李提領處	baggage claim area
失物招領處	lost and found
海關	customs
海關檢查	customs inspection
應稅物品	dutiable articles
免稅物品	duty-free articles
違禁物品	contraband
飛機	airplane
起飛	takeoff
降落	landing
準時	on time
誤點	delay
預定出發時間	estimated time of departure (= ETD)
預定到達時間	estimated time of arrival (= ETA)
直飛	direct flight
轉機	connecting flight
中途停留	stopover
頭等艙	first class
商務艙	business class
經濟艙	economy class

機艙內相關單字

乘客	passenger
機長	captain
副機師	first officer
空服員	flight attendant
呼叫鈴	call button
安全帶	seatbelt
暈機藥	medicine
嘔吐袋	barf bag

枕頭	pillow
毛毯	blanket
餐點	meal
機艙	cabin
座位上方置物箱	overhead compartment
亂流	turbulence
緊急逃生口	emergency exit
救生衣	life vest
廁所有人	occupied
廁所沒人	vacant
洗手間	lavatory

Part 18

出差旅行：旅館篇

At the Hotel

出差旅行：旅館篇

AT THE HOTEL

MP3 018

情境會話

旅館　櫃台人員　忘了房卡

Mr. Yang	I left my room card in my room.
Receptionist	May I have your room number, please?
Mr. Yang	My room number is 301.
Receptionist	Excuse me, can you show me the ID offered when you checked in?
Mr. Yang	Sure.
Receptionist	Room 301. OK. Mr. Yang. Please hold on a second. Our staff will open the door for you.
Mr. Yang	Thank you very much.

Mr. Yang：　我把房卡（鑰匙）忘在房間了。
Receptionist：請問您住在幾號房？
Mr. Yang：　我住 301 號房。
Receptionist：方便請您出示住房時登記的身分證件嗎？
Mr. Yang：　沒問題。
Receptionist：301 號房…有了。楊先生，請您稍後，我的同事會替您開門。
Mr. Yang：　謝謝。

旅館訂房

請問貴旅館的房間類型？

What kind of rooms do you have at your hotel?

- 我們提供單人房、雙人房、雙床房、家庭房、商務套房和總統套房。
  We have single rooms, double rooms, twin rooms, family rooms, executive suites, and the presidential suites.

請問商務套房一晚多少錢？

How much is the executive suite for one night?

- 例假日兩百美元，平日七折優惠。
  On weekends and holidays, it's 200 dollars, and on weekdays it's 30% off.

- 兩百美元。有 VIP 卡可以打八折。
  200 dollars a night. If you have a VIP card, you can take 20% off.

我要預約十月五日的單人房一間。

I'd like to make a reservation for a single room on October 5th.

◎ make a reservation = 預約（房間、位置等）。

- 抱歉，那天房間全都訂滿了。
  I'm sorry. All the rooms are full on that day.

- 抱歉，單人房已經客滿。請問商務套房可以嗎？
  I'm sorry, but the single rooms are all booked. How about the executive suite?

- 好。請問預計住幾晚？
  OK. How many nights will you be staying?

我預計住一個星期。

I plan to stay for one week.

先想好要住的房型和天數，並準備好相關證件，就能讓訂房過程更順利喔。

入住 & 退房

[先生 / 女士]，我能替您效勞嗎？	[Sir / Madam], can I help you?
我想要登記入住。	I'd like to check in, please.
我用楊威利的名字訂房間。	I have a reservation under the name of Weili Yang. 請問您姓名的拼法？ How do you spell your name?
我想住高一點的樓層。	I'd like to stay in a room on a higher floor.
請給我有景觀的房間。	Please give me a room with a view.
我要再多住兩晚。	I'd like to stay another two nights.
請填寫這張住宿登記表。	Please fill in this registration form.
加床需要額外付多少錢？	How much more would it cost to add another bed?
請問幾點前要辦理退房？	What time do I have to check out?
請問有附設酒吧或咖啡廳嗎？	Do you have your own bar or café?
請讓我影印您的護照。	Please present your passport and allow me to photocopy it. ◎ photocopy (v.) = 影印。
請稍等。這是您房間的鑰匙。	Please wait a moment. Here are your room key.
請問您要刷卡還是付現？	Are you going to use your credit card or pay in cash?

這是您的帳單。請在此簽名。	Here's your bill. Please sign here.
我要辦理退房。	I'd like to check out.
請問可以寄放行李嗎？我大概 5 點左右回來拿。	Can I leave my baggage here? I'll pick it up at about 5 o'clock.

入住旅館時，可以向櫃台詢問旅遊資訊，譬如附近有名的景點、餐廳等，或許會有意外的發現哦。

旅館服務

抱歉，我搞丟房卡了。	Excuse me. I lost my room key card.
早餐時間是幾點呢？	What time is breakfast?
可以幫我叫計程車嗎？	Can you call a taxi for me?
請問有衣服送洗服務嗎？	Do you have laundry service?
明天早上七點請打電話叫我起床。	I'd like a wake-up call at 7 tomorrow morning.
這裡是 301 號房。我想要點義大利麵和柳橙汁。	This is room 301. I'd like to order a pasta and an orange juice.
請送兩瓶紅酒到 568 號房。	Please send 2 bottles of red wine to room 568.
食物還沒送來。	The food hasn't come yet.

請問房間有什麼問題呢？

Are there any problems with the room?

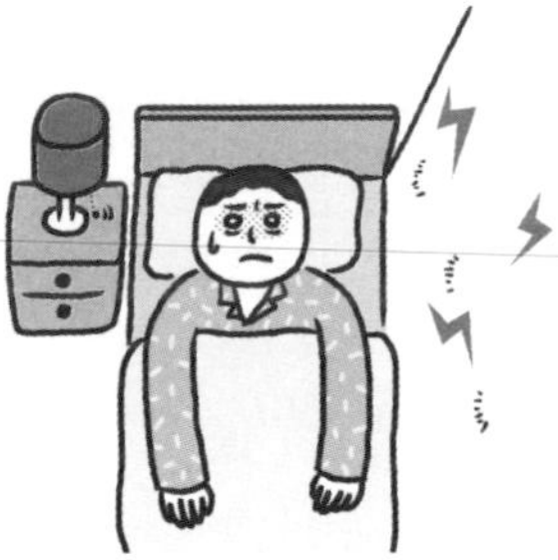

- 房門無法上鎖。
  I can't lock the door.
- 房間還沒打掃。
  The room hasn't been cleaned.
- 這個房間有潮濕的味道。我想要換房間。
  This room has a musty smell. I'd like to change rooms.
- 隔壁太吵，請幫我換房間。
  The neighbors are too noisy. Please help me change rooms.
- 衛浴用品沒有換新。
  The toiletries haven't been changed.
- 房間的水龍頭漏水，請派人修理。
  This room's faucet is leaking, please send someone to fix it.
  ◎ leak (v.) = 漏水。
- 電燈不會亮。
  I can't turn on the light.
- 蓮蓬頭壞掉了。
  The shower head is broken.
- 浴室沒有吹風機。
  There is no hair dryer in the bathroom.

請問要怎麼使用房間內的保險箱？

Excuse me, how do you use the safe in the room?

請勿打擾。

Please don't disturb.

◎ disturb (v.) = 打擾。

入住旅館時，若發現房間有問題，不該勉強接受，應盡快通知飯店人員處理，以免造成不必要的糾紛。

練習問題

選擇題　請選出正確的答案。

A) with a view	F) another two nights
B) hair dryer	G) fix it
C) check out	H) fill in
D) laundry service	I) any problems
E) under the name of	J) disturb

1. 我用楊威利的名字預訂房間。
   I have a reservation ________ Weili Yang.

2. 請勿打擾。
   Please do not ________ .

3. 請給我有景觀的房間。
   Please give me a room ________ .

4. 房間的水龍頭漏水，請派人修理。
   This room's faucet is leaking; please send someone to ________ .

5. 請問有衣服送洗服務嗎？
   Do you have ________ ?

6. 請填寫這張住宿登記表。
   Please ________ this registration form.

7. 浴室沒有吹風機。
   There is no ________ in the bathroom.

8. 我要再多住兩晚。

I'd like to stay ________ .

9. 我要辦理退房。

I'd like to ________ .

10. 請問房間有什麼問題嗎？

Are there ________ with the room?

單字填空 請填入適當的單字。

1. 我要預約十月五日的單人房一間。

I'd like to ________ for a single room on October 5th.

2. 我預計在旅館住一星期。

I ________ stay at the hotel for one week.

3. 隔壁太吵，請幫我換房。

The neighbors' are ________ . Please help me change rooms.

4. 請問商務套房一晚多少錢？

How much is the executive suite ________ one night?

5. 可以幫我叫計程車嗎？

Can you ________ for me?

6. 這是您的帳單。請在此簽名。

Here's your bill. Please ________ here.

7. 這個房間有潮濕味道。

This room has a ________ .

8. 明天早上七點請打電話叫我起床。

I'd like a ________ at 7 tomorrow morning.

9. 請送兩瓶紅酒到 568 號房。

Please ________ 2 bottles of red wine ________ room 568.

10. 抱歉，單人房已經客滿。請問商務套房可以嗎？

I'm sorry, but the ________ are all booked.

• 答案 •

Ⓐ 單字填空

① E ⑥ H

② J ⑦ B

③ A ⑧ F

④ G ⑨ C

⑤ D ⑩ I

Ⓐ 單字填空

① make a reservation ⑥ sign

② plan to ⑦ musty smell

③ too loud ⑧ wake-up call

④ for ⑨ send; to

⑤ call a taxi ⑩ single rooms

不怕一萬，只怕萬一

到外地差旅時，最好將投宿飯店、開會地點的名字、地址、電話等聯絡方式影印或抄一份下來隨身攜帶，如果可以的話最好也將周遭的環境或地標記起來，這樣子當行李遭竊或遺失，或是迷路手機又沒收訊時，就可以直接請人幫忙，就不用擔心要整天流浪街頭了。

公事辦完後若還有時間，不妨請飯店推薦附近好吃或好玩的景點，到處走走逛逛，順便為自己以及親朋好友挑選獨一無二的紀念品，犒賞一下認真工作的自己。

出差旅行：在旅館

旅館相關單字

大廳	lobby
門童	doorman
服務台人員	concierge
接待人員	receptionist
出納員	cashier
經理	manager
清潔人員	housekeeping staff

房間相關單字

床單	bed sheet
枕頭	pillow
棉被	comforter
水龍頭	faucet
吹風機	hair dryer
洗衣服務	laundry service
電燈	light
房卡	room key card
客房服務	room service
保險箱	safe
蓮蓬頭	shower head
衛浴用品	toiletry
毛巾	towel

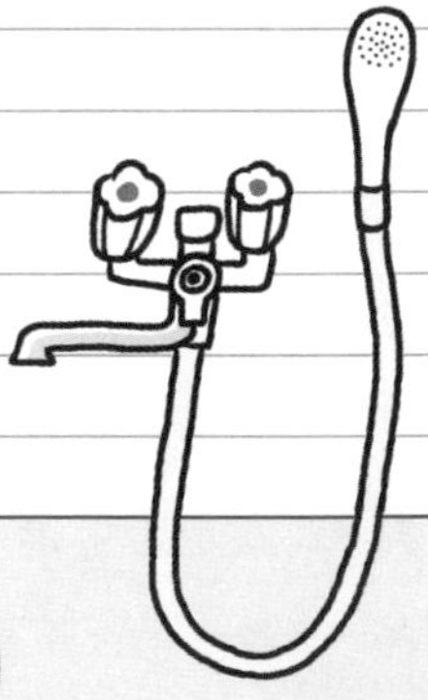

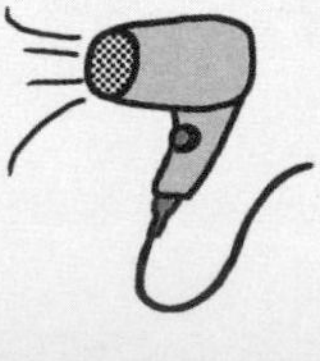

Part 19

出差旅行：觀光篇

Tourism

出差旅行：觀光篇

TOURISM

MP3 019

情境會話

國外 新朋友 搭訕

Terry	Hi, where do you come from?
Jane	I am from Taiwan.
Terry	Taiwan? What coincidence! I went to Taiwan last summer. My name is Terry.
Jane	I'm Jane.
Terry	Do you have time now? I'll treat you to afternoon tea.
Jane	Great! I just wanted to ask someone if there are any private tourist organizations around here.
Terry	You can ask me. I can show you where to hang out around the area.

Terry：嗨，你從哪裡來？
Jane：我來自台灣。
Terry：台灣？好巧，我去年夏天才去過台灣。我叫泰瑞。
Jane：我是珍。
Terry：你有空嗎？我請你喝杯茶。
Jane：好啊，剛好想問人這附近有什麼私房景點。
Terry：問我就對了，我能帶你逛逛這一區。

觀光旅遊

可以請你幫我們拍照嗎？	Could you please take a photo of us?
我們明天要去參觀自由女神。	We're going to see the Statue of Liberty tomorrow. 文 *S+ be going to +Vr⋯= 某人將做⋯，是未來式的用法。*
我們想去第五大道逛街。	We want to go shopping on 5th Avenue. ◎ go shopping = 逛街。 ★ go + Ving = 去做某事。例：go running = 去跑步。go camping = 去露營。
這附近有什麼著名的景點嗎？	Are there any famous tourism spots around here?
請問大都會博物館要怎麼走？	Excuse me, do you know how to get to the Metropolitan Museum? ◎ Excuse me, do you know how to get to ⋯? 不好意思，請問您知道怎麼去⋯嗎？
中央公園在這附近嗎？	Is Central Park close by? ◎ close by = 附近。
請問附近有中餐廳嗎？	Excuse me, is there a Chinese restaurant nearby?
請問最近的 [地鐵站 / 火車站] 怎麼走？	How do I get to the nearest [subway / train] station?
[地鐵站 / 火車站] 在哪裡？	Where is the [subway / train] station?

地鐵站的入口就在前面轉角。	The subway entrance is right at the corner. ◎ entrance (n.) = 入口。
我不太清楚怎麼搭地鐵。	I don't really know how to take the subway.
這班車是到百老匯的嗎？	Is this train for Broadway?
到博物館要在哪裡下車呢？	Where do I get off for the museum? ◎ get off = 下車 反 get on = 上車。
下一班到華盛頓的車何時出發？	When does the next train leave for Washington? 再五分鐘。 In five minutes. 這是最後一班車。 This is the last train.
我要到哪個月台搭車？	On which platform should I board the train?
我想買下午五點到曼徹斯特的火車票。	I'd like to buy a seat on the 5 o'clock train to Manchester.
你要坐吸菸區，還是禁菸區呢？	Do you want to sit in the smoking or non-smoking section? ◎ section (n.) = 區域。
這裡搭公車很方便又省錢。	Taking the bus from here is cheap and convenient.
叫計程車的電話是多少？	What's the number for the taxi service?

請載我到假日飯店。	Please take me to the Holiday Inn.
從這裡到旅館要多久？	How long will it take to get to the hotel from here?
這艘船何時出發到歐胡島？	When does this boat leave for Oahu?
坐渡輪到埃利斯島要多少錢？	How much is it to take the ferry to Ellis Island?
我們坐船需要預約位置嗎？	Do we need to make reservations for the boat?

旅行時難免會遇到交通問題，若能先熟悉基本問句以及各種交通工具的名稱，旅行就能更順利。

旅途中大小狀況

我想將台幣兌換成美金。	I'd like to exchange NT Dollars into US Dollars. ◎ exchange A into B = 把 A 換成 B。
請問這附近哪裡可以兌換外幣？	Excuse me, where can I exchange money around here? ◎ exchange (v.) = 兌換。
請問現在的匯率多少？	How much is the exchange rate of dollars now? ◎ exchange rate (n.) = 匯率。
你要兌換什麼面額？	How would you like the money? 全部換成十元。 I want them all in tens.

	五張二十元，五張十元，十張五元。 Five twenties, five tens, and ten fives please.
這是您兌換的錢。	Here you go.
[先生 / 女士]，這張信用卡不能用。	[Sir / Madam], we don't accept this credit card. 這不可能啊，一定是哪裡出了問題。 It's impossible. It must be something wrong. ◎ impossible (a.) = 不可能的。 請試試看這張卡。 Please try this credit card.
[先生 / 女士]，您的卡刷不過。	[Sir / Madam], I'm sorry but your credit card won't go through.
[先生 / 女士]，您的卡有問題。	[Sir / Madam], I'm sorry, but there is a problem with your credit card.
我忘記帶信用卡了。	I forgot to bring my credit card.
我忘了提款卡的密碼。	I forgot my password for my ATM card.
我找不到我的護照。	I can't find my passport.
我的行李不見了。	I lost my baggage. ◎ lose (v.) = 遺失，過去式為 lost。
航空公司把我的行李弄丟了。	The airlines lost my luggage.
我被搶劫了。	I was robbed.

糟糕，我竟然在大街上迷路了。	Shoot, I am actually lost even though I'm on this main road.
你有旅館的電話號碼嗎？	Do you have the hotel's phone number?
這是我住的旅館的地址。	Here's my hotel's address.
請問貴餐廳收旅行支票嗎？	Excuse me,do you accept traveler's checks in your restaurant?
我的旅行支票忘了簽名。	I forgot to sign my traveler's checks.

旅行中碰到突發狀況時，切記冷靜為上策。

購買伴手禮

請問禮品店在哪裡？	Excuse me, where is the gift shop?
請問這附近有什麼特色小店嗎？	Excuse me, are there any special shops around here?
我想買個包包送我老婆。	I want to buy a handbag for my wife.
我要買些伴手禮回去給同事。	I need to buy some souvenirs for my colleague. ◎ souvenir (n.) = 紀念品。
每次買伴手禮都要猶豫好久。	I hesitate about the souvenirs every time.

到底要買什麼給朋友才好呢？	What should I buy for my friends after all? 你可以買當地的特產啊。 You can buy local specialties. ◎ specialty (n.) = 名產 。 別想那麼多，禮輕情意重，買些飾品就好了。 Don't think too much. I think the thought that counts. You can just buy some accessories.
糟糕，忘了買伴手禮了。	Oops, I forgot to buy souvenirs. 你可以在機場的免稅商店購買。 You can purchase at the duty-free stores in the airport.
我從法國帶回來的紅酒和巧克力很特別喔。	The red wine and chocolate I bought in France is very special.

出差回來時帶些零食點心或小禮物慰勞同事，有助於增進彼此的情誼。當然也別忘了想到家人。

"Adventure is worthwhile in itself."

– Amelia Earhart, Aviator

「探險本身就是值得的。」

～ 愛蜜莉亞· 艾爾哈特（飛行員）

練習問題

選擇題　請選出正確的答案。

A) What's the number	F) exchange
B) famous tourism	G) get off
C) nearby	H) in
D) credit card	I) entrance
E) exchange money	J) souvenirs

1. 這附近有任何著名景點嗎？

   Are there any ________ spots around here?

2. 到博物館要在哪裡下車呢？

   Where do I ________ for the museum?

3. 請問這附近哪裡可以兌換外幣？

   Excuse me, where can I ________ around here?

4. 地鐵站的入口就在前面轉角。

   The subway ________ is right at the corner.

5. 叫計程車的電話是多少？

   ________ for the taxi service?

6. 全部換成十元。

   I want them all ________ tens.

7. 先生，您這張信用卡不能用。

   Sir, we don't accept this ________ .

8. 請問附近有中餐廳嗎？

Excuse me, is there a Chinese restaurant ________ ?

9. 我想將台幣兌換成美金。

I'd like to ________ NT Dollars into US Dollars.

10. 還要買些伴手禮回去給同事。

I need to buy some ________ for my colleague.

單字填空 請填入適當的單字。

1. 這不可能啊，一定是哪裡出了問題。

________ . It must be something wrong.

2. 這裡搭公車很方便又省錢。

Taking the bus from here is cheap and ________ .

3. 請問貴餐廳收旅行支票嗎？

Excuse me,do you accept ________ in your restaurant?

4. 我要到哪個月台搭車？

On ________ should I board the train?

5. 我不太知道怎麼搭地鐵。

I don't really know how to ________ the subway.

6. 可以請你幫我們拍照嗎？

Could you please ________ of us?

7. 我忘了提款卡的密碼。

I forgot ________ for my ATM card.

8. 請問現在的匯率多少？

How much is the exchange ________ of dollars now?

9. 我找不到我的護照。

________ my passport.

10. 這班車是到百老匯的嗎？

Is this train ________ Broadway?

• 答案 •

Ⓐ 單字填空

① B　⑥ H

② G　⑦ D

③ E　⑧ C

④ I　⑨ F

⑤ A　⑩ J

Ⓐ 單字填空

① It's impossible　⑥ take a photo

② convenient　⑦ my password

③ traveler's checks　⑧ rate

④ which platform　⑨ I can't find

⑤ take　⑩ for

別把雞蛋放在同一個籃子

到歐洲旅遊時，別把所有錢財、護照、機票等帶在身上，萬一遇到強盜或騙子，東西被偷了不要緊，回不了國才是最麻煩的事。為了避免這種情況，可以採取下列方法：

① 抵達目的地後先到飯店 check-in，將貴重物品鎖在飯店保險箱，或請飯店櫃台幫忙保管，再不行就鎖行李箱裡。

② 大鈔、信用卡藏在貼身衣物裡，只帶一點錢在小零錢包裡。

③ 隨時注意隨身物品是否拉上拉鍊，人多時更要將包包背緊。

④ 有人朝你走來向你問話或要求拍照等一律不理，盡量遠離對方。

⑤ 不亂撿錢財或物品。

⑥ 不落單、不走小路。

⑦ 不大剌剌的背名牌包。

⑧ 搭車時盡量不坐門邊，容易被搶劫。

⑨ 盡量不在地鐵上拿出數位產品。

⑩ 若怕遺失護照，建議多影印幾份放行李箱及包包裡（甚至放一份在貼身衣物裡）。多預備一份電子檔案也是很好的選擇。

出差旅行：觀光篇

付款方式

現金	cash
支票	check
旅行支票	traveler's check
信用卡	credit card
提款卡	ATM card
借記卡	debit card （類似台灣的 VISA 金融卡）
電子錢包	digital wallet

常見景觀

世界遺產	world heritage
博物館	museum
美術館	art museum
畫廊	gallery
圖書館	library
基金會	foundation
廣場	square
教堂	church
廟宇	temple
清真寺	mosque
國家公園	national park
遊樂園	amusement park

動物園	zoo
水族館	aquarium
花園	garden
鐵塔	tower
金字塔	pyramid
紀念碑	monument
雕塑	sculpture
噴泉	fountain

memo

Part 20

出差旅行：旅費申請

Travel Expenses Reimbursement

出差旅行：旅費申請

TRAVEL EXPENSES REIMBURSEMENT MP3 020

情境會話

公司 會計 旅費申請

Emma	I've filled out the reimbursement form for my travel expenses. I also attached my invoice and receipts. To whom should I give the information ?
Accountant	You can just hand them to me.
Emma	When can I reimburse for my travel expenses?
Accountant	It takes almost a week. If everything is ok after checking your documents, it will be transferred to your account.

Emma： 我已經填好旅費申請表，也附上發票和收據了。應該把資料交給誰呢？
Accountant：交給我就可以了。
Emma： 我大概何時會拿到旅費呢？
Accountant：通常要一個禮拜左右，核對過沒問題就會轉入你的戶頭。

旅費申請報帳

我的旅費需要報帳。	I'd like to request my travel reimbursement. ◎ reimbursement (n.) = 退款。
申報旅費要填什麼表格呢？	Which form should I fill out to get my travel reimbursement?
你的表格填寫不完整。	Your form is not completed.
旅費報帳要附上發票或收據。	If you want to get reimbursed for your travel expenses, you will need to attach invoices and receipts.
我沒有發票，也沒有收據。	I don't have invoices, and I don't have receipts, either.
沒有發票或收據沒辦法報帳。	You can't apply for reimbursement without a receipt.
有其他證明嗎？	Do you have any evidence? ◎ evidence (n.) = 證明。
手續這麼麻煩喔。	The procedures are so inconvenient. ◎ procedure (n.) = 手續。
我的旅費總共七萬兩千元。	My travel expenses are totally NT$72,000.
你的住宿費過高，可能無法全額申請。	Your accommodation fee is too high. You may not get the full application back. ◎ accommodation (n.) = 住宿。

練習問題

選擇題　請選出正確的答案。

A) evidence
B) apply for
C) procedures
D) accommodation fee
E) without a receipt

1. 你好，我的旅費需要報帳。
   Hello, I'd like to ________ reimbursement for my travel expenses.

2. 沒有收據沒辦法報帳。
   You can't apply for reimbursement ________ .

3. 有其他證明嗎？
   Do you have any ________ ?

4. 你的住宿費過高，可能無法全額申請。
   Your ________ is too high. You may not get the full application back.

5. 手續這麼麻煩喔。
   The ________ are so inconvenient.

單字填空　請填入適當的單字。

1. 我沒有發票，也沒有收據。
   I don't have ________ , and I don't have ________ , either.

2. 申請旅費要填什麼表格呢？
   Which form should I ________ to get my travel reimbursement?

3. 手續這麼麻煩喔。

The procedures are so ________ .

4. 我的旅費總共七萬兩千元。

My ________ are totally NT$72,000.

5. 你的表格填寫不完整。

Your form is not ________ .

• 答案 •

Ⓐ 單字填空

① B

② E

③ A

④ D

⑤ C

Ⓐ 單字填空

① invoices; receipts

② fill out

③ inconvenient

④ travel expenses

⑤ completed

差旅費用

因公出差時，公司通常會補助一定金額的差旅費。差旅費通常分成交通費、生活費、辦公費、業務費、雜費等支出，有些費用需要依規定事先申請，有些則是事後憑收據、發票請款，請務必確認所有細節，例如每天補助幾餐？餐費上限？團體租車費用如何報銷？外幣匯率如何換算？遇到緊急狀況時怎麼處理？等問題，以免無法請款或超出預算，必須自掏腰包。另外，到國外差旅時，若想和店家索取收據，可以說：「May I have a receipt?（我可以要一張收據嗎？）」

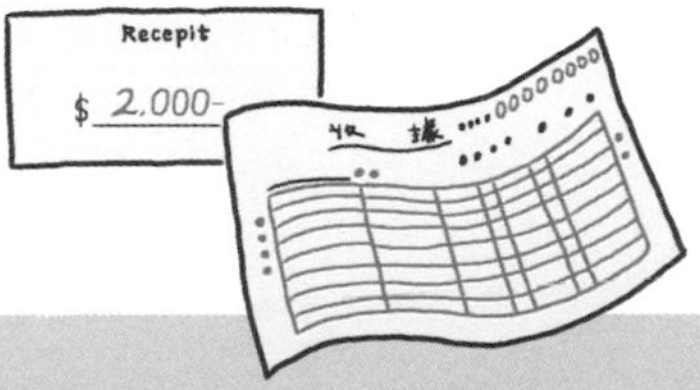

memo

Part 21

職場進修

Training

職場進修

TRAINING

MP3 021

情境會話

捷運上 朋友 閒聊

Andrew	How about going to the movies after work?
Sally	Sorry. I will go to a class after work today.
Andrew	Class? What kind of class?
Sally	It's about marketing and sales management.
Andrew	I didn't know you are that hard-working.
Sally	I have no choice. My boss requires all employees to take this course.
Andrew	Fine. How about Wednesday night? Are you free?

Andrew：今天下班後要不要去看電影？
Sally：我下班後要去上課。
Andrew：上課？上什麼課？
Sally：有關市場行銷的課程。
Andrew：你什麼時候那麼認真了？
Sally：沒辦法，老闆規定所有員工都要上這堂課。
Andrew：好吧，那星期三晚上你有空嗎？

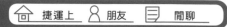

語言相關

英文是最重要的國際語言。	English is the most important international language.
公司希望研發人員懂英文和日文。	The company wants their research and development employees to know English and Japanese.
這份工作要求法語流利。	This job requires candidates to be fluent in French. ◎ be fluent in + 語言 = 精通某種語言。
總經理要求所有員工都要通過全民英檢初級。	The president requires all employees to pass the GEPT Elementary level.
我的目標是通過全民英檢中高級。	My goal is to pass the GEPT High-Intermediate level.
如果通過全民英檢中高級，公司會給獎金三千元。	If I pass the GEPT High-Intermediate level, the company will give me a grant of NT$3,000.
我已經報名了美語補習班。	I've already registered for American English classes. ◎ register (v.) = 登記、註冊。
老師上課全程講英文。	During class, the teacher only speaks English.

你每個星期要上幾次課？	How many times a week do you have class? ◎ How many times a week …? = 每星期…幾次？ 💬 每星期 [兩次 / 三次]。 [Twice / Third times] a week.
這次多益考試結果如何？	What did you get on the TOEIC this time? 💬 我以為我的表現會更好。 I thought my performance would be better.
你會買英語參考書嗎？	Do you buy any English reference books? ◎ reference book = 參考書。
我一個月花一千元以上買英文書。	I spend more than NT$1,000 a month on English books.
我最近在試著看原文書。	I'm trying to read books in their original language recently. ◎ original (a.) = 原始的。
日文有越來越重要的趨勢。	Japanese is becoming a more important language to learn.
日文可以增加我的競爭力。	Knowing Japanese will make me more competitive. ◎ competitive (a.) = 競爭的。
我以前學過日文，可是現在幾乎忘光了。	I learned Japanese before, but I have basically forgotten all of my Japanese. ◎ basically (ad.) = 基本上。

我不久後要去義大利出差。	I'm going on a business trip soon to Italy.
我需要一位義大利語家教。	I need an Italian language tutor.
我星期一和星期三晚上 7 點到 9 點上義大利文。	I take Italian classes on Mondays and Wednesdays, from 7-9 P.M.

無論是哪個行業，要求員工學習第二外語的公司越來越多，語言儼然是找工作不可或缺的條件之一了。若能多學一種語言，等於多了一項優勢喔。

電腦相關

取得證照讓你有優勢。	It will be an advantage for you once you get the certificate. ◎ certificate (n.) = 證書、證照。
懂 InDesign 對找工作有幫助。	Getting the know-how about InDesign is helpful for you to find a job. ◎ know-how (n.) = 技術；竅門。 ◎ helpful (a.) = 有幫助的。
老闆要我學會用 PowerPoint 做簡報。	My boss wants me to learn how to give presentations on PowerPoint.
我想要進修 Excel 方面的課程，補習費一個月五千元。	I would like to take a course on Excel, and the course costs NT$5,000 a month. ◎ take a course = 選修課程。

兩人同行還可以打八折。	If a friend joins too, they'll give us 20% off. 文 *假設句句型：If + S + V, S +will + Vr+⋯，是指未來可能發生的事情。*
那是免費課程，只需要付教材費。	That's a free class. You only have to pay for textbooks. ◎ pay for ⋯ = 付錢買⋯。
用 Word 做文書編輯很簡單。	It's easy to use Word to edit text. ◎ It's easy to ⋯ = ⋯很容易。
Access 沒有想像中那麼困難。	Access isn't as hard as you think.
我對影像處理很有興趣。	I'm very interested in image processing. ◎ be interested in ⋯= 對⋯有興趣。
Illustrator 是常用的繪圖工具。	Illustrator is a commonly used drawing tool.
你有聽過 CorelDRAW 這個軟體嗎？	Have you heard of the software CorelDRAW?
你們有插畫和設計的課程嗎？	Do you have courses about illustration and design?
程式設計的課程比其他的貴很多。	The computer programming courses are a lot more expensive than other ones.
我目前最想學 Flash 動畫。	I want to learn Adobe Flash the most at present.

程式設計有基礎入門和專業進階的課程。	There are introductory and advanced computer programming classes. ◎ introductory (a.) = 入門的。advanced (a.) = 進階的。
我最近報名了 AutoCAD 製圖課程。	I recently registered for an AutoCAD class.

如果真的沒時間進修，至少學會最基本的辦公室軟體吧！

"I am always ready to learn, although I do not always like being taught."

— Winston Churchill

「我隨時做好準備要學習，雖然我不見得喜歡被訓話。」

～ 邱吉爾（英國前首相）

練習問題

選擇題　請選出正確的答案。

A) is helpful for	F) fluent in
B) as hard as	G) an advantage for
C) international language	H) registered for
D) interested in	I) give presentations
E) business trip	J) commonly used

1. 英文是最重要的國際語言。

   English is the most important ________ .

2. 我不久後要去義大利出差。

   I'm going on a ________ soon to Italy.

3. 我已經報名了美語補習班。

   I've already ________ American English classes.

4. 老闆要我學會用 PowerPoint 做簡報。

   My boss wants me to learn how to ________ on PowerPoint.

5. 懂 InDesign 對找工作有幫助。

   Getting the know-how about InDesign ________ you to find a job.

6. 這份工作要求法語流利。

   This job requires candidates to be ________ French.

7. Access 沒有想像中那麼困難喔。

   Access isn't ________ you think.

8. 我對影像處理很有興趣。

I'm very ________ image processing.

9. Illustrator 是常用的繪圖工具。

Illustrator is a ________ drawing tool.

10. 拿到證照會讓你有優勢。

It will be ________ you once you get the certificate.

單字填空 請填入適當的單字。

1. 我每星期上兩堂電腦課。

I ________ two computer classes a week.

2. 你有聽過 CorelDRAW 這個軟體嗎？

Have you heard of the ________ CorelDRAW?

3. 我的目標是通過全民英檢中高級考試。

My ________ is to pass the GEPT High-Intermediate level.

4. 總經理要求所有員工都要通過全民英檢初級。

The president ________ all employees to pass the GEPT Elementary level.

5. 我需要一位義大利語家教。

I need an Italian language ________ .

6. 我一個月花一千元以上買英文書。

I spend more than NT$1,000 a month ________ English books.

7. 我以前學過德文，可是幾乎忘光了。

I learned German before, but I have basically ________ all of my Japanese.

8. 英語可以增加我的競爭力。

Knowing English will make me more ________ .

9. 你們有插畫設計的課程嗎？

Do you have ________ about illustration and design?

10. 我最近報名 AutoCAD 製圖課程。

I recently ________ an AutoCAD class.

• 答案 •

Ⓐ 單字填空

①C ⑥F

②E ⑦B

③H ⑧D

④I ⑨J

⑤A ⑩G

Ⓐ 單字填空

① take ⑥ on

② software ⑦ forgotten

③ goal ⑧ competitive

④ requires ⑨ courses

⑤ tutor ⑩ registered for

善用零碎時間

每天回到家就累到只想癱在床上？工作都做不完了哪有時間進修？扣掉工作和吃飯、睡覺的時間，所剩的時間不到八個小時，更別提還要交際應酬了。

在學習資源豐富的今日，想要充實自己沒那麼困難，也不一定要去補習班，只要稍微減少漫無目的上網、玩手機、看電視的時間，就算一天只花15分鐘學習、閱讀，積沙成塔，一年累積下來也是很可觀的。現在開始，試著善用自己的零碎時間吧！

上班族常用單字匯總

職場進修

語言相關

亞洲語系

國語	Mandarin
客語	Hakka
台語	Taiwanese
日語	Japanese
韓語	Korean
粵語	Cantonese
泰語	Thai
越南語	Vietnamese
菲律賓語	Filipino
印尼語	Indonesian
馬來西亞語	Malay
阿拉伯語	Arabic

歐美語系

英語	English
西班牙語	Spanish
法語	French
葡萄牙語	Portuguese
德語	German
義大利語	Italian
俄語	Russian
荷蘭語	Dutch
芬蘭語	Finnish
瑞典語	Swedish
冰島語	Icelandic
捷克語	Czech

其他課程

課程	class
課程	course
工作坊	workshop
網頁設計	web design
程式設計	computer programming
行動 app 設計	mobile app design
商用書信	business writing
溝通技巧	communication skills
領袖課程	leadership
公眾演説	public speaking
時間管理	time management

設計	design
平面設計	graphic design
插畫	illustration
繪畫	painting
攝影	photography
影像處理	image processing
珠寶設計	jewelry design
金工	metalsmithing
花藝	floral design
陶藝	pottery
烹飪	cooking

memo

Part 22

求職面試

Applying & Interviewing

求職面試

APPLYING & INTERVIEWING

MP3 022

情境會話

餐廳　朋友　面試後

Annie	How was your interview today? Did everything go OK?
Olivia	I think I didn't behave myself well. I was too nervous.
Annie	Don't always think the worst. Everyone gets nervous when they have an interview.
Olivia	I hope so. I really look forward to working in the company.
Annie	When will you know the result?
Olivia	They will send me the result by email.
Annie	You are all qualified. You will get the job.

Annie：今天的面試怎麼樣？一切還好嗎？
Olivia：我覺得自己表現得不夠好，我太緊張了。
Annie：別老往壞處想，大家面試都會緊張。
Olivia：希望如此。我真的很想進這間公司。
Annie：什麼時候會知道結果？
Olivia：一個禮拜內會以 E-mail 通知。
Annie：你符合所有條件，一定沒問題的。

面試問答—經歷與特質

請在三分鐘之內介紹自己。

Please introduce yourself in three minutes or less.

請用英文和日文自我介紹。

Please introduce yourself in English and Japanese.

請談談你之前的工作經驗。

Please talk about your previous work experience.

◎ previous (adj.) = 先前的。

我之前當了兩年行政助理。
I've been an administrative assistant for two years.

我之前從事業務工作三年。
I have worked as a salesperson for three years.

我之前是研發人員。
I worked in research and development.

我之前是兒童美語老師。
I was an ESL teacher to kids.

你有英語證照嗎？

Do you have any English language certifications?

你會其他外語嗎？

Do you know any foreign languages?

你有幾年的工作經驗？

How many years of work experience do you have?

你一分鐘可以打幾個字？

How many words can you type per minute?

請形容你自己的個性。	Please describe your personality. ◎ describe (v.) = 描述。
談談你的家庭狀況。	Tell me about your family.
請長話短說，謝謝。	Please tell me the short version, thank you.
請簡略說明前份工作一天的行程。	Please describe a typical day at your last job.
之前的工作，你最不喜歡的部分是？	What did you like the least about your last job?
請說明你上份工作離職的原因。	Please tell me the reason why you left your last job. ◎ leave (v.) = 離開，left 為過去式。

我被公司資遣。
I was laid off.
★ laid 的原形動詞是 lay。lay 的相關片語：lay on⋯ = 把⋯歸於。lay with / on = 打賭。

我另有生涯規劃。
I had a different career plan.

我覺得發展受限。
There was a limit to my growth there.

我不滿意薪水。
I was dissatisfied with the salary.
◎ be dissatisfied with⋯ = 對⋯不滿意。

公司的氣氛不好。
The atmosphere at the company was bad.
◎ atmosphere (n.) = 氣氛。

你的生涯規劃為何？	What is your career plan? ◎ career plan = 生涯規劃。
你的座右銘是？	What are your mottos? 失敗為成功之母。 Failure leads to success. 我思故我在。 I think; therefore I am.
你為什麼失業這麼久？	Why have you been unemployed for so long? ◎ unemployed (adj.) = 失業的。
請談談你遭遇失敗的例子。	Please tell me about a time when you failed.
你最大的缺點是什麼？	What is your biggest flaw? ◎ flaw (n.) = 缺點、瑕疵。

投了好幾份履歷，終於得到面試機會了。好好準備，讓面試官留下良好的第一印象，進而從面試中脫穎而出吧！

面試問答—公司與展望

你對於本公司的看法？	What do you think about our company?
你和同事相處情形如何？	How do you get along with your coworkers?

你為什麼選擇我們公司？	Why did you choose our company? 💬 貴公司讓我有發揮的空間。 Your company will give me space to develop. 💬 貴公司的福利和制度很健全。 Your company's benefits and policies are very sound. ◎ benefit (n.) = 福利。 policy (n.) = 政策。 💬 我對貴公司的前景很有信心。 I believe in your company's prospects. ◎ prospect (n.) = 前景。
你認為你對公司能有何貢獻？	What do you think you will contribute to our company? ◎ contribute (v.) = 貢獻、出力。
和上司意見不合，你會怎麼解決？	What are you going to do about your disagreement with your supervisor? ◎ disagreement with… = 和…意見不合。 💬 我會和上司溝通。 I'm going to talk to him about it. 💬 我會聽上司的意見。 I'm going to listen to what he has to say. 💬 我會耐心解釋我的意見。 I will patiently explain my opinion.
你希望三年後會有何發展？	Which position do you want to be after three years? ◎ position (n.) = 職位。
你可以配合加班嗎？	Are you willing to work overtime?

你最無法忍受哪種同事？

What kind of coworker do you have the least amount of tolerance for?

◎ tolerance (n.) = 容忍。

自私的人。
Selfish ones.

不負責任的人。
Irresponsible people.

喜歡打小報告的人。
People who tattle tale to the boss.

沒有效率的人。
Inefficient people.

這份工作最吸引你的地方是什麼？

What attracts you most about this position?

你們的工作態度讓我印象深刻。
Your attitudes at work have left a deep impression on me.
★ leave a good impression on + 人 = 給…留下好印象。under the impression that = 以為是。

這裡的同事都很認真。
Everyone here seems to work hard.

我喜歡這裡的工作氣氛。
I like the atmosphere at work.

你介意調到國外嗎？

Do you mind being sent abroad?

◎ Do you mind +Ving…?= 你介意…嗎？

你對本公司有什麼問題呢？

Do you have any other questions about our company?

- 請問貴公司的福利制度？
  What kind of benefits do you provide at your company?
- 請問貴公司有試用期嗎？
  Does your company have a probationary period?
  ◎ probationary period = 試用期。
- 未來公司有新的發展計畫嗎？
  Does the company have any plans for new developments or projects in the future?
- 公司對於員工下班後進修有什麼政策嗎？
  Does the company have any policy on employees taking classes after work?
- 請問貴公司的升遷管道？
  Can you tell me the typical career path at your company?
  ◎ career (n.) = 職業。
- 會外派到其他國家嗎？
  Does this job require international travel?

面試前一定要事先做足準備，瞭解該公司的文化背景以及所應徵的工作內容。否則即使背景或學歷再優秀，當問到對公司的看法卻一問三不知時，仍然會讓面試官留下不好的印象。

其他狀況

面試前要先打電話確認。	You should call to confirm your interview before going.
面試最忌諱遲到。	You should avoid being late for an interview. ◎ avoid + Ving= 避免⋯。be late to/for = 遲到。
面試時要關手機。	Turn off your cell phone during the interview. ◎ during (prep.) = 在⋯期間。
面試時間臨時更改。	They switched the interview time all of a sudden. ◎ all of a sudden = 突然地。
面試臨時取消。	The interview was cancelled at the last minute.
面試時間已經結束了。	The time for interview is over.
經理正在開會，請稍等十分鐘。	The manager is in a meeting, so please wait for about 10 minutes.
我忘了帶履歷表。	I forgot to bring my resume. ◎ bring (v.) = 帶來。
你的回答跟問題無關。	Your answer is irrelevant to the question. ◎ irrelevant (a.) = 無關的。
你的衣著太隨意了。	You are dressed too casually.
你的眼神飄忽不定。	You don't make eye contact.

你的氣燄太高。	You're too haughty. ◎ haughty (a.) = 高傲的。
除了學經歷，待人處世也很重要。	Besides education and experience, the ability of associating with people is also very important.
你對本公司完全不了解。	You do not know anything about our company.
我們會在一週內通知你。	We will contact you within one week. ◎ within (prep.) = 在…之內。
你被錄用了。	You've been hired.

經過重重關卡，總算錄取了，通常錄取後還有 1 ～ 3 個月的試用期（有些公司甚至有職前訓練），一定要謹言慎行，多表現自己的優點，讓公司覺得你是有能力的，加油！

"The beginning is the most important part of the work."

– Plato, Philosopher

「開始階段是工作裡最重要的部份。」

～ 柏拉圖（古希臘哲學家）

練習問題

選擇題　請選出正確的答案。

A) short version	F) get along with
B) contribute to	G) work experience
C) disagreement with	H) for an interview
D) being sent abroad	I) all of a sudden
E) Turn off	J) patiently explain

1. 面試時間臨時更改。
   They switched the interview time ________ .

2. 面試最忌諱遲到。
   You should avoid being late ________ .

3. 面試時要關手機。
   ________ your cell phone during the interview.

4. 你有幾年的工作經驗？
   How many years of ________ do you have?

5. 請長話短說，謝謝。
   Please tell me the ________ , thanks.

6. 你介意出差或調到國外嗎？
   Do you mind travelling or ________ ?

7. 我會耐心解釋我的意見。
   I will ________ my opinion.

8. 你和同事相處情形如何？

How do you _________ your coworkers?

9. 你認為你對公司能有何貢獻？

What do you think you will _________ our company?

10. 和上司意見不何，你會怎麼解決？

What are you going to do about your _________ your supervisor?

單字填空 請填入適當的單字。

1. 你會其他外語嗎？

Do you know any _________ languages?

2. 請簡略說明前份工作一天的行程。

Please _________ typical day at your last job.

3. 我另有生涯規劃。

I had a different _________ plan.

4. 貴公司讓我有發揮的空間。

Your company will give me _________ to develop.

5. 貴公司的福利和制度很健全。

Your company's _________ and policies are very sound.

6. 請形容你自己的個性。

Please describe your _________ .

7. 請在三分鐘之內，介紹自己。

Please _________ yourself in three minutes or less.

8. 請談談你之前的工作經驗。

Please talk about your ________ work experience.

9. 你為何失業這麼久的時間？

Why have you been ________ for so long?

10. 我們會在一週內通知你。

We will contact you ________ one week.

• 答案 •

Ⓐ 單字填空

①I ⑥D

②H ⑦J

③E ⑧F

④G ⑨B

⑤A ⑩C

Ⓐ 單字填空

① foreign ⑥ personality

② describe ⑦ introduce

③ career ⑧ previous

④ space ⑨ unemployed

⑤ benefits ⑩ within

求職面試要注意

求職面試一定要注意以下六點：

① 準時或早到：遲到等於將機會往外推，再好的學經歷都沒用。

② 打扮得宜：穿著打扮要得體，切勿穿拖鞋去面試。

③ 講話適當：過度冗長只會讓人想睡。

④ 切忌抱怨：抱怨是很不好的行為，尤其是抱怨前公司。不管對前公司再怎麼感冒，也不要在面試時說出來。

⑤ 切入重點：面試時適時表現優點，展現出自己的技能和經驗。

⑥ 態度誠懇：傲慢或不食人間煙火的態度只會讓人反感。

求職面試

各行各業

正式員工	full-time employee / regular employee
約聘派遣人員	contractor
實習生	intern
兼職員工	part-time worker
臨時工	temporary worker
秘書	secretary
企劃	planner
行政人員	administrative staff
採購專員	procurement specialist
銷售員 / 業務員	salesperson
會計師	accountant
保險專員	insurance agent
工程師	engineer
工人	worker
網頁設計師	web designer
程式設計工程師	programmer
建築師	architect
空間設計師	space designer
平面設計師	graphic designer
法官	judge
律師	lawyer
編輯	editor
譯者	translator
口譯員	interpreter
圖書館員	librarian
教師	teacher
家教	tutor
醫師	doctor

護士	nurse
藥師	pharmacist
獸醫	vet
木匠	carpenter
水電工	plumber
警察	policeman
消防員	fire fighter
藝術家	artist
音樂家	musician
插畫家	illustrator
導演	director
製片 / 製作人	producer
動畫師	animator
演員	actor
歌手	singer
舞者	dancer
攝影師	photographer
服裝設計師	dress designer
模特兒	model
新聞主播	newscaster
記者	reporter
新聞工作者	journalist
科學家	scientist
股票經紀人	stockbroker
導遊	tourist guide
飛行員	pilot
計程車司機	taxi driver
救生員	lifeguard
政治人物	politician
警衛 / 保全	security guard
清潔隊員	refuse collector
收銀員	cashier
店員	clerk

服務生	waiter / waitress
攤販	vendor
廚師	cook
麵包師傅	baker
調酒師 / 酒保	bartender
農夫	farmer
漁夫	fisherman
園藝人員 / 園丁	gardener
家庭主婦	housewife
太空人	astronaut
私家偵探	private eye
偵探	detective
牧師 / 神父	priest
保母	nanny / babysitter

求職常見單字

應徵者	applicant
找工作	job hunting
職缺	job opening
職務說明	job description
職位	position
職責	responsibilities
工作條件	requirements

福利制度	benefits
學歷	education
背景	background
工作經驗	work experience
履歷	resume / CV (=curriculum vitae)
面試	interview

Part 23

薪資待遇

Salaries & Benefits

薪資待遇

SALARIES & BENEFITS

MP3 023

情境會話

居酒屋　同事　抱怨薪水

Jennifer	Everything is more expensive, only the salary never changes.
Alex	It's because of economic hardship.
Jennifer	You know what? I haven't had a raise for five years.
Alex	Oh? Have you discussed this with the boss?
Jennifer	Of course. But it doesn't work. The boss always agrees to raise my salary, but he just makes empty promises.
Alex	It comes as no surprise. The boss is stingy.
Jennifer	Everyone is not very satisfied with the salary.
Alex	Right. Fortunately, we still have holiday bonuses (three Chinese festival gifts) and a year- end bonus.

Jennifer：什麼都漲，只有薪水不漲。
Alex：經濟不景氣嘛！
Jennifer：你知道嗎？我已經 5 年沒調薪了！
Alex：是哦，你有和老闆反映過嗎？
Jennifer：當然，但沒有用。老闆每次答應幫我調薪，結果都是說說。
Alex：不意外。老闆本來就很小氣。
Jennifer：每個人都對薪水不滿意。
Alex：對啊。幸好還有三節和年終獎金。

薪資待遇

你的希望待遇是多少？

What are your salary expectations?

◎ expectation (n.) = 期待。

依公司規定。
Depends on the company.

月薪三萬五千元。
NT$35,000 per month.

你要求的待遇太高了。

Your salary requirement is too high.

這份工作的薪水多少？

What is the salary for this position?

月薪三萬，獎金視績效而定。
Thirty thousand a month, bonuses depend on performance.
◎ dependent on = 視…而定。
◎ performance (n.) = 表現 。

底薪兩萬五千元，全勤獎金兩千元。
Base salary is NT$25,000, and your perfect attendance bonus is NT$2,000.
◎ perfect attendance (n.) = 全勤。

除了薪資外，外加分紅。
Besides the salary, you will also receive the dividend.
◎ besides (prerp.) = 除…之外。

保障一年十四個月。
Salary will be paid for 14 months a year.

底薪十二個月，外加年終三個月。
Base salary is for 12 months, and you will get a 3 month bonus.

請問有加班費嗎？	Does the company pay for overtime work?
請問加班費多少錢？	How much is the overtime pay?
一切依勞動法規定。	Everything is in accordance with the labor laws. ◎in accordance with=根據（法律、合約等）。
本公司的薪資公平合理，以績效為原則。	Our company's salary is based on performance, and is fair and reasonable.
本公司採責任制。	Our company follows the system of job responsibility.
試用期三個月。	There is a three month probationary period.
本公司有三節獎金。	We get bonuses for three holidays a year.
每半年調一次薪。	There is a company review every 6 months.
遲到半小時扣薪五十元。	If you are late for half an hour, we will deduct NT$50 from your paycheck. ◎ deduct (v.)= 扣除。
加班會供餐。	We will provide you with a meal if you work overtime.
實習生的薪資比較低。	Intern salaries are lower.

碩士的起薪比大學生高。	People with master's degrees get higher pay than those with bachelor's degrees.
課長級以上，發放公司股票。	If you are a grade above the section manager, then you will get company stocks. ◎ stock (n.)= 股票；庫存。
主管級以上有額外補貼。	There are special subsidies for the upper management. ◎ subsidy = 津貼。
補貼部分包含電話費和誤餐費。	The subsidies include telephone and overtime meal allowances.
部門主管每個月補助交通費五千元。	Departmental managers are provided with transportation allowances of NT$5,000 a month.
高階主管享有家庭旅遊補助。	The senior managers get family travel allowances.
補助費最高可以領多少？	What's the maximum amount for subsidies? 實支實付。 You can be reimbursed for all your expenses. 最多兩萬元。 NT$20,000 at most.

雖然薪資待遇是敏感的問題，最好還是面試時先弄清楚，以免損失自己的權益。

討論斡旋

我的薪資似乎有問題。	It seems that there is some problems with my salary. ◎ It seems …= 似乎…。
這個月少算全勤獎金給我。	I didn't get my bonus for perfect attendance this month. ◎ bonus (n.) = 獎金。
我的加班時數好像怪怪的。	There is something strange about my overtime hours. 怎麼會呢？時數是照打卡算的。 How can it be? It's in accordance with what's on the employee timesheet.
我的業績獎金比上個月少。	My incentive pay is less than last month. ◎ incentive pay= 獎金。
我想和你談談薪資的問題。	I'd like to discuss my salary with you.
我對我的薪資不太滿意。	I'm not very satisfied with my salary. ◎ be satisfied with… = 對…滿意。
我已經工作五年了，從未加過薪。	I've been working for 5 years already, and I've never had a pay raise.
我認為我的表現可以加薪。	I believe that I deserve a raise based on my performance. 文 *have/has been + Ving 是現在完成進行式的句型。* ◎ raise = 加薪。

下個月起，公司全體員工減薪百分之十。	Starting next month, we will cut salaries by 10 percent across the board. ◎ across the board = 總括、全面地。
我沒辦法接受減薪。	I can't accept a pay cut.
我可以先預支薪水嗎？	Can I get an advance on my salary? ◎ advance (n.) = 預付。 ★ an advance of + 錢 = 預支多少錢。
你的考績只有 C。	Your employee review got a "C".
你的工作態度欠佳。	Your attitude at work is undesirable.
你不適任這份工作。	You're not suited to this job.

薪資有問題時一定要說出口。曾經有人發現薪水比之前少，卻不好意思詢問，直到某天發現是會計出問題，才補發了少算的薪水。

"Time is the coin of your life. It is the only coin you have, and only you can determine how it will be spent. Be careful lest you let other people spend it for you."

— Carl Sandburg, Writer

「時間是你人生的錢幣，它是你唯一的錢幣，只有你能決定將怎麼使用它。
要小心，以免其它人替你使用。」

～ 卡爾 ‧ 桑德堡 (文學作家)

練習問題

選擇題　請選出正確的答案。

A)	based on	F)	allowances
B)	can't accept	G)	suited to
C)	special subsidies	H)	for this position
D)	probationary period	I)	salary expectations
E)	Base salary	J)	Depends on

1. 你不適任這份工作。

   You're not ________ this job.

2. 主管級以上有額外補貼。

   There are ________ for the upper management.

3. 補貼部分包含電話費和誤餐費。

   The subsidies include telephone and overtime meal ________ .

4. 你的希望待遇是多少？

   What are your ________ ?

5. 依公司規定。

   ________ the company.

6. 這份工作的薪水多少？

   What is the salary ________ ?

7. 我們公司的薪資公平合理，以績效為原則。

   Our company's salary is ____________ performance, and is fair and reasonable.

8. 試用期三個月。

There is a three month ________ .

9. 我沒辦法接受減薪。

I ________ a pay cut.

10. 底薪十二個月，外加年終三個月。

________ is for 12 months, and you will get a 3 month bonus.

單字填空 請填入適當的單字。

1. 遲到半小時扣薪五十元。

If you are late for ________ an hour, we will deduct NT$50 from your paycheck.

2. 我想要談談調薪的問題。

I'd like to ________ my salary with you.

3. 課長級以上，發放公司股票。

If you are a grade above the section manager, then you will get company ________ .

4. 我的加班時數好像怪怪的。

There is something strange about my ________ hours.

5. 補助費最高可以領多少？

What's the ________ amount for subsidies?

6. 我已經工作五年了，從未加過薪。

I've been working for 5 years already, and I've never had a ________ .

7. 我對我的薪資不太滿意。

I'm not very ________ with my salary.

8. 實習生的薪資會比較低。

_________ salaries are lower.

9. 每半年調一次薪水。

There is a company _________ every 6 months.

10. 底薪兩萬五千元，全勤獎金兩千元。

Your base salary is NT$25,000, and your perfect ___________ bonus is NT$2000.

• 答案 •

Ⓐ 單字填空

① G ⑥ H

② C ⑦ A

③ F ⑧ D

④ I ⑨ B

⑤ J ⑩ E

Ⓐ 單字填空

① half ⑥ raise

② discuss ⑦ satisfied

③ stocks ⑧ Intern

④ overtime ⑨ review

⑤ maximum ⑩ attendance

談錢傷感情?

談錢是很多人不擅長的事，很多人在面試被問到希望待遇時，總是怕會太直接而不好意思講明也不敢多問關於公司福利的細節，甚至到進了公司後薪水被少發也不敢吭聲。其實這都是自己的權益，應該勇敢提出，好好討論。但也請注意不要胡亂喊價，有些剛畢業、毫無經驗的新鮮人，期望待遇居然是五、六萬起跳，又不願意加班或出差，當然很難找到理想的工作。

薪資待遇

薪水相關單字

收入	income
基本薪資	base salary
起薪	starting salary
薪水	pay
薪水	wage（時、日、週薪）
薪水	salary （月薪）
案件計酬	paid by the piece
加薪	pay raise
減薪	pay cut
扣薪	deduct
加班費	overtime pay
補貼	allowance
額外津貼	perk
分紅	dividend
獎金	bonus
佣金	commission
全勤獎金	[perfect / full] attendance bonus
薪資支票	paycheck
薪資條	pay slip
發薪日	payday
所得稅	income tax

memo

Part 24

下班後的休閒娛樂

After Work

下班後的休閒娛樂

AFTER WORK

MP3 024

情境會話

咖啡廳　朋友　月光族

Annie　I become a Moonlight Clan this month.

Bill　Are you kidding? It is just the middle of the month. What have you spent your money on?

Annie　I am not sure. Maybe I spent too much money collecting dolls.

Bill　You should control your shopping habits and spend money wisely.

Annie　I understand, but the limited edition dolls that they sell in the market are only 100. If I hesitate, they will be sold out.

Bill　How dare you talk like this. I don't want to waste my time talking to you anymore.

Annie：哎，我這個月又要當月光族了。
Bill：　不會吧？才月中而已。你都把錢花在哪了？
Annie：我也不清楚。也許我花太多錢收藏公仔了。
Bill：　你要有所節制。錢要花在刀口上。
Annie：我也知道，但最近推出的公仔全球限量 100 個，晚了就買不到了。
Bill：　虧你說的出這種話，我懶得和你說了。

逛街購物

十一月九日到二十日是快樂百貨週年慶。	November 9 to 20 is Happy Department Store's anniversary sale. ◎ anniversary (n.) = 週年。
快樂百貨全館三折起。	Everything at Happy Department Store is 70% off and up.
下班後我們一起去逛街吧！我要買我妹的生日禮物。	Let's go shopping after work. I have to buy a birthday present for my younger sister. ◎ let's + Vr = 我們…吧，後面接原形動詞。例：Let's play basketball. (我們去打籃球吧。) 好阿，但我得先去 ATM 領錢。 OK. But first I need to withdraw some money from an ATM. ◎ withdraw (v.) = 領錢。
這家百貨公司頂樓有電影院。	This department store has a movie theater on the top floor.
我們買完東西後可以順便看電影。	We can go to a movie after shopping.
你多久逛一次街？	How often do you go shopping? 幾乎每週六都會去逛。 Almost every Saturday. 不一定。 It depends. 我很少逛街。 Not much.

我這個月已經超支了。	I went over my budget this month. ◎ budget (n.) = 預算。over budget = 超出預算。
我快把信用卡刷爆了。	I nearly maxed out my credit cards. ◎ max out = 刷爆（信用卡）。
信用卡真是邪惡，讓我不考慮後果就花了一堆錢。	The credit card is evil. It makes me spend a lot of money without thinking about the consequences. 這就是為什麼我都付現金。 That's why I always use cash.
我這個月買衣服已經花了一萬元。	I've already spent NT$10,000 on clothes this month. 真敗家。 Spoiled brat. 你不該花那麼多錢。 You shouldn't spend so much money. 我花得比你還多。 I've spent more than you. ◎ more than …= 比…多。
全館滿千送百。	If you spend 1000 dollars in the store, you'll get a 100 dollar gift certificate.
牛仔褲買一送一。	Jeans are buy one get one free.
大衣兩件打六折。	If you buy two coats, you'll get 40% off.
靴子第二雙五折。	The boots can buy one get the second one half off.

我想買件襯衫。	I want to buy a shirt.
我逛得腳很痠。	My feet are sore from shopping.
我喜歡自己一個人逛街。	I like to go shopping alone. ◎ alone (a.) = 獨自的。
我喜歡和大家一起逛街。	I like to go shopping with other people.

百貨公司週年慶時，折扣下殺好幾折，刷卡又能分期付款和累積點數，不買實在可惜，你是否也因此衝動購物了呢？切記，只買有需要且會用到的商品，否則收到驚人的卡費帳單時可就笑不出來囉。

體育運動

你有在做什麼運動嗎？	Do you play any sports? 我打羽毛球。 I play badminton. ★ play + 球類運動 = 打…球。
你喜歡什麼運動？	What kind of sports do you like? 我喜歡打高爾夫球。 I like to play golf.
你喜歡游泳嗎？	Do you like swimming?
我很會打籃球喔。	I'm good at basketball. ◎ be good at = 擅長做某事。例：be good at cooking = 擅長烹飪。

露營是很有趣的活動。	Camping is a really interesting activity. ◎ activity (n.) =活動。 文 *Ving 當主詞時，動詞要用第三人稱單數。*
我們星期天要去露營，一起去吧。	We're going camping on Sunday. Why don't you come with us? ◎ Why don't you …? = 何不…？
我每星期日都會去爬山。	I go hiking every Sunday.
水上摩托車很刺激。	Riding a jet ski is exciting. ◎ exciting (a.) = 刺激。 ★ exciting 用來形容某事物很刺激。如果是人感到興奮，要用 excited。
你有騎馬的經驗嗎？	Do you have experience of riding horses? 沒有，我不敢騎馬。 Never, I even don't dare to ride horses. I'm scared of riding horses. 我曾經從馬上摔下來。 Yes. I was thrown off a horse once.
我喜歡戶外活動。	I like outdoor activities. ◎ outdoor (a.) = 戶外的、露天的。
我們下星期五一起去爬山。	We're going hiking next Friday.
爬山很累可是很有成就感。	Hiking is really tiring, but comes with a sense of accomplishment. ◎ accomplishment (n.) = 成就。
我覺得泛舟好像很危險。	I think white water rafting seems dangerous.

我喜歡和朋友一起浮潛。	I like to go snorkeling with my friends.
騎腳踏車是很好的運動。	Riding a bike is a really good exercise.
溜直排輪很容易受傷。	It's easy to hurt yourself rollerblading. ◎ rollerblading (n.) = 直排輪。
飛盤很簡單又好玩。	Playing Frisbee is easy and it's fun.
放風箏需要技巧。	It takes some skill to fly a kite.

上班族每天坐辦公室，身體活動的時間少得可憐。等察覺過來時身材早已像吹氣球胖了好幾公斤。就算沒有要減重，為了健康著想，開始運動吧。

影視音樂

這部電影叫好又叫座。	This movie is good and it's doing well in the box office.
你喜歡看什麼電影？	What kind of movies do you like? 喜劇片。 Comedies.
你一個月去看幾次電影？	How many times do you go to the movies a month? 大概一個月一次。 About once a month.
現在最熱門的電影是哪部？	What's the hottest movie out right now?

你平常都看什麼電視節目？

What kind of TV programs do you usually watch?

我常看日 / 韓劇。
I usually watch Korean/Japanese dramas.

我總是看新聞。
I always watch the news.

你有看最新的偶像劇嗎？

Did you watch the latest idol drama?

◎ idol drama (n.) = 偶像劇。

我每天看兩小時的電視。

I watch about 2 hours of TV a day.

我對那些鄉土劇已經厭煩了。

I'm fed up with all those native soap operas.

◎ soap opera (n.) = 肥皂劇。

電視節目愈來愈無聊了。

TV programming is more and more boring.

◎ more and more + 形容詞 = 越來越…。

你喜歡什麼音樂？

What kind of music do you like?

搖滾樂 / 爵士樂。
Rock n' Roll. /Jazz.

你喜歡古典音樂嗎？

Do you like classical music?

◎ classical (adj.) = 古典的。

非常喜歡。
I like it a lot.

不怎麼喜歡。我聽古典樂會想睡覺。
Not really. Listening to classical music makes me sleepy.

我習慣邊看書邊聽音樂。	I usually listen to music while reading. ◎ while (conj.) = 當…的時候。
你有買 CD 的習慣嗎？	Do you buy CDs?
這張 CD 已經絕版了。	This CD is already out of print. ◎ out of print = 絕版。

興趣嗜好

我假日會去唱卡拉 OK。	I go sing karaoke when I have time off.
我蒐集玩具車已經有一年了。	I've had a toy car collection for a year already.
集郵是很有趣的嗜好。	Collecting stamps is an interesting hobby. 文 *物 / 事 +be+ interesting = 某事很有趣 。人 + be+ interested in = 某人對…感到興趣。* ◎ hobby (n.) = 嗜好。
集郵會花很多錢嗎？	Does it cost much to collect stamps?
我很熱衷於烹飪。	I'm really keen on cooking. ◎ be keen on = 熱衷於…。
我每天一定要上網。	I surf the Internet every day. ◎ surf the Internet = 上網。
打電動也可以動腦。	Playing video games can also exercise your wits.

玩線上遊戲很容易沉迷。	Playing online games is really addictive. ◎ addictive (a.) = 沉溺的。
我喜歡網路購物，可是很難控制購物慾。	I like online shopping, but it's hard to control my desire to shop.
園藝是我的喜好之一。	Gardening is one of my interests.
釣魚是我最喜歡做的事。	Fishing is my favorite activity.
我有空時喜歡看書。	When I have time, I like to read.
我喜歡旅行，我每年出國一次。	I love travel. I travel abroad once a year.
我每個月旅行兩次。	I take a trip somewhere twice a month. ◎ take a trip = 旅行。 ★ take 的相關片語：take a rest = 休息；take a shower= 洗澡；take a break = 休息一下 。
夏天我喜歡去海邊玩。	During the summer, I like to go to the beach. ◎ during + 時間 = 在…時間。

你有培養出自己的嗜好嗎？要是沒有的話，從現在起慢慢開發自己的興趣吧。

"Life isn't about finding yourself. Life is about creating yourself."

– George Bernard Shaw

「生命不在於找尋自我，在於創造自我。」

～ 喬治 ‧ 蕭伯納，劇作家

練習問題

選擇題　請選出正確的答案。

A) go shopping	F) keen on
B) while	G) went over my budget
C) fed up with	H) maxed out
D) out of print	I) anniversary sale
E) good exercise	J) sense of accomplishment

1. 爬山很累，可是很有成就感。

   Hiking is really tiring, but comes with a ________ .

2. 我快把信用卡刷爆了。

   I nearly ________ my credit cards.

3. 我這個月已經超支了。

   I ________ this month.

4. 我對那些鄉土劇已經厭煩了。

   I'm ________ all those native soap operas.

5. 這張 CD 已經絕版了。

   This CD is already ________ .

6. 我對於烹飪很熱衷。

   I'm really ________ cooking.

7. 十一月九日到二十日是快樂百貨週年慶。

   November 9 to 20 is Happy Department Store's ________ .

8. 下班後我們一起去逛街吧！

Let's ________ after work!

9. 我習慣邊看書邊聽音樂。

I usually listen to music ________ reading.

10. 騎腳踏車是很好的運動。

Riding a bike is a really ________ .

單字填空 請填入適當的單字。

1. 水上摩托車很刺激。

Riding a jet ski is ________ .

2. 你多久逛一次街？

How ________ do you go shopping?

3. 我這個月買衣服已經花了一萬元。

I've already ________ NT$10,000 on clothes this month.

4. 這就是為什麼我都付現金。

That's why I always use ________ .

5. 我們買完東西後可以順便看電影。

We can ________ after shopping.

6. 我曾經從馬上摔下來。

I was thrown ________ a horse once.

7. 你有騎馬的經驗嗎？

Do you have experience of ________ horses?

8. 我們星期天要去露營，一起去吧。

We're going ________ on Sunday, why don't you come with us?

9. 我很會打籃球喔。

I'm ________ basketball.

10. 我得先去 ATM 領錢。

I need to ________ some money from an ATM.

• 答案 •

Ⓐ 單字填空

① J	⑥ F
② H	⑦ I
③ G	⑧ A
④ C	⑨ B
⑤ D	⑩ E

Ⓐ 單字填空

① exciting	⑥ off
② often	⑦ ridding
③ spent	⑧ camping
④ cash	⑨ good at
⑤ go to a movie	⑩ withdraw

無法自拔

如何用英文表達沉迷某樣事物呢？可以用 addict 及其衍伸的單字。addict 指的是「沉迷～的人」； addiction 有「成癮」的意思；片語 be addicted to～ 則是表達「沉迷於～」。此外，字尾 -oholic/-aholic 是「～狂」的意思。

・**addict（名）沉迷於～的人**

a drug addict　癮君子　a gambling addict 賭徒

a TV addict　電視迷　a computer addict　電腦迷

・**addiction（名）成癮**

Internet addiction 網路成癮

Smartphone addiction 手機成癮（低頭族）

・**be addicted to… 沉迷於～**

I'm addicted to love. 我沉溺於愛情。

・**-oholic / -aholic ～狂**

alcoholic　酒鬼　shopaholic　購物狂

workaholic 工作狂　chocoholic　巧克力狂

下班後的休閒娛樂

電影、電視相關單字

文藝愛情片	romance
劇情片	drama
喜劇片	comedy
科幻片	Sci-Fi (=science fiction)
冒險片	adventure
驚悚片	thriller
恐怖片	horror
動作片	action
動畫片	animation / cartoon
懸疑片	mystery
紀錄片	documentary
電視影集	television series
迷你影集	mini-series
電視劇	television drama
連續劇	television serial
情境喜劇	sitcom
肥皂劇	soap opera
偶像劇	idol drama / trendy drama
音樂節目	music
綜藝節目	variety show
脫口秀、談話節目	talk show
單人脫口秀	stand-up comedy
遊戲節目	game show
真人實境秀	reality show
黃金時段	prime time
連續劇的一集	episode
罐頭笑聲	canned laughter / laugh track

memo

Part 25

家庭生活

Family Life

家庭生活

FAMILY LIFE

MP3 025

情境會話

員工餐廳　朋友　家庭日

Christina	Do you have family day?
Bruce	Yes. We will go out for dinner or take a trip.
Christina	Sounds great. My family always watches TV or plays computer games all day long on holidays.
Bruce	You can invite them out.
Christina	I've tried, but they are not interested in going.
Bruce	You should try a few more times, and you will be successful.
Christina	All right. I will try again.

Christina：你們家有家庭日嗎？
Bruce：　有啊，我們每個月都會去餐廳吃飯或出遊。
Christina：那真不錯，我們家的人一放假就整天悶在家看電視、玩電腦。
Bruce：　你可以邀他們出去走走。
Christina：我試過了，大家都沒興趣。
Bruce：　多試幾次總會成功。
Christina：好吧，我再試試。

家庭生活

你月薪多少？	How much do you make a month? ★薪水是個人隱私，無論在台灣或國外，直接問對方的薪水都是不太禮貌的。
你一個月的花費大概多少？	What are your monthly expenses?
你老婆有上班嗎？	Does your wife work?
你老公常常加班嗎？	Does your husband often work overtime?
現在很多雙薪家庭。	There are a lot of double income families now. ◎ a lot of +N = 很多的。
我先生是一般的上班族。	My husband is just a regular office worker. ◎ regular (a.) = 一般的。
我媽媽是家庭主婦。	My mom is a housewife.
我姊姊在百貨公司上班。	My older sister works at a department store.
我妹妹從事程式設計。	My younger sister works as a computer programmer.
我表弟在竹科工作。	My younger cousin works in the Hsinchu Science Park.
我先生的工作十分穩定。	My husband's work is perfectly stable. ◎ stable (a.) = 穩定的。

我先生最近被減薪了。	My husband got a salary reduction recently. ◎ salary = 薪水。
我哥最近升遷了。	My older brother got a promotion recently. ◎ promotion (n.) = 升職。
你家住哪一區？	What area do you live in?
你平常的休閒是什麼？	What do you usually do for fun?
你們放假時會去野餐嗎？	Do you go on a picnic on your day off?
我們放假時喜歡到郊外走走。	We like to get out of the city during the holidays.
我們週末常到餐廳吃飯。	We often dine out at restaurants on weekends.
星期天我們通常會去教會。	We usually go to church on Sundays.

"A man should never neglect his family for business."

— Walt Disney

「永遠不要為了事業忽略家庭。」

～ 華特・迪士尼

練習問題

選擇題 請選出正確的答案。

A)	double income
B)	got a promotion
C)	monthly expenses
D)	day off
E)	housewife

1. 你一個月的花費大概多少？
   What are your ________ ?
2. 現在很多都是雙薪家庭。
   There are a lot of ________ families now.
3. 我媽媽是家庭主婦。
   My mom is a ________ .
4. 我哥最近升遷了。
   My older brother ________ recently.
5. 你們放假時會去野餐嗎？
   Do you go on a picnic on your ________ ?

單字填空 請填入適當的單字。

1. 我先生是一般的上班族。
   My husband is just a regular ________ .
2. 你老公常常加班嗎？
   Does your husband often ________ ?

3. 我先生的工作十分穩定。

My husband's work is perfectly ________ .

4. 我妹從事程式設計師。

My younger sister works as a ________ .

5. 我們放假時喜歡到郊外走走。

We like to get out of the city ________ .

• 答案 •

Ⓐ 單字填空

① C

② A

③ E

④ B

⑤ D

Ⓐ 單字填空

① office worker

② work overtime

③ stable

④ computer programmer

⑤ during the holidays

再忙也別忘了家人

無論工作再忙再累，也不要忘了家人。有些人外表光鮮亮麗，回到家後卻判若兩人，生活習慣很差、對家人愛理不理、甚至把工作壓力發洩在家人身上。請記得，幸福的家庭是要用心經營的，家人不是免費幫傭，更不是出氣筒。偶爾花時間關心一下家人吧！

家庭生活

家族成員

雙親	parents
爸爸	father / dad
媽媽	mother / mom
繼父	stepfather
繼母	stepmother
小孩	child 複 children / kid 複 kids
兒子	son
女兒	daughter
養子	foster child 複 foster children
養子	foster son
養女	foster daughter
孫子	grandchild 複 grandchildren
孫子	grandson
孫女	granddaughter
祖父母	grandparents
祖父	grandfather / grandpa
祖母	grandmother / grandma
岳父 / 丈人	father-in-law
岳母 / 婆婆	mother-in-law
大嫂 / 小姑	sister-in-law
大伯 / 小叔	brother-in-law
叔叔 / 舅舅	uncle
嬸嬸 / 舅媽	aunt
堂親表親	cousin
姪子	nephew
姪女	niece
親戚	relative

memo

Part 26

衣著打扮

Dressing up

衣著打扮

DRESSING UP

MP3 026

情境會話

公司 同事 討論穿搭

Julie: I don't know what to wear to work every day.

William: Are you serious? I think your clothes are appropriate and pretty.

Julie: Thank you. I spend a lot of time on it. I think men are better. They only need to wear suits.

William: You are wrong. Picking up a suitable suit is not as easy as you think. A good quality suit is not cheap. Moreover, wearing a suit in summer is pretty hot.

Julie: Oh. It seems there are many tips for wearing clothes.

William: Exactly.

Julie： 每天上班都不知道要穿什麼。

William：會嗎？我覺得你穿著得體又好看呀。

Julie： 謝謝。我花了很多時間在上面。還是男生比較吃香，穿套西裝就好了。

William：你錯了。要挑到合適的西裝不容易，質料好的也不便宜。而且夏天穿西裝很熱。

Julie： 是哦，看來穿衣服真是門學問。

William：沒錯。

平日衣著

老闆要求秘書要穿套裝。	The boss requires his secretaries to wear suits.
上班不該穿得太隨便。	You shouldn't dress too casually at the office.
我覺得穿 T 恤不太適合。	I don't think it is appropriate to wear T-shirts. ◎ appropriate (a.) = 適合的。
這件襯衫好看耶，很適合你。	That's a great shirt. It fits you well. 謝謝，是我太太幫我挑的啦。 Thanks. My wife picked it out for me. ◎ pick out = 挑選。 謝啦，我也喜歡你的 polo 衫。 Thank you. I like your polo shirt, too.
你的領帶和襯衫不搭。	Your tie does not match your shirt. ◎ match (v.) = 和…相配。
你褲子太鬆，需要繫皮帶。	Your pants are too loose; you need to wear a belt.
瑪莉總是打扮的很有型。	Mary always dresses in style.
她穿衣服很有品味。	She has great taste when it comes to clothes. ◎ when it comes to… = 談到…、提及…。
她的靴子看起來很時尚。	Her boots are really fashionable. ◎ fashionable (a.) = 時尚的。
她的手提包很漂亮。	Her handbag is pretty.

她的包包是義大利製造的。	Her bag is made in Italy.
你都買哪個牌子的衣服？	What brand clothes do you usually buy? 不一定耶，喜歡就買。 It depends; I just buy whatever I like. ◎ It depends. = 視情況而定。 我都買名牌。 I always buy brand names.
你一個月治裝費多少？	How much do you spend on clothes a month? 大概二到五千元。 About NT$2,000 to NT$5,000. 低於兩千元。 Less than NT$2,000.
不要迷信名牌。	Don't be a fool for brand names.
路邊攤也可以穿出自我風格。	You can create your own personal style from buying clothes at the street stalls, too.
珍妮的衣著一成不變。	Jenny dresses the same all the time. ◎ all the time = 一直。
她每天都穿長褲和襯衫。	She wears slacks and dress shirts every day.
她連冬天都穿涼鞋。	She wears sandals even in winter.

上班族服裝因職業而異，如果同事都穿套裝，就不要只穿 T 恤、牛仔褲和運動鞋。

特殊場合

正式場合請注意穿著。	Please dress appropriately in formal occasions. ◎ occasion (n.) = 場合；時刻。
穿著短褲和T恤無法進入這間餐廳。	You can't enter this restaurant wearing shorts and a T-shirt.
明天的典禮要穿著得體。	You have to dress appropriately for tomorrow's ceremony. ◎ ceremony (n.) = 典禮。
明天的派對規定要穿什麼？	Do you know the dress code for tomorrow's party? 女性要穿洋裝。 Women should wear dresses. 男性要穿西裝。 Men should wear suits.
萬聖節派對要變裝打扮。	We got to dress up in a costume for the Halloween party.
明天的舞會你要穿什麼衣服？	What are you going to wear to tomorrow's party?
珍妮佛的婚禮我想穿藍色的洋裝。	I want to wear a blue dress to Jennifer's wedding.
後天聚餐你要穿粉紅色的長裙嗎？	Are you going to wear that long pink skirt to the dinner the day after tomorrow?

特殊場合需要穿不同於平日的服裝，拿不定主意時不妨先與同事討論。

練習問題

選擇題　請選出正確的答案。

A)	Less than	F)	it's appropriate
B)	in formal occasions	G)	dress too casually
C)	own personal style	H)	in style
D)	great taste	I)	all the time
E)	It depends	J)	made in

1. 不一定耶，喜歡就買。

   ________ ; I just buy whatever I like.

2. 低於兩千元。

   ________ NT$2,000.

3. 你穿衣服很有品味。

   You have ________ when it comes to clothes.

4. 上班不要穿得太隨便。

   You shouldn't ________ at the office.

5. 她的衣著一成不變。

   She dresses the same ________ .

6. Mary 的打扮總是很有型。

   Mary always dresses ________ .

7. 路邊攤也可以穿出自我風格。

   You can create your ________ from buying clothes at the street stalls too.

8. 我的包包是義大利製造的。

My bag is ________ Italy.

9. 正式場合請注意穿著。

Please dress appropriately ________ .

10. 我覺得穿 T 恤不太適合。

I don't think ________ to wear T-shirts.

單字填空 請填入適當的單字。

1. 老闆要求秘書要穿套裝。

The boss requires his secretaries to wear ________ .

2. 你褲子太鬆，需要繫皮帶。

Your pants are too loose; you need to wear a ________ .

3. Jennifer 的婚禮我想穿藍色洋裝。

I want to wear a blue dress to Jennifer's ________ .

4. 看心情而定。

Depends on my ________ .

5. 不要迷信名牌。

Don't be a ________ for brand names.

6. 妳的手提包很漂亮。

Your ________ is pretty.

7. 明天的派對規定要穿什麼？

Do you know the dress ________ for the party tomorrow?

8. 你的領帶和襯衫不搭。

Your tie does not ________ your shirt.

9. 明天的典禮要穿著得體。

You have to dress appropriately for tomorrow's ________ .

10. 她的馬靴看起來很時尚。

Her boots are really ________ .

• 答案 •

Ⓐ 單字填空

① E ⑥ H

② A ⑦ C

③ D ⑧ J

④ G ⑨ B

⑤ I ⑩ F

Ⓐ 單字填空

① suits ⑥ handbag

② belt ⑦ code

③ wedding ⑧ match

④ mood ⑨ ceremony

⑤ fool ⑩ fashionale

人要衣裝

懂得看場合打扮也是上班族需要注意的部分，這不僅代表你個人，有時也代表了公司的形象。雖然許多公司沒有明文規定服裝，但也不代表可以亂穿。穿著得體可以帶給別人專業的印象，進而展開後續合作，甚至會影響到一個人的長期發展。那麼，到底要怎麼打扮才好呢？大家都很休閒，只有我很正式怎麼辦？其實不用想太多，可以參考下面幾個原則：不穿過份休閒、不穿奇裝異服、不穿太裸露、乾淨的妝容、定期修剪鬍子與指甲、保持整潔。如果還是很擔心，不妨觀察其他同事的穿著打扮再慢慢調整。

衣著打扮

服裝相關單字

上衣

上衣	top
短上衣 / 罩衫	blouse
背心	vest
T 恤	T-shirt
襯衫	shirt
正式襯衫	dress shirt
毛衣	sweater
洋裝	dress
西裝	suit
兩件式西裝（外套、長褲）	two-piece suit
三件式西裝（外套、背心、長褲）	three-piece suit
西裝背心	waistcoat
西裝外套	blazer
外套 / 大衣	coat
長大衣	overcoat
夾克	jacket
斗篷	cape

褲、裙

牛仔褲	jeans
長褲	trousers / pants
寬鬆長褲	slacks
內搭褲	leggings

短褲	shorts
裙子	skirt
褲裙	culottes

包包

錢包	purse	公事包	briefcase
皮夾	wallet	手提包	handbag
皮包	handbag	托特包	tote

鞋、襪

鞋子	shoes	楔型鞋	wedge heels
馬靴	boots	涼鞋	sandals
平底鞋	flats	運動鞋	sneakers
皮鞋	leather shoes	絲襪	pantyhose
高跟鞋	high heels	襪子	socks
淺口高跟鞋	pumps	褲襪	tights

其他配件

帽子	hat	領帶	necktie
皮帶	belt	領帶夾	tie-pin
珠寶	jewelry	項鍊	necklace
絲巾	scarf	手錶	watch
太陽眼鏡	sunglasses	配件	accessory

Part 27

健康話題

Topics about Health

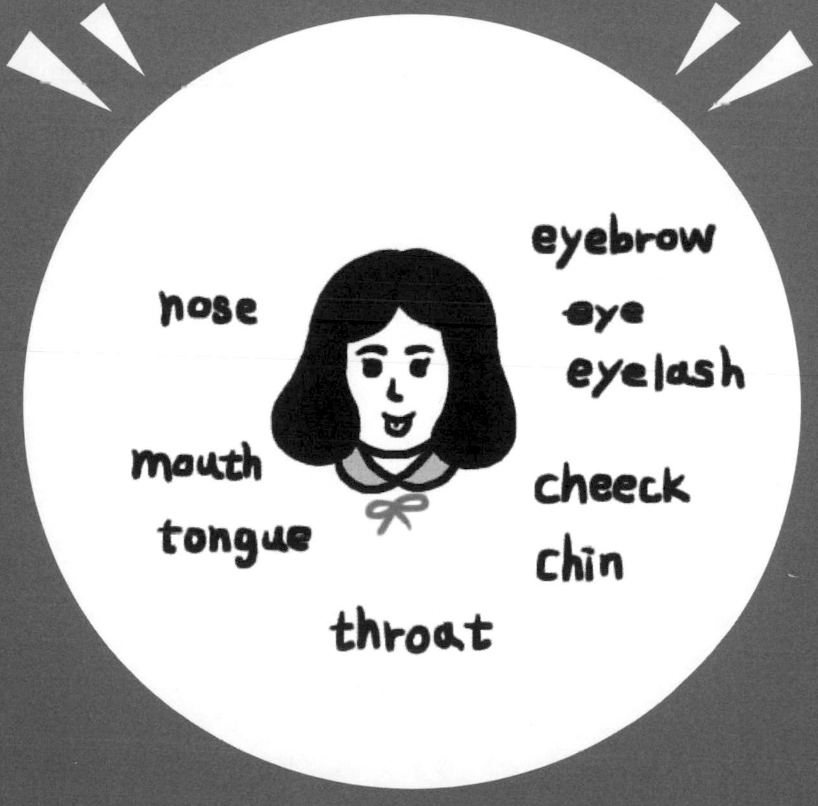

健康話題

TOPICS ABOUT HEALTH

MP3 027

情境會話

茶水間　同事　閒聊

Alex	Your skin looks better. How do you take care of your skin?
Kate	Thank you. I've started going to bed before 11 pm since last month.
Alex	That's it ? I go to bed at 10:30 pm, but I am still pimply.
Kate	Moreover, I am addicted to running. I go jogging in the morning for thirty to sixty minutes.
Alex	The real reason is exercise. No wonder you are in better shape.
Kate	Exercising is good for your health. Do you want to go running with me?

Alex：你皮膚變好了。你怎麼保養的？
Kate：謝謝。我上個月開始每天晚上 11 點前上床睡覺。
Alex：就這樣嗎？那我每天 10 點半睡覺怎麼還是滿臉痘痘。
Kate：還有我最近迷上跑步，每天早上都會晨跑 30 分鐘到 1 個小時。
Alex：原來是運動的關係，難怪你身材也變好了。
Kate：運動對健康真的好處多多，你要和我一起跑步嗎？

健康資訊

用餐時請細嚼慢嚥。	You should chew slowly when you eat.
飯後請勿立刻洗澡。	Don't shower right after you eat.
多吃蔬果對身體有幫助。	Eating more fruits and vegetables can improve your health.
吃素對身體很好。	Being vegetarian is good for you.
維他命吃多對身體不一定好。	Eating more vitamins doesn't necessarily guarantee better health.
多喝水可預防皮膚乾燥。	Drink more water to keep your skin from drying out.
喝綠茶有益健康。	Green tea is good for your health. ◎ be good for … = 有益…。
一天不能喝超過兩杯咖啡。	You shouldn't drink more than 2 cups of coffee a day.
喝太多咖啡會得骨質疏鬆症。	Drinking too much coffee can give you osteoporosis. ◎ osteoporosis (n.) = 骨質疏鬆症。
每天喝珍珠奶茶容易發胖。	It's easy to gain weight by drinking bubble tea every day.
需要久坐的工作會讓屁股變大。	Sedentary work leads to big bottoms. ◎ sedentary (a.) = 坐著的、需要久坐的。

吃藥減肥是不好的。	Diet pills aren't good for you.
抽菸有害身體健康。	Smoking is bad for your health.
吸二手菸更容易罹患癌症。	Second hand smoke increases the risk of cancer.
防曬係數愈高，安全日曬愈久。	The higher the SPF is, the longer it is safe to be out in the sun.
憂鬱症可用藥物治癒。	There are some kinds of medications that treat depression.
你有聽過雞尾酒治療法嗎？	Have you heard of cocktail therapy? ◎ therapy (n.) = 治療法。
頭痛的原因有很多種。	There could be many reasons for a headache.
整晚熬夜對身體不好。	It's not good for you to stay up all night. ◎ stay up = 熬夜。
最佳睡眠時間是晚上十一點。	The best time to go to bed is at 11pm.
魚類有豐富的鈣質。	Fish is a good source of calcium. ◎ calcium(n.) = 鈣質。
網站上健康資訊很豐富。	You can find a lot of health information on the internet.

健康資訊日新月異，不妨定期閱讀報章雜誌或看新聞吸收新知。

健康與美容

仰臥起坐可以讓腹部結實。	Sit-ups can tighten your stomach muscles.
伏地挺身很困難。	Push-ups are hard.
你變年輕了。	You've gotten younger.
你似乎變胖了。	You seem to have gained weight.
你如何保持苗條呢？ 你的秘訣是什麼？	How do you stay slim? What's your secret?
你看起來體弱多病。	You look frail and sickly.
你應該要戒菸了。	You should quit smoking.
減重有什麼好方法？	How do I lose weight? 做運動。 Exercise. 少吃甜食。 Don't eat so many sweets. 不要吃油膩的食物。 Don't eat greasy foods. ◎ greasy (a.) = 油膩的。 晚上八點後不要進食。 Don't eat anything after 8pm.
我已經報名健身房會員了。	I've already signed up for a gym membership. ◎ sign up = 報名。

健身房一年要花兩萬元以上。	I need to pay over NT$20,000 a year for my gym membership.
我們可以去慢跑。	What kind of skin care products do you buy?
這組美白花了我五千元。	This whitening set cost me NT$5,000.
聽說美白保養品效果只有五成。	I heard that whitening products are only 50% effective.
這是最新的抗皺霜。	This is the latest anti-wrinkle cream.
今年很流行這個眼影顏色。	This eye shadow shade is hot this year.
我不習慣用腮紅。	I'm not used to using blush.
你的洗髮精味道很好聞。	Your shampoo smells great.

身體不適

我這星期很容易感到疲勞。	I've been easily fatigued this week.
我壓力過大。	I am under too much pressure.
我最近常失眠。	Lately I've had trouble sleeping.
昨天晚睡，今天頭好痛。	I went to bed late last night and I have a bad headache today.
我眼睛好像發炎了。	I think I have an infection in my eye. ◎ infection(n.) = 感染。

我的腳很痠。	My legs are sore.
我腰痠背痛。	My back hurts. 因為你長期坐著。 It's because you are sedentary. 因為你坐姿不良。 You have bad posture. ◎ posture (n.) = 姿勢。 可能因為你長期穿高跟鞋。 Maybe it is because you often wear high heels.
你好像是食物中毒。	You seem to have food poisoning.
你昨天有吃什麼東西嗎？	Did you eat anything yesterday?
這是腸胃炎症狀。	There is an inflammation of the stomach and intestines.
飯後要吃藥。	Take your medicine after meals. ◎ take medicine = 吃藥，不要寫成 eat。
我不想打針。	I don't want to get a shot.

身體不適或感冒絕對不能一拖再拖，請好好休息或盡快就醫。

練習問題

選擇題　請選出正確的答案。

A) food poisoning	F) drying out
B) a good source of	G) stay up all night
C) easily fatigued	H) greasy foods
D) is bad for	I) lose weight
E) Second hand smoke	J) quit smoking

1. 你好像是食物中毒。
   You seem to have ________ .

2. 吸二手菸更容易罹患癌症。
   ________ increases the risk of cancer.

3. 多喝水可預防皮膚乾燥。
   Drink more water to keep your skin from ________ .

4. 晚熬夜對身體不好。
   It's not good for you to ________ .

5. 魚類有豐富的鈣質。
   Fish is ________ calcium.

6. 抽菸有害身體健康。
   Smoking ________ your health.

7. 你應該要戒菸了。
   You should ________ .

8. 減重有什麼好方法？

How do I _________ ?

9. 這星期很容易感到疲勞。

I've been _________ this week.

10. 不要吃油膩的食物。

Don't eat _________ .

單字填空 請填入適當的單字。

1. 你如何保持苗條呢？

How do you stay _________ ?

2. 健身房一年要花兩萬元以上。

I need to pay over NT$20,000 a year for my gym _________ .

3. 聽說美白保養品效果只有五成。

I heard that whitening products are only 50% _________ .

4. 飯後要吃藥。

_________ your medicine after meals.

5. 你似乎變胖了。

You seem to have _________ weight.

6. 最近腸胃脹氣。

I've had flatulence _________ .

7. 我不想打針。

I don't want to get a _________ .

8. 憂鬱症可用藥物治癒。

There are some kinds of medications that treat ________ .

9. 我壓力過大。

I am under too much ________ .

10. 我昨天晚睡今天頭好痛。

I went to bed late last night and I have a bad ________ today.

• 答案 •

Ⓐ 單字填空

①A ⑥D

②E ⑦J

③F ⑧I

④G ⑨C

⑤B ⑩H

Ⓐ 單字填空

① slim ⑥ recently

② membership ⑦ shot

③ effective ⑧ depression

④ Take ⑨ pressure

⑤ gained ⑩ headache

休息是為了走更長遠的路

健康是人類最大的本錢，身體不好不但無法盡全力工作，也不能縱情玩樂。所以，平時就要多了解健康新知，養成早睡早起、少吃垃圾食物、多運動的習慣。此外，也要注意不要忽略了身體所發出來的警訊，如果身體不適的症狀超過一個星期，務必盡快找時間就醫。身體只有一個，如果沒有健康習慣，不管在職場上多麼呼風喚雨，哪天突然因為過勞而倒下，先前的努力可能也都白費了。

上班族常用單字匯總

健康話題

身體各部位

頭	head
頭髮	hair
臉	face
額頭	forehead
眼睛	eye
眉毛	eyebrow
睫毛	eyelash
耳朵	ear
鼻子	nose
嘴巴	mouth
嘴唇	lip
牙齒	tooth 複 teeth
舌頭	tongue
臉頰	cheeck
下巴	chin
脖子	neck
喉嚨	throat

肩膀	shoulder
胸部	chest
胸部（乳房）	breast
肚子	stomach
肚擠	bellybutton / navel
手臂	arm
手肘	elbow
手	hand
手指	finger
背部	back
腰部	lower back
腿	leg
膝蓋	knee
臀部	buttocks
腳	foot 複 feet
腳趾	toe
指甲	nail

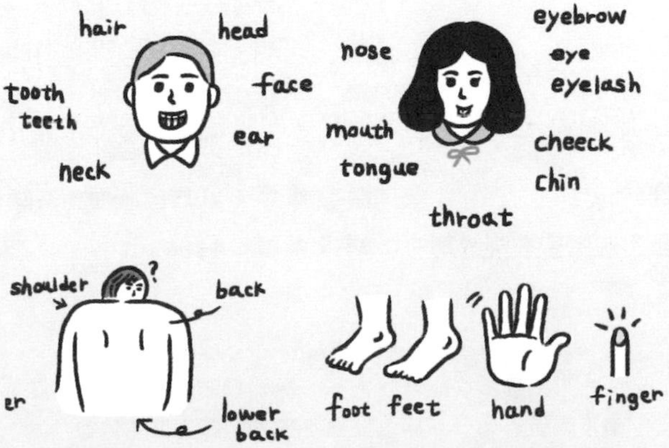

國家圖書館出版品預行編目(CIP)資料

Everyday English!每日生活英語會話 / Carolyn G. Choong著. -- 初版. -- 臺北市 : 笛藤, 2017.03
面 ;　公分
ISBN 978-957-710-689-6(平裝附光碟片)
1.英語 2.會話
805.188　　106003814

2017年4月9日　初版 第1刷　定價430元

著　　者	Carolyn G. Choong	地　　址	台北市重慶南路三段1號3樓-1
特約編著	席菈(Sheila)	電　　話	(02)2358-3891
封面設計	王舒玗	傳　　真	(02)2358-3902
插　　畫	Aikoberry	總 經 銷	聯合發行股份有限公司
總 編 輯	賴巧凌	電　　話	(02)2917-8022 · (02)2917-8042
編　　輯	伍曉玥・林子鈺・徐一巧	製 版 廠	造極彩色印刷製版股份有限公司
發 行 人	林建仲	劃撥帳戶	八方出版股份有限公司
發 行 所	笛藤出版圖書有限公司	劃撥帳號	19809050